JUST DOWN THE HALL

ALESSANDRA THOMAS

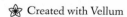 Created with Vellum

For every amazing journalist who paid their dues in one crazy way or another. Thank you for hanging in there. We need you now more than ever.

CHAPTER 1

JORDAN

I SHOVED the last of my luggage into the back of my SUV, then did one last check of the straps holding my mattress and a solitary book shelf to the top of the roof. If anyone could do a good job packing a life into a mid-sized car, it was someone headed off to start his PhD candidacy in the Aerospace Engineering department of the University of Pennsylvania. Me.

I hugged my kid sister Kiera - even though, at twenty-two years old, she was hardly a kid anymore—and swung her around by the waist for a quick selfie. I tapped at the screen to send it off to our mom, who couldn't be here to see me off since she had to work an early shift at the hospital. She'd seemed a little choked up about it last night, but I'd reminded her that Philly wasn't really that far away from home, anyway.

Pittsburgh—the home I was escaping from for another three or four years—was on the opposite side of the state from Philly. That was just barely far enough.

I shouldered my way into the car, glad that Mom had been willing to switch mine with hers. That little Honda Civic might have been okay for when I was a scrawny seventeen-year-old trying to figure out how to live off student loans in California, but six years had brought six more inches and thirty pounds of muscle to my body.

Yeah, I worked out. I wasn't cocky about it, but as soon as I realized, as a junior in the Aero Engineering program, that I actually did want to be an astronaut when I grew up, I'd started working out. I ran with the guys from my classes, trained with the free weight jockeys at the student health center, ate right and then worked out some more on my own. A lot of people in the program said they were going to fly up to the moon in a space ship, but I knew that with my brains, a lot of hard work, good timing, and some serious luck, I might actually have a shot at it.

Besides that, only fourteen black astronauts had ever flown in space in the entire history of NASA, out of more than five hundred astronauts in total. I intended to fly to outer space in a rocket ship and help that number reach twenty. Our mother told us every day of our childhood that it wasn't enough to hope for true racial equality and black representation – if we wanted it, it was our responsibility to work toward it. My sister had been the only black female statistics major in most of her college classes. I had been one of a handful of black men in the engineering department.

Our mother told me how proud we made her every time we talked on the phone, in every greeting card she sent, in every social media post she made. But the stubborn little boy inside of me told me that I wouldn't be successful until I made it up into space.

Earning a degree in aerospace engineering wasn't easy for a kid who had grown up poor and had to work extra hard for every scholarship and grant dime he got. After I graduated with honors from Stanford, I thought I'd be able to take my pick of programs. I was right, but only halfway. The goddamn economy meant that programs were being cut way back. I worked a job for a couple years at an airplane parts manufacturing plant before applying for grad school, hoping that the extra experience would help my chances. It did – I got offers of admission from a couple amazing schools. Problem was, I couldn't afford any of the schools that would agree to take me on for a PhD in Engineering and Applied Aerodynamics with an emphasis in Biochem - a fucking dream trifecta for NASA's candidate program - except for Carnegie Mellon. The only reason CMU was doable is that I would be able to move back home with my mom.

It was far from ideal—really far from it. The best job I'd be able to get with a degree from CMU was a cushy position with Boeing, but I wanted to fly rocket ships, not make airplanes. I'd accepted, though—what else was I going to do?

Well, fate had the surprise of my life in store for me.

UPenn had rejected my application back in April, which was why the letter I received five days ago, during the first week of June, was such a surprise. I'd torn it open, with Kiera bouncing and squealing in the background. A spot had opened up and they wanted me to fill it. There was even a stipend. After a little internet research, I realized I could probably make the money stretch just far enough if I found a cheap place and a roommate.

There was just one problem. They wanted me to start a week later — mid-June. I knew damn well that the housing market in Philly was booked up at least six months in advance, not to mention crazy expensive, and that was for studios I wouldn't have to depend on anyone else to split rent with.

Dammit. I was just explaining all this to Kiera and working out whether I could defer UPenn for a semester or even a year when Kiera checked her phone and screamed again.

"You have got to stop that, KiKi," I complained, rubbing the patch of skin behind my ear. I was going to go deaf staying here.

"Shut *up!*" she said. "I literally just got a text from Lizzie. This is perfect."

"Lizzie? Like, your high school best friend Lizzie?"

"Yes, moron. The one who lives in Philadelphia. She just got dumped by her boyfriend who she was supposed to move in with next week. She thought he was going to propose and now he pulls this shit."

"So why are you so smiley?" I eyed Kiera suspiciously. That girl was always a step ahead of me when it came to planning my future life.

"Because," she said, rolling her eyes like it was obvious, "She's devastated and freaking out about her future and her options especially because her new job pays like shit and now she doesn't have a roommate. You get me?" Kiera raised her eyebrows and stared me down while dialing Lizzie blind. "God, sometimes I swear rocket scientists are the dumbest people on earth," she muttered under her breath as she tapped at her phone, then held it at arm's length, fixing her hair for a video call.

"Lizzie? *Lizzie.* Okay okay okay, I know this is a shitty day for you, but I am going to make it a hundred times better! You ready?"

A soft, deep laugh answered Kiera, and instinct tugged me to her side. Something about just that hint of her voice made me desperate to get a look at her.

I popped my head over Kiera's shoulder, hoping she'd decided to FaceTime with Lizzie. I was a red-blooded American man, after all, and everyone from my mom to my Aero Engineering professor knew I had a thing for pretty girls. My curiosity over whether Lizzie had had a run-in with the hotness fairy pulled my eyes to the screen.

No such luck.

Her voice, though, held an oddly familiar tone – a little

raspy, her vowels drawn out just a little longer than anyone else's. Six years had deepened it, but it was definitely the Lizzie I'd known as an annoying brace-faced kid. I listened as Kiera summarized my situation, and registered the cadence of Lizzie's voice as she responded to basic questions about location and price. With every word she spoke, familiarity for Lizzie washed over me in waves.

Yeah, I remembered her - as a kid, she'd always had her eyes glued to her phone, and spent the time when she didn't gossiping about this guy or that teacher from school. Everywhere she walked, she left a trial of detritus behind her - gum wrappers, scraps of notebook paper, hair ties. Her outfits were always some weird mishmash of the latest trends, like she'd relied on a handful of pages randomly torn from fashion magazines to dress her in the morning.

I also remembered how she'd rolled her eyes at me every time she saw me, and how I'd distinctly heard her call me a dweeb as I walked by at least once. Maybe twice.

But, hey. We were all grown up now. Obviously. I had certainly matured, and it only stood to reason that Lizzie had changed too.

"Really, JJ?" Lizzie's voice pulled me out of my nostalgic thoughts.

"Um...what?" I stammered as her stark question pulled me away from my wandering thoughts.

The last time talking to some girl had made me lose my train of thought, I was a freshman at Stanford about to lose my virginity. What the hell was going on?

"You really wouldn't mind moving in with me? It would be..." she let out a shuddering breath and turned her head to the side for a moment, blinking hard. "Sorry, it's just a surprise. I had no idea this was going to happen. But I'm so glad you're moving here. If you're really up for it, then I'll at least be living with someone I know I can trust."

"You sure you don't have someone else you'd rather call?"

She let out another sigh. "All my friends are either moving somewhere else or already have a place in the city. It's damn near impossible to find a decent place here and...yeah."

I could tell her voice was on the edge of breaking. I suddenly felt an urge to make her smile, or laugh, or something to stop the tears from falling. It was certainly more deep and intense than the last time I listened to a girl cry - two months ago, when I'd dumped my last girlfriend. Also over the phone.

I'd given myself a pass for that one. My last jerky move at the end of a pretty decent college dating career.

I probably felt so connected to Lizzie because I'd known her as a kid. Just hearing her voice couldn't make me attached to a girl. It was the familiarity I already had with her, and my sister's enthusiasm, which had her practically bouncing off the walls at the idea of Lizzie and I living together. That had to be it.

Regardless, it seemed that Lizzie Palmer, the annoying sideshow to a kid sister I tolerated, had turned into quite a woman. She'd made it through college at UPenn and found a job on the other end. Yeah, she was probably a disaster after her fuck-tard boyfriend dumped her and left her hanging with half an apartment lease to fill, but I was certainly not going to complain about that.

As I pulled away from Pittsburgh and onto the turnpike toward Philly, I thought of Lizzie for about the thousandth time since I'd seen her face on the phone five days ago. She was just Lizzie Palmer, and I was just Jordan Jacobs. Two nice kids from Pittsburgh who'd grown up together. We'd fallen into this situation almost like fate had guided us there.

What could possibly go wrong?

CHAPTER 2

LIZ

"WHAT COULD POSSIBLY GO WRONG?" I asked the saner half of myself as I unpacked what had to be one of the last boxes in this never ending stack of brown cardboard ridiculousness the movers had dumped into my new apartment in University City. There was no way I had this much stuff. With every box I unpacked, I told myself there had to be a mistake, that they must have unloaded some other girl's boxes in addition to my own, but every single box I opened held something that I only then remembered deciding I absolutely, positively needed in my post-grad life.

Thank God Dad had paid the movers.

This box, unfortunately, held two things I really didn't want to see. First, the industrial sized box of condoms I'd picked up before the first time Josh and I had had sex over a year ago, and only managed to use half of. I'd done the deed with a couple of guys before Josh, but I figured doing it with a guy I loved would feel more like fun and less of a messy, awkward chore.

I'd been wrong.

I slung those to the corner of the room, hoping I could just throw a dirty sweatshirt over them where they wouldn't see the light of day for a good long while.

Then, there were the picture frames. Fortunately, I hadn't packed these before Josh broke up with me and completely ruined the surprise I had for him - the fact that I'd found us a totally darling fully-furnished apartment close to UPenn Law, where he was about to start his third year. With tears dripping from my cheeks, I'd yanked out every framed photo of the two of us - dressed up for the Barrister's Ball, face-painted for an Eagles football game, and, finally, me in a graduation cap and gown with his arm draped loosely around my waist - and pulled the prints from their frames.

A couple days later, I'd texted Kiera and convinced her to send me some old pictures with both Jordan and I from high school. I'd grinned, sent them right to the drugstore, and filled those same damn frames with pictures of me and my new roomie as soon as I got home.

At least I'd been able to find a roommate so quickly. I'd never be able to thank Kiera enough for that. I held one of the frames gently in my hands, running my thumb over the face of Kiera's scrawny, goofy big brother, who had his arm slung around my shoulders like he was about to pull me down for a headlock.

Come to think of it, he probably had right after Kiera snapped it.

God, Jordan was a dweeb. I moved to the coffee table, a fairly solid if boring piece that had come with the furnished apartment, and set down a couple of the frames, brushing over more of the photos with my fingertips. I lingered on one of their family when he and Kiera were little, before their dad passed away. His blond hair was a shock against the other three heads of sprawling curls. I knew that I'd meet Kiera just a few years after this picture had been taken, on the playground at Kindergarten. Our lives had nearly always been entwined.

I moved on to another frame. Teenaged Jordan was skinny as a toothpick, his hair was a huge puffy mess, and his thick black glasses were always falling down his nose. In this pic, he had on a NASA t-shirt under a navy and white track jacket, and his chin was tipped up, making the smug curve of his lips look slightly wider than it actually was. He was too smart for his own good, and I'd lost count of how many times Kiera and I had to help him get out of some locker he'd been stuffed in or buy him a second lunch after some asshole dumped his on the floor of the cafeteria.

"But you were always a nice dweeb," I mused in a soft voice, smiling at the memory of how he gave us a ride home from school any time we asked. He really didn't have to talk to some giggly sixteen-year-old brace-faces who'd barely gotten their shit together to test for our learner's permits, let alone figure out how to get a driver's license. I'd been happy for him when he'd graduated a year early and scored a sweet all-inclusive full ride to Stanford. I'd been happy for myself, too, when Kiera and I had all that extra space to spread out when he moved away.

"God, are you still calling me that?" A deep voice, rich and soft as velvet, curled in through the crack of the new apartment door. The first thing I saw follow it was a very distinctive head of black curls, no longer nearly as puffy as it used to be, but definitely belonging to Jordan Jacobs.

"Jordan!" I cried, replacing the picture and hustling over to the door. He pushed it the rest of the way open and stood there, grinning, with a huge duffle bag slung over each shoulder.

I'd assumed 23-year-old Jordan would look exactly like 17-year-old Jordan.

Hot damn. I'd assumed so freaking wrong.

I stopped in my tracks.

It was uncanny, really. He was wearing those same thick black frames he'd had in high school, only his jaw and cheekbones had somehow found themselves some serious contour and chisel at Stanford University, not to mention a truly manly scatter of stubble. His style had changed since high school, too. Jordan had always seemed lost in terms of clothing choices, going through phases where he only wore baggy jeans and shirts, or graphic tees and sweats, or track suits with bucket hats. Back then, he'd always looked like he was trying on someone else's life by walking around in a costume. Now, though, he just looked casual, comfortable, and pulled together, wearing slightly worn dark wash jeans, vintage-colored Air Jordans, and a button-down shirt.

But the most noticeable change took my breath away. Grownup Jordan filled my *–our–*doorframe with a body at least six inches taller than the last one I'd laid eyes on.

Plus, you know, the voice. It was no longer squeaky and quiet, and it slid beautifully over his tongue and past his brace-free, straight, white teeth.

I stood there gaping for some good, long seconds before Jordan waved his hand in front of my eyes. "Lizzie? You okay?"

"Oh my God, yes!" *No.* "Come in," I said, reaching for one of his duffle bags. "Just tired, you know, finishing up with the unpacking and -" The bag thunked to the ground as soon as he relinquished it, taking my shoulder with it. I grunted and stumbled.

"Whoa there!" he laughed. "Sorry about that." Jordan dropped the other duffle beside the first.

"Well," he said, running his hand back through his curls, which had lost some puff and gained some shine, "This is—I can't tell you how much I appreciate this. Really."

"No, no, I'm the one who's grateful," I babbled. "Well, to Kiera and to you. This could have turned out to be really shitty for me, but..." I let my eyes take in the whole new-and-improved Jordan package one more time "but it didn't."

"Same," he said, flashing that white grin at me again. "Uh, speaking of Kiera—would you mind shooting her a text to let her know I got here? It's already five and I kind of want to get unloaded and parked before dark."

"Yeah. I'll keep the door open," I said, before he turned and left to get some more of his stuff. With wide eyes and a shaking head, I punched in a call to Kiera. My head whirred while I listened to the phone ring.

"Hey, Lizzie!" she practically sang into the phone when she picked up. "Did JJ make it to your place?"

"He goes by JJ now?" I asked.

"Yeah. Didn't I tell you that?"

I could tell by the way she asked that she was probably trying to watch a TV show and paint her nails at the same time she was holding a conversation with me. "No, you didn't tell me that. You also didn't tell me that he's so..."

"What? Annoying? Cocky? Self-satisfied? Biggest head in the tri-state area?"

"Tall," I substituted, trying to collect my thoughts. "And he seems perfectly friendly."

Kiera scoffed. "Of course he's tall. You haven't seen him in six years. He hit a late growth spurt. And you think he's friendly? Just wait."

What, so now he wasn't friendly? She'd sworn up and down that he'd be a great roommate just a few days ago . "What did you get me into, Kiera?" I practically growled. "You told me I'd be fine with him living here."

"Oh my God, no, nothing serious. Just, you know. Jordan being a total obnoxious dweeb of a big brother, like he's always been. You know I love him. Nothing new. Just don't bug him and he won't bug you, I'm sure."

"Okay. He's just...he, um...he also got his braces off," I finished lamely.

"Lizzie. Yes. He no longer wears braces. He's a twenty-five-year old man. What's so surprising about that?"

That was when I heard his footsteps coming back up the stairs. "Maybe this place was available at the last minute because the elevator's busted," he called from one flight down. When he got to the top, though, I saw that he was smiling. "Good thing I'm an engineer. If I can fix it, maybe they'll take some off our rent, huh?"

Ah. So *there* was a little bit of that cockiness.

"Gotta go, Kiki," I breathed into the phone. She clicked off the call before I even finished the sentence.

"She didn't have time to say hi to me, huh?" Jordan said, grunting as he dropped a box right inside his bedroom door.

"No, and actually," I said, flashing him my most winning job-interview smile, "neither do I. You gonna be okay doing this unloading? I have a dinner date."

"Really," Jordan said, his eyebrows tenting up. "You must be pretty popular around here. Thought you and what's-his-face broke up like a week ago. Was there like a line of guys waiting for you, or something?" I didn't miss the quick up-down look he gave me as I bent at the knees to pick up my handbag.

I'd grown up quite a bit in six years, too, I realized. I'd figured out how to get rid of the stubborn frizz and flyaways that plagued my hair, found out which jeans made my ass look great without cutting off my circulation, learned about flattering vs. Drag queen-esque makeup, and grown a couple of cup sizes. Realizing all that gave me a burst of confidence, and I looked into his eyes while flashing him a giant smile. "With my old roommates," I said. "I've gotta get the keys back to them, and it's ladies' night at our favorite sushi place."

"Cool," Jordan said, moving back toward the door. "Well, if I crash before you get home…"

"See you tomorrow," I said, as breezily as I could manage, with a brush of my fingertips against his shoulder.

I sincerely hoped he was crashed out by the time I got home, I thought as I ducked into the Uber I ordered on my way down the stairs. I didn't think I wanted to know what slightly-tipsy Elizabeth Palmer would do when faced with a newly-hot Jordan Jacobs now living just one door away.

Just like old times.

CHAPTER 3

JORDAN

CHILL THE FUCK OUT, JJ. It was just Elizabeth Palmer. Generic, insipid, self-involved Lizzie P from Bertram Public High.

It turned out that if you fast-forwarded six years that little Lizzie Palmer turned totally fucking hot. Somehow the visual confirmation had hit me like a Mack truck, probably. I could hardly believe it, but something about seeing her again had my knees slightly weak. A cliché, but one hundred percent true.

Before I could think twice, I picked up my phone to text Kiera.

Jordan: You didn't tell me about Lizzie.

Kiera: Didn't tell you what? What did she do? She wasn't a crying mess, was she?

Jordan: No. Not at all.

Kiera: Please don't tell me that you are also surprised that she's aged six years.

Jordan: ...what does that mean? "Also?"
Kiera: ...
Kiera: ...
Kiera: Nothing.
Jordan: She's just different. You're right. Nothing.
Kiera: Okay big guy. Whatever you say.

Dammit. I could practically hear my kid sister teasing me from all the way across the state. She was probably singing the "Lizzie and JJ, sittin' in a tree" song in her head.

It only took another hour to haul the rest of my stuff up from the car. From the looks of Liz's boxes, she'd had a whole truckload of shit, and I felt damn proud of myself for keeping my possessions so minimal.

That observation only helped me take my thoughts on Lizzie back to acceptable territory the next time they strayed. She may have gotten hotter, and there may have been an undeniable spark between us when we saw each other again, but that didn't mean that it was going to be a good idea in any sense of the term to develop a crush on my new roommate, for God's sake.

Not to mention that there was absolutely nothing to indicate that she'd changed at all from when I'd known her in high school.

Still, my traitorous brain kept arguing with me. She'd graduated with a B.A. from UPenn—an Ivy League college. She couldn't have done that if she was brainless. And even though her dad worked for the biggest newspaper in Pittsburgh, she'd probably had to do something at least a little impressive to get an internship at Philly Illustrated in this economy.

I reminded myself as I sweated up and down the stairs, and then through the annoying process of putting sheets on my bed and locating my comforter, that none of it meant anything. I'd dated my fair share of girls at Stanford, and slept with a good handful. I was picky, too. I'd taken the smartest girls in our dorm out to dinner, bought drinks for only the brightest rising stars in the pre-med and pre-law programs. The reason I hadn't had a long term relationship with any of them was simple – none of them held my attention long enough. At the same time, I'd never dated anyone that made me feel like I could let my guard down. I wanted someone who interested me and made me feel at home, all at the same time. Though I was convinced it would happen eventually, at only twenty-five years old, I hadn't yet felt the need to rush into anything serious. What were the chances that I was moving in with the one girl who would be any different?

The last thing I hefted up from the car was my collection of weights and resistance bands. Yeah, I knew it was annoying to girls and pretty much everyone else when a guy kept weight equipment in his room, but I couldn't help it if my academic program was demanding. It wasn't my fault that NASA prioritized astronaut candidates in only the very best physical shape, and that the only time I had to work out some weeks was late at night while simultaneously looking through my textbooks.

Actually, maybe I could get a quick workout in now.

The whole time I jogged a few blocks' perimeter around my new place, I reminded myself that girls were a distraction, especially girls who wanted more of my time than I was willing or able to give them. Every time I thought that, though, another pesky image pushed rationality away. First, the silky swish of Lizzie's hair as it was freed from the strap of my duffel bag. The scent of it as it brushed against my shoulder. That smile, so bright and wide and, hell, *beautiful* now that she didn't have braces anymore.

Dammit. I could not have a crush on my roommate. Could. Not.

I sweated through some bicep curls and grunted out a couple hundred sit ups, the whole time trying to purge the image of the way Liz's tits peeked out of the upper hem of her shirt, just enough for me to see the very tops. The hundred pushups I did had no effect on the persistent picture of the tulip-curve of her hips in those form fitting jeans.

When I gave up and stripped down to shower, my dick sprung out of my shorts like Lizzie was spread out naked on my bed, wanting me, instead of just a fully-clothed picture in my mind. I groaned as I pulled the curtain shut, grateful that Liz had a plastic liner set up between it and the highly-stainable fabric, and took my dick in hand.

We'd only talked face to face for a few minutes, but hell if it wasn't enough to jack off to. I thanked heaven and all the angels that Lizzie wasn't home as I gripped myself in earnest, letting my thumb flick over the head and slide that little bit of precum all the way down my shaft. I imagined what that shiny-soft honey-colored hair would feel like brushing down over my stomach and pooling over my balls, how I could slide my fingers through it and grip her scalp gently as she took me in her mouth. Would I be able to smell its intoxicating perfume while she wrapped those perfect lips around me, licking and sucking like I was the most delicious thing she'd ever tasted?

Just the thought of it got me twice as hard, and I hadn't even soaped up yet. I unhanded myself just long enough to get some suds going, but when the memory of her voice popped into my head, so much deeper than the little-girl tone I remembered, I was right back in my own fantasy world. I could picture exactly how hot it would be for her to suck me off - she'd get an incredible rhythm going and work me over till I was nearly out of my mind. And then, when I finally slid inside her - those golden-brown and green eyes sparkled in that way that just made a guy want to look straight into them when he came, and her long, smooth neck would be incredible for nibbling right up until the moment that I was almost at my peak. More than that, Lizzie wasn't the kind of girl that made you want to shoot off and then roll over and say goodnight to.

No. I knew from the second she spoke to me, Liz had grown into the kind of woman who saw what she wanted and grabbed it like it had been hers all along. And in this shower fantasy, right here, right now, what that gorgeous girl wanted was me. Not just my dick in her mouth, but my body working inside hers, rasping against every ridge and playing across every tiny, miraculous muscle in that tight little channel of hers like a goddamn grand piano.

I felt myself harden even more against my palm, and I groaned at the thought of how wet she would feel under my fingers as I reached between us to thumb at her. That would be when she'd start to beg.

I imagined her heels digging into my calves and her nails piercing the skin of my back. God, I was almost there. I'd give her everything I had and then some, because holy Christ, I couldn't remember wanting anything as bad as I wanted her..

If anyone had told me jerking off could be better than half the real-life sex I'd had with actual women, I would have called them an idiot. But in that moment, I realized it was possible.

Apparently, all I had to do was imagine getting into bed with my kid sister's best friend.

Interesting, considering those partners of mine were so educated in human biology, and I was only barely acquainted with the all-grown-up and impossibly curvy Elizabeth Harriet Palmer.

I found a clean towel, wrapped it around my waist, and hastily swiped some of the steam off the mirror. I took a good look at my reflection - bags under my eyes from a long drive, sagging shoulders sore from hauling all that shit up three flights of stairs, an impromptu workout, and, of course, fucking myself silly in my brand new shower. I gave my reflection a withering look. "Nice job, Jacobs. You're eighteen years old again, huh?"

It didn't make much sense to me why the image of someone I'd just seen for the first time in six years would do a better job of getting me off than a real live girl. What I knew for sure, though, was that in my imagination had to be the only place I got to fuck Lizzie. I could not lose this apartment, because you couldn't be homeless and do well in the PhD. program at UPenn, and if we started dating and things got weird, I had to imagine that Liz kicking me out of our place would follow soon enough. Hell, my sister would probably drive out just to help her kick both my butt cheeks at once.

Luckily, I'd managed to exhaust myself enough that I drifted off into a dark, dreamless sleep. Seemed like I had more than one thing to thank Lizzie for today.

CHAPTER 4

LIZ

"YOU WANT ME TO DO WHAT?"

My first day at Philly Illustrated was not turning out to be the sunshine-filled dreamland I had, well, dreamed it would be.

"Listen, honey, you know we hired you as a favor to your dad, right? I mean, not that you're not qualified, but...."

This woman was dressed like a freaking Chico's catalog with a bit of fortune-teller chic thrown in for variety, yet she gave me the disdainful up-and-down eye raking that someone would normally give a prostitute that crashed a posh country club. I bit down on my lip, trying to quell any tears or curse words from breaking free.

"No, I know, and I'm totally willing to do anything. Honestly, I figured I'd be working on a story about garbage collectors or something...

"Yeah, but stories about garbage collectors don't fulfill this little affiliate piece we promised we'd write with funding from Cosmo. Now do they?"

I should have been grateful for the opportunity to write a piece for Philly Illustrated, a struggling but marginally well-known Philadelphia lifestyle publication, with Cosmo's name on it. It was just that the idea of it was so...smarmy.

"Listen, honey, you're cheap. Okay?"

My brow furrowed at her. I hoped I didn't live to regret being so transparent with my emotions.

Luckily, Monica didn't seem to notice. She shook her head, waving her manicured shiny-red talons in the air at me dismissively. "Not like a *slut*, that's not what I'm saying."

Thanks for that.

"It's just that we can't afford to hire *another* new girl specifically for this project, and all our writers are either dating, married, or gay. You can't expect me to assign the story about dating in Philly to one of *them*, now can you?"

Monica was my supervisor in my shiny new staff writer position at Philly Illustrated. She was excellent at steamrolling newbies into agreement with her before they even saw it coming.

I struggled to find words. "I guess not, but I -"

"And you told me yourself in our little chat over coffee that you and your boyfriend had just broken up, and I figured when you didn't flood your goddamn latte with tears of despair, you'd be okay maybe branching out a little bit. Aren't you? Four months of dates on us! Who knows, if you meet Mr. Right maybe we can spin it into sponsorships! Engagement rings! Wedding dresses! Free honeymoons! You could be just like Philly's own discount bachelorette!"

The image clarified in my mind - Liz Palmer, B-list Bachelorette of Philadelphia. Great.

I could see how Monica had gotten a job like this now, managing a magazine whose stories, realistically, barely passed as "journalism." Every sentence out of her mouth was like a freight train, and you either had to grab on to survive or get the hell out of the way. Without really realizing what I was doing, I bobbed my head at her words.

Even though I didn't agree with this idea. Not one bit.

"Okay, but it's not just dating, right?" I said. "The readers are gonna choose the guys I date?"

"We'll vet every choice first, honey. It'll be fine."

I'd only worked at this magazine for six hours, but my mind was already running wild imagining what Monica's idea of vetting someone was. If I was going to be Philly's discount bachelorette - which, yuck - then the guys she was going to choose would be discount bachelors - ridiculous caricatures of America's single men, specifically chosen to get readers to buy the slim daily paper.

Oh my God. This was going to be awful.

"Well..." I said, trying hard to infuse my voice with confidence in Monica's choices. "Could I get a seat at the vetting table?"

"Sure, honey. But listen. I just want you to focus on having fun and writing fabulous stories about these guys. Everything will be perfectly safe. Our girl Deanna will be with you taking pictures, okay?"

"Pictures? But I..."

"Enjoy yourself! Nice meals out on the town and maybe we can even get you set up with some cute outfits! Jewels, maybe! This is every single girl's dream, and you're gonna be the one to live it and write about it!"

Maybe Monica somehow had her finger on the pulse of every single girl's dream, but if that was true, then I was definitely a freak among my people. Besides the fact that I still hated thinking about myself as a single girl - with all my old college friends already light years ahead of me, settling into lifelong relationships or on the fast track to dream careers, this just made me feel pathetic. Like a sad, sad freak who was going to have to put herself on dating display for all of Philadelphia because she couldn't find another job, because she'd only gotten this one as a favor to her semi-powerful Daddy on the other side of the state.

Yeah. I had to suck it up.

So, I nodded again, swallowed back a lump in my throat, plastered a smile on my face, and said, "Okay. When do we start?"

"Right after you sign this little stack of papers," Monica said, hefting a small stack of pages filled with fine print onto her desk. "You know. Liability reasons. Non-disclosure agreements, waivers, stuff like that. You understand."

Oh, God. I was gonna be sick.

Luckily, most of the staff at Philly Illustrated, or Phill-Ill for short, seemed to leave the office by 6 PM. I'd never really considered how exhausting it would be to move from a few hours of classes every day to nine hours in an office. So many things were just sapping every ounce of energy out of me - smiling at every freaking person who made eye contact with me, constantly checking to make sure my hair, clothes, and makeup were in good shape, trying to master the ins and outs of the creaky desktop computer I'd been asked to use - security reasons, Monica was sure I'd understand - in a musty corner of a rather sparsely-outfitted third floor office.

Yeah. I was definitely not working at Vogue. Or even Seventeen Magazine.

All I'd wanted since I was a kid was to be a journalist reporting on politics. I'd somehow seen one episode of The West Wing, and I'd been hooked. The way so many people worked tirelessly, day after day, for the greater good was an inspiration. The fact that the press corps was so close to the process, and sometimes even influential, all the while keeping the President and his staff honest? Well, that was where I wanted to be. On Air Force One, in the bullpen, trading jabs with the White House Press Secretary.

I'd proven it in school, too. I'd worked my ass off and been the editor for UPenn's student paper, and even won an award or two. My professors swore I'd get a prime position at one of the biggest papers in the country when I graduated.

The shitty economy, and the decline it had caused in print media revenue, disagreed.

I trudged up the three flights of stairs to my new place - *our* new place - wincing with each step. Who the hell knew that three-inch heels got exponentially painful with every hour you walked on them? I made a halfhearted mental note to call the landlord about fixing the freaking elevator, knowing full well that I probably wouldn't get to it. Instead, I'd turn into one of those ladies who packed sneakers and socks in her work bag, looking like a tool the whole commute home.

God, I was old. Maybe I did need help finding dates.

One thing I knew for sure is that I probably wouldn't be able to open my own door when sharp knives of pain were shooting up from my stiletto heels up through my calves. Did they use these things as torture devices? They should. Need to get info from someone? Make her walk around in three-inch spike heels for ten hours. Done. She'll break every time. I shoved my new key into the lock and grunted when it didn't give a single bit of give in the lock. I jiggled, pushed in, and tried again.

Nothing. Dammit. The worst first day of anything I'd ever had to date and I couldn't even go into my half-put-together, unfamiliar place with no cable, no internet, and no food in the fridge.

My forehead fell into the cold metal door with faux-wood

covering, and I groaned in frustrated pain. Not even my freaking door was constructed from what I expected it to be. I planned to try the key again after allowing myself a few seconds of self-pity, but I didn't get the chance. The grind-and-click sound of the lock opening from the inside caused me to take in a deep breath of relief.

Jordan. Bless him, he was home.

I hurriedly stood up straight, shoved my feet back into my heels, and smoothed my hair. I hadn't forgotten how unexpectedly attractive Jordan had looked after six years and a six-hour drive down the Pennsylvania turnpike. Maybe he'd be as unexpectedly sweet and non-dweeby as he had been hot, and we could bond over my horrible experience.

He opened the door, wearing the same jeans and shoes as yesterday with a different colored shirt- red heather, today. It clung to his body a little tighter than yesterday's, though. I swallowed as I dragged my eyes up to his, somehow bright behind his thick glasses. He gave a soft chuckle at the sight of me, which immediately set me on the defensive. "What?" I grumped.

"Nothing," he said, his smile soft now. "You okay?"

I swallowed again. "Yeah." God, those eyes. I'd never thought dark eyes could be so multifaceted, so mesmerizing. "Just...thirsty."

"Hungry too, I hope," he said, stepping back and motioning for me to come in. "My stop at the UPenn office was shorter than I expected this morning, so I went shopping. And then I cooked."

The smell in our new place was freaking heavenly. I hadn't really eaten lunch - nobody had offered to take me out, like I imagined - *expected* - they would - and I obviously hadn't packed anything. But the other surprises of the day must have blocked out how absolutely ravenous I was. "Oh my God. Did you roast a chicken?"

Jordan nodded. "And some potatoes and my mom's famous collard greens."

My mouth watered. "You know how to make those?" Mama Jacobs – all the neighborhood kids had called her that – made the best collard greens I'd ever tasted.

"Don't sound so surprised. I've changed a lot since six years ago, you know. I asked her to teach me a couple years ago. Made her cry. It's my great grandmother's recipe." He shrugged. "I guess I'm not such a *dweeb* anymore. " The sparkle in his eyes when he emphasized that name I used to exclusively call him created a funny feeling in my gut - something between guilt and self-consciousness.

I stepped out of my shoes again and groaned. "Oh, God. I'm so sorry about-"

"No worries," he said, laughing and motioning for me to hand him my bag. "I *was* a dweeb at eighteen. And you were obnoxious at sixteen."

"Hey!" I said, feeling only a small sting before realizing how right he was. I mean, I must have been such a pain in the ass, always swooning over stupid fashion magazines and giggling about boys and school gossip, but I couldn't remember a single time that Jordan was ever truly mean to me and Kiera. He'd always been just a really good guy.

"Well," I said, unable to stop my eyes from raking down his body again. "I guess we've both grown up."

"Yeah. We really have." There was no mistaking that he held my gaze for just a moment longer than absolutely necessary when he said that. I tried to ignore the warmth gathering in my belly and cleared my throat again. Geez, he'd probably think I was contagious now or something.

God, Elizabeth, get some chill. You are an adult. You just broke up with your boyfriend. Control yourself.

The thing causing the heat, though, was more than just

Jordan's unexpected attractiveness. It was that being near him was making me feel things that I'd never felt around Josh, or any of the boyfriends that had come before him, for that matter. It was a magnetism that made me want to get closer and closer to him - which was exactly what I'd been doing, I realized. He'd walked around into our small little kitchen area to check on the chicken, and I realized with horror that I was practically standing on his heels. Abruptly, I turned and walked back to the loveseat in our little living room and plopped down.

This was the first time I'd sat on the furniture that had come with the place, and for a second, I was unbearably grateful that it didn't seem to be moldy or decrepit or gross. Between coming home to dinner being cooked for me and finally collapsing onto a clean, comfortable couch, I was beginning to think that, behind my faux wood door, in this little apartment with my new-old-totally-cute friend from my childhood, I'd actually get to feel at home.

"I guess Philly apartments don't really have room for dining room tables, huh?" Jordan called from the kitchen.

"I thought about finding a small one Josh and I could squeeze into that corner right by the front door but..." I trailed off, feeling my cheeks go pink, even though there was absolutely no reason for them to. Maybe I was ashamed of myself, for being so used to that pesky pre-planned future where Josh and I hosted dinner parties and played house in this little apartment until he graduated, got a well-paying job, letting me get paid next to nothing chasing stories, and bought me a real house.

"Well, hopefully coffee table dinner with JJ is a decent substitute." He stepped out of the kitchen, two plates in hand. I had literally never had a guy serve me homemade dinner at the end of a long day, but oh my God, I could get used to this.

I wrinkled my nose. "Do you always speak in the third person?"

Jordan laughed. "Actually, I don't think I *ever* do. Maybe the exhaustion of this crazy week is finally getting to me."

I met his eyes with a smile and murmured a "Thank you," before I leaned over my plate and dug in.

"So, the ex. Josh. Total dick, huh? Or is your heart really broken?"

I nearly choked on my first mouthful, and Jordan leaned over to slap me on the back. By the time I swallowed it down, thankfully without spitting anything onto my shirt, I'd at least figured out what to say. "Total dick," I said, pounding my chest and clearing my throat one more time. "I mean, you saw me. I was upset, but it was more about my future plans getting messed up than losing him."

"You don't miss him?"

I shrugged. "Miss what? Making sure he paid his rent on time? Being his designated driver at parties? Dealing with his stuck-up parents? Cooking him dinner? Nah," I said, leaning forward and taking a long drink from the glass of water that Jordan had plunked down next to my plate, letting a ring form on the cheap wood laminate. "I mean," I finished after I'd swallowed. "He never cooked for me. Ever."

I took another bite, taking my time chewing, savoring the spices. It was the most heavenly thing I'd ever tasted. Truly. Even including the Morimoto's sushi I treated myself to after I'd landed the internship.

Suddenly, I felt even more a need to explain myself. Namely, the version of me that had been so convinced that Josh and I would be together forever that I felt confident finding us an apartment to share.

"I know he doesn't sound like a gem," I blurted. "But he was exactly what I had pictured. You know? There was a path that my life would take, I'd imagined all of it, and when I met Josh…

he was exactly what I had imagined. He fit the picture. Perfectly."

Jordan's eyebrow ticked up, and instantly, I was mortified. I knew full well that Jordan and Kiera, being two of a very small number of kids with a black parent in our high school, sometimes met resistance from parents in our suburb when trying to date classmates. "That's not what I meant. I mean...not how he looked," I explained, hating the heat seeping into my cheeks. "He *was* white," I jabbered. "Is white. But that's not what it was. He was going to be a lawyer. He wanted to get a steady job and settle down and have kids. He never told me that, but it was just...part of the way he was brought up. Part of him. It's hard to explain, but when I saw him, it was like I'd found a puzzle piece I'd been hunting for. Even if the picture of my life is different from how I'd imagined it years ago, I still wanted to grab that piece. Then that made me want to make him fit into my life, even if he was never supposed to. You know?"

"

Jordan just nodded, observing me, like I was a perplexing painting in a gallery that he was enjoying trying to interpret. As a kid, he had been so reactionary, so self-conscious. Six years seemed to have changed all of that.

We ate in silence for a few minutes until Jordan leaned back against the couch, opposite me. "Either that chicken is incredible or you had a really long day, judging by the moans coming from over there."

My eyes went wide and I snapped my gaze to his. I had been *moaning*? Over *chicken*? God, this day just got more and more embarrassing, didn't it? But a wide smile from Jordan helped diffuse my mortification, and I gratefully returned it.

"Both," I said into my napkin, grabbing at any excuse to hide while I recovered. "Dinner tastes amazing, and yes, it was the shittiest day ever."

"Well, if you want to tell me all about it, I've got nothin' but time. We don't even have internet yet so I can't subject you to my Netflix queue."

I snorted and shook my head. "I can just guess what shows an engineer has on his list." I sighed. "You really want to hear it? I mean, I am lucky to have a job, and this really amounts to one extended First World Problem, but..."

"Seriously, Liz." Jordan pushed up from his seat and strode toward the kitchen, and I couldn't ignore the pang of worry that he was done talking to me for the night. But he pulled open the fridge, grabbed a bottle of red and a six-pack of IPA, and returned to his seat. "Have a drink with me. Tell me a story, before I get so bored that I would rather clean up the kitchen."

So I did. As he poured me a plastic glass of wine, I told him the whole awful day, from beginning to end. The shitty desk and computer, the condescending dismissiveness from Monica, and, finally, the details of my first and only assignment - the one that might also be my last, if I refused it or screwed it up.

"So that's it," I said, staring mournfully at the bottom of my now-empty glass "My job is to go out on dates with guys that Philadelphia votes on, and write about them."

"Okay, here's what gets me," Jordan said as he stacked our scraped-clean plates and utensils in a neat pile on the coffee table. "You don't even get to choose. That hardly seems...appropriate. Like, in terms of consent."

I scoffed. "It's definitely not. But, I mean, what Monica said is true. I'm lucky to have a job at all, it's an opportunity to get my name out there if I do a good job, and...I *am* single now. I guess."

"Maybe it'll be a good excuse for you to get back out there," Jordan said, suddenly examining the label on his beer bottle intently. "Although, I gotta say - and this may be the beers talking, so pardon me if I'm overstepping - but you seem pretty okay considering you were planning on eventually marrying this Josh guy."

I put my plastic cup down with perhaps a little too much force. "Did Kiera tell you that? God, so embarrassing," I moaned. "I mean, yes, half of my friends got engaged to their boyfriends right after graduation, and yes I had pipedreams about it, but honestly, that's mostly because I hate dating. *Hate it*, Jordan. And I just...Josh was so *perfect*, you know? Right career. Right friends. Right family. So cute. I mean. *So* cute. My parents loved him."

"Kiera didn't," Jordan muttered.

"Oh, Kiera." I waved him off, not even surprised to hear him say it. I knew how to tell when Kiera liked someone—the way she squealed my ear off on the phone, the way she made a interest board to plan an entire future—and she had never liked Josh. "She never thought anyone was good enough for me."

"Maybe nobody was," Jordan said, his gaze fixed on one of the baseboards. Then, like he was snapping out of a trance, he cleared his throat. "Whatever. Jerky Josh is out of the picture. You're starting a new chapter."

"I guess," I said, grimacing at Jordan's lame nickname for my ex. "But...you went to school wanting to be an astronaut, right? And here you are, getting a PhD in astronaut stuff. Your undergrad wasn't a colossal waste like mine was. You're here, learning what you love."

Jordan chuckled. "If only it were that simple. Actually becoming an astronaut is as much a pipe dream for me as becoming editor of the New York Times is for you."

"But...with the workouts and the perfect grades and your acceptance here, I thought it was pretty much a sure thing. Dream job on the horizon, and all that," I finished, realizing how simplistic the whole thing sounded only as the words left my mouth.

"Nah," he said, letting out a slow breath. "I've known since space camp when I was fourteen – remember that?"

"I do," I replied. "I remember trying to steal that hat you brought home and write "Nerd" above "Space" on the design."

"And I knew you would. Slept in that damn hat for weeks so Kiera couldn't snatch it."

I giggled at the memory. I'd been so stressed with adult life that remembering what it was like to be a kid was actually kind of a relief.

"Anyway," Jordan continued, "They always told us that if we wanted to go to space one day, it would take a whole lot of hard work and even more luck. Actually, the first piece of luck was not getting too tall. You have to be under six foot three."

"And you are..."

"Six foot two and a half," Jordan said. I could swear he adjusted in his seat then, sitting just a little taller. "And then it was school, school, and more school. Excellent grades in anything having to do with chem, math, engineering. Hundreds of hours of flight training, and then—"

"Wait, wait. You've flown a plane?" Something about the image of Jordan in a cockpit, headset arching over his short, springy curls and his hands commanding the controls, set every part of my body on edge.

"Yep. Solo. I could take you up some time if you want. Also went through SCUBA training and certification." He watched my reaction with an easy smile.

Had he just winked at me? I blinked hard and busied myself with crumpling up my napkin. Kiera hadn't told me any of this about Jordan. Not that I had asked her.

"So how do they get chosen? Astronauts?"

"After I get my PhD, I'll work for a while — two or three years max, because they don't want you to be too old when you fly up in space," Jordan said. "And then I'll apply for NASA

Candidate School. That's where the luck comes in. Every applicant will be just as qualified as I am, lots of them in almost exactly the same ways. Last year, there were six thousand applicants."

Just picturing six thousand literal rocket scientists and their collective brain power had my head spinning. "And how many slots are there?"

"Eight," Jordan said, his jaw setting into a hard angle.

"Eight hundred?"

"No hundred. Just eight. Half will be women, so that leaves my chances at about one in fifteen hundred. If my application is good enough. Just have to keep my eyes on the prize, you know? It's stupid, but I've had a checklist of things I need to do in order to become an astronaut since I was eight. Still have the original. Every time I check one thing off...I don't know. It keeps me going." He shrugged like it was no big deal.

"Wow," I said, feeling a sense of awe settle over me at the realization that Jordan's odds of actually traveling to space were nearly impossible, and that he was dead set on that goal anyway. "You are amazing." The words slipped out of my mouth before I could even put a check on the breathy voice that accompanied them.

Jordan hummed, shaking his head, as he settled back into his seat. He'd finished two beers but hadn't had anything to drink since then, half an hour ago.

"Really, besides a decent career," I continued, my tongue just a little loose and my head a tiny bit spinny with the wine, "I just want someone to come home to, I think. You can't come home to some rando that a few thousand giggling Philly women picked for you when they were bored online."

"Well, that's what I'm here for," Jordan said, that gorgeous bright smile stretching across his face again. "I mean...oh, God, that came out wrong...I wasn't trying to say...um, that is—I'm happy to cook dinner sometimes and keep you company. I'm not bringing up anything... more."

Maybe it was how soft the floor lamp lighting was in the dimming apartment, or maybe it was my happy belly and slightly tipsy head. But he was so cute right now, looking all warm and happy and rumpled. And... was he *blushing*? At this point, I was just trying hard not to crack up at how flustered he was. "You know what, Jordan?" I said, standing up to grab the plates and walk them into the kitchen. It was harder to stand up from the super-cushy couch than I would have thought, and I pitched toward the plates, tripping over my own feet.

"Whoa there, Lizzie P!" Jordan chuckled, catching me around the waist and guiding me back down to the couch. To his side of the couch. Our legs touched from knee to hip, his fingers trailed across my lower back as he loosened his grip on me, and his breath blew, warm and earthy-smelling, against my cheek. Our eyes met, and my breath caught. "What were you going to tell me, before you got up?"

My voice was distinctively breathier than it had been just seconds ago. "Oh. Um. Just...the good things is that at least I don't have to have sex with them. The guys I'm dating for work. I mean, just based on the setup of the whole thing, there won't be any expectations, you know? It wouldn't be fair to the other guys over the six months, and they all know what they signed up for, so..."

Jordan's left eyebrow arched up. "I guess that's something, but... you make it sound like a chore, or something."

"What? Sex?" The alcohol must have settled comfortably into my blood stream, because usually, when I talked about sex, I automatically lowered my voice. It wasn't that I was embarrassed, exactly, but sex talk felt like one of those deep, private aspects of someone's life not appropriate for casual discussion. For some reason, though, the words came out bold and challenging this time. Maybe...a little flirty? "I mean, okay, not to insult your entire gender, but... Jordan, come on." I forced a short chuckle. "It's not like my idea of a party."

"I honestly don't get it," he said, and the deepening furrow in his brow told me he was genuinely confused.

"Well, you know," I said, waving my heavier-than-normal feeling arm in the air at nothing. "It's like this: Kiss, tongue, grab, grope, squeeze boobs, maybe give a little blow job, pull down panties, get in position, in, out, in, out, *ohhh I'm gonna commmmmme*, stop, extract, roll over, go to sleep."

Jordan's mouth dropped open slightly, then closed again as he turned fully toward me. "I'm sorry. Are you saying that's what all sex is like? Just, like, robotic and...boring?"

I let out a little laugh and nodded like he was an idiot, until I realized that his shock had turned to disbelief. "I mean," I mumbled, "I've only done it with four guys. One in high school, a couple boyfriends here at UPenn, and then a one-night stand. But, yeah. That's pretty much the experience, at least on my end."

"No," Jordan said, rubbing a hand at the back of his ear and scooting back, away from me, putting distance between us. Oh, God. What had I said?

CHAPTER 5

JORDAN

"NO FUCKING WAY." I honestly couldn't believe my ears. Was this beautiful, cheerful girl seriously telling me that she'd basically been used as a sex toy for every single guy she'd ever slept with? Okay, that sounded crude, but seriously - what kind of an asshole doesn't at least stop to consider whether his girl is having a good time?

"Did I say something wrong?" Lizzie's eyes darted around the room, probably looking for an excuse to extract herself from this awkward conversation. Jesus, now I'd really fucked it up.

"No, no," I said, reaching out to grab her hand, half to keep her sitting there and half to let her know that I wasn't upset with her at all. I smoothed my thumb over the back of her hand, and I could swear I felt a little sighing gust of air rush past her lips. "No, I'm just saying - okay, I'm no expert. I'm not saying that." I shook my head, thanking everything holy that the dark tan hue of my skin rarely showed a blush. "It's just that, every time I've been, you know, *with* someone, half the fun has come from making sure she enjoys herself. You know?"

She scoffed, looking everywhere but at me. "Well, you know. It's not like I had a horrible time, I just—"

"Would rather have been watching TV?"

Liz looked down at where my thumb rubbed over her hand, bumping over her delicate wrist bone on every pass. "Maybe," she said. She pulled her plump bottom lip between her teeth, and I had to bite back a groan. How did girls do these impossibly sexy things without even trying to?

Or maybe she *was* trying. Suddenly, every single pornographic scene I'd imagined during last night's shower flooded my brain again, and every bit of blood rushed downward. Just feeling the soft skin of Lizzie's hip when I'd reached out to keep her from falling had gotten me half-hard, but now my cock was getting damn uncomfortable the more it strained against the zipper of my jeans. I peered down to look into Lizzie's eyes, and she looked up at me with wide doe-eyes. That look could have meant nothing, but maybe, just maybe, it meant an open door.

What the hell? Might as well go for it.

"How many of these guys you dated took the time to make sure you came before they did, Lizzie?"

She shrugged and looked up, eyes heavy-lidded and staring steadily into mine. Her soft smile was laced with curiosity, maybe a little playfulness. "None of them. That's unfortunately always been up to me. And I don't know if I ever have, you know—,during."

I shook my head back and forth slowly, squeezing her hand. "That's... well that's just a damn shame."

Lizzie arched an eyebrow, managed another barely-there shrug. Her body said she'd accepted the sad fact that no guy had ever had the pleasure of having her come undone around his fingers, that none of them had run their tongues over her sweet heat and sucked her clit until she screamed. But her eyes were still wide. Wondering. Challenging. "Guess there's nothing to be done about it now," she said softly, her voice rasping on the last word. "Not for a while, at least." She licked her lips and, somehow, I managed to speak.

"I could do something about it," I said, leaning forward just enough so that her shuddering breath brushed my cheek, just enough that she could probably sense my frantic heartbeat and twitching fingers.

Then, so fast I barely realized what was happening, her mouth tipped up to mine, her lips latching on like they'd been molded to fit there. Warmth flooded me and I groaned as I pushed my fingers back through her hair. After just a second or two, though, she pulled away, chest heaving, eyes wide with trepidation. "God, I'm sorry, Jordan."

I ran my palm up the outside of her thigh, desperate to keep her close to me, dying to touch her again. She might be pulling back, but I refused to mirror it. "For what? That was..."

"...amazing, I know. And if we keep going, I won't want to stop, and the last thing I want is for things to get weird. For so many reasons."

"Roommates," I nodded, keeping the unfortunate distance between us at a minimum.

"And Kiera. And work. God," she groaned, and I couldn't help thinking of her making the same noise while her body writhed under me. "I'm supposed to be professionally dating and reporting on it for the next four months and I can't have..."

I decided to be brave. If she was teetering on the edge of doing this, I wanted to give her stronger footing. She was right - this was a big decision, and I didn't want her to regret it one bit. I reached out and let my fingers graze the line of her jaw, tipping her face up to look at me. "You have to know I would never, ever hurt you. Never take advantage of you. Never make you do something you don't want to do."

She nodded slowly, not breaking eye contact, but not speaking, either. So, I took a deep breath and continued, "The only people that need to be involved in whatever happens between you and me are you," I leaned in, kissing the corner of her mouth, "...and me." I pulled back, leaving significantly less space between us than there had been before. Her breath ghosted out over my lips. "It doesn't have to be anything but a night with someone you know. Someone you trust."

"I want to," Lizzie whispered, her breaths growing heavier, faster.

I leaned down, pressing my forehead to hers, smiling before brushing our lips together and threading my fingers through the hair at the nape of her neck. "Then do," I managed before she closed the distance between us once again and kissed me, licking her way into my mouth almost immediately.

God, she really was thirsty. And I was going to give her exactly what she needed.

My hand slid easily up to her waist, and I dug my fingers in. This was one of the things I loved most about girls - the smooth, delicate feel of the clothes they wore, and how they gave way to soft, hot curves underneath. I had her blouse tugged out of her skirt within seconds, and she arched her back, pushing her chest ever closer to me in response.

Her kisses were firm and eager, each one carefully aimed for maximum contact as she cupped my jaw with her delicate fingers and guided my mouth to tip one way, then another, against hers.

My palms continued their path north until my thumbs brushed the underside of her breasts, dimly registering the lacy cotton that held them perfectly in place. There was no padding or pushing up here - her curves were one hundred percent, genuine Lizzie. I swiped my thumb up over her right breast. We both groaned when it rasped against her nipple, which already stood at attention, hard as a little pebble.

"Christ, Lizzie," I managed. "I want to see you."

She nodded, tugging her bottom lip between her teeth in what I was now one hundred percent sure was her demure lust-filled goddess signature move. "Bedroom?" She definitely wasn't a shy girl, but I still didn't expect the wicked flash in her eyes when she smiled at me.

I grinned in response and jumped to my feet in a second. In the next breath I bent down, slid one arm under her shoulder blades and another in the bends of her knees, and swept her up in a cradle hold.

She stretched out her neck and started mouthing at mine like she'd been wandering though the desert and had finally found an oasis in my skin.

My legs couldn't get us to my room fast enough, even though the rock-hardness of my dick was now making any kind of movement at all damn near impossible. I'd bought new high thread count, stone-gray sheets and a duvet set in a deeper steel color the day after I found out I'd gotten into UPenn. I'd done a lot of growing up in my five years at Stanford, for sure, but I'd never owned a stitch of adult bedding.

I honestly never thought I'd break it in this soon. Liz's grin up at me as I dropped her onto the mattress was pure sunshine, and I couldn't get my hands back on her body quickly enough. It was too bad she had entirely too many clothes on. "I want to see you," I repeated, my words thick with lust this time.

"The feeling is mutual," she said, all open confidence, before pushing herself up on her elbows and hooking her hands into the front of my jeans. "Shirt. Off."

"Yes ma'am," I said, grabbing the hem of my t-shirt and starting to tug it up. Then I paused. "But only if you'll let me help you with yours."

I hadn't slept with *that* many girls - a dozen or so - but I'd quickly learned that one of my favorite parts of this whole process was getting her shirt off. My theory was that girls tended to be a lot more confident about their top half than their bottom half. They knew their collarbones were beautiful, and they knew their breasts were generally a fan favorite of guys. They spread lotion over their shoulders and breastbones, they wore gorgeous underthings to perfectly cradle and frame their chests. They wanted guys to appreciate that part of their bodies, to take their time, to drink them in and admire and enjoy.

I'd never been more eager to do exactly that than I was in this moment.

Lizzie nodded with another of those impossibly sexy lip bites, and my shirt was off and tossed to the side in seconds. Then I planted a knee on either side of her waist, settled my weight over her, and got to work.

CHAPTER 6

LIZ

JORDAN'S FINGERS WERE CAREFUL, gentle, and deter-mined all at the same time. I was wearing a blouse with at least ten delicate little buttons holding it together, obscuring all but a tiny bit of my cleavage. Most guys would have been frustrated, struggled with the freaking thing so much that they tore it, and then made me do it myself. *He's an engineer,* I giddily reminded myself as he deftly flicked each little mother-of-pearl button from its fastener. I shivered at every brush of his fingers against my body, marveling how sensitive the skin just under my collar-bone and at the swell of my breast was to his touch. Finally, he reached the very last button on my top. When his thumb dipped into my navel in what had to be a deliberate move, I felt a sudden swell between my thighs, followed by a rush of slickness.

Unconsciously, I pushed my shoulders back into the bedding - the very soft, very grown-up bedding, I'd noticed. The movement caused my chest to rise up and my torso to dip, stretching my abs and basically laying out my body for Jordan like dinner on a silver platter.

Yeah, I'd noticed how unexpectedly hot he was when he'd

walked into my life - into our apartment - just twenty-four hours ago. But if anyone had told me yesterday that I'd want him this badly, I wouldn't have believed it.

Now, though, as he ran his fingers down the opening of my blouse, skin hot through my camisole, I would have done just about anything for more of Jordan Jacobs touching more of me. The warm mocha tone of his skin only looked better when the lean sinews of his biceps and abs were uncovered and bathed in the dim light from our hallway, and I reached out to run my hands from his lightly defined pecs down over his stomach. I didn't bother to stop my fingers when they ran into the light spray of hair that only got thicker as it disappeared into his jeans.

The very same jeans that teased me with a view of that little muscle that framed a guy's hips. They had to come off. Now.

I whimpered as I tugged on the waistband, but he slid his fingers under my palms and gently removed them. "Patience," he murmured as he lowered himself over me, pressing a long, soft kiss to my lips. "We have all night. Right?"

I swept my tongue over his bottom lip before I answered him, desperate to taste more and more of him. "Yeah, but..."

"Let me do what no other guy has bothered to do for you, okay? Let me take care of you. Let me show you what it can be like."

My heart swelled with such unexpected warmth then, but it was quickly replaced by burning lust when he skimmed my camisole up my torso and over my head, letting it fall in a soft heap on the floor. I pulled him back to me for another long, hard kiss. Within seconds, it turned heated, his tongue sweeping my mouth before he pulled away, lightly tugging my bottom lip between his teeth. I sighed and let my cheek fall against his cool pillowcase. "That's good," I murmured, squeezing my thighs together to try to dull some of the insistent - and surprising -

need gathering there. His tongue danced along the curve just behind my ear, following the hot veins of my neck down, down, down, until he locked his lips around the end of my collarbone and sucked there, ending with a nip of his teeth and one more swipe of his tongue to soothe the little hurt there.

A satisfied moan rumbled deep in my throat, and I swore he smirked before running his finger along my bra strap while kissing even further down, hovering tantalizingly over the swell of my breast. Millimeter by agonizing millimeter, he edged the strap down so that my shoulder was bare, then gazed at it with a soft, satisfied smile. "Absolutely gorgeous," he said, the low, reverent tone in his voice taking my breath away. I squirmed, trying to reach my hands around to undo the bra completely, growling in frustration.

"Liz," he said in that deep, smooth voice, "Let me. Remember?" He slid back up, gliding his arms under me and lapping at the edges of my mouth like he was parched for more.

While his tongue dipped languidly between my lips, his fingers wriggled under my back and deftly snapped open my bra.

"Where did you learn how to do that?" I asked, surprised at how soft and low my voice was, like I was subconsciously changing to match him.

"I went to college for five years?" he answered with a chuckle. "Besides, I'm an engineer. I know how to make complicated machinery with lots of parts work exactly the way I want it to." His fingers brushed smooth lines over my ribs and under the wire of my bra, lifting it away and dropping it to the floor like he was performing some kind of holy act.

Now, every girl on the planet knows how her boobs look best, and my particular rack was not flattered much by lying down. So I pushed up on my elbows, forcing Jordan to sit up completely. His eyes danced as he watched me, then maneuvered to sitting on his heels, clutched at my waist, and pulled me to him so my thighs were wrapped around his hips. He stretched his neck up to kiss me again, and I moaned into his mouth. Somehow, with one of his thumbs digging in just under my hip bone and another reaching up to tease at my nipple, I felt more powerful than I had ever imagined I could in the bedroom.

He dipped his lips down until his nose brushed against the underside of my breast, and it was like he'd flipped a switch inside me. I wanted his mouth doing more than licking, brushing, whispering against me - I wanted him to devour me. I thrust my chest forward and he growled, sucking one nipple deep into his mouth, and twisting the other into a hard, tight peak within seconds.

I'd had a few guys pay attention to my chest, but never like this - most wanted to lick my tits like an ice cream cone, like they were playthings; little fidget toys dangling from my body they could amuse themselves with until the main event. Jordan was different from the beginning. At the slightest encouragement, he gave me more of what made me moan - his teeth gently scraping against my areola as he laved his tongue along the lower swoop of each breast, palm hot as he lifted and squeezed the other.

Whatever fullness I'd felt between my legs when he'd first taken me to bed had expanded to an almost unbearable tension between my thighs. I'd heard of girls begging in bed, heard that it turned some guys on, but I'd never been brought the precipice of something enticing enough to beg for. Tonight was different.

"Please, Jordan," I managed to rasp out. "Touch me."

I felt his growl of agreement deep in his chest, and my lips twitched up through my panting breaths at the thought that, as much as Jordan swore this was for me, he seemed to be enjoying himself at least as much as I was.

He pushed up on his knees, dropping me back with a soft

thud onto the mattress, sending my hair splaying out against the pillows and making me feel enticing as an ice cream sundae on a hot summer day. My skirt was gone in the next instant, victim to his clever hands. He licked his lips as he crawled toward me on the mattress, then dropped to his side next to me and pressed a hot, rough kiss to my mouth. His palm dragged down between my breasts, over my stomach, and he wiggled his fingers ever so slightly as he went, a preview what he had in store for me.

They pushed past the band of my panties, raked through the trimmed curls underneath, and slid between my legs like that had been their anticipated destination this whole time. A grunt of satisfaction rumbled from his throat. "Jesus, you're so wet."

After a few moments of slicking his fingers through my wetness, his kisses grew harder, faster, and then all of a sudden, he pulled away, growling, then mouthing at my shoulders, chest, and ribs again. I was about to ask what was wrong before I realized that he was kissing a determined path down to where his hand had just been.

Apprehension twisted in my gut, threatening to dispel the arousal growing there.

"This is, uh..." I cleared my throat. "It's a first for me."

"Which part?" he mumbled against my hip bone as he let his lips take the same path his fingers had. He nipped at the small protrusion of bone from the curve of my hip, then licked at it. He was so close to where I wanted him, yet entirely too far away. My hips twitched upward, desperate to have him, any part of him, working against the unbearable swell at my core.

"All of it," I moaned, letting my hips push just a bit farther, hoping he got it this time. "But especially your mouth. There."

His lips tugged up into a tiny smile, then he dipped his head and kissed a line along where my thigh met my pussy. I could feel his breath on my clit, and with how worked up I already was, it was almost enough to send me into a frenzy.

"Jordan, please," I said, my words more a desperate whimper than anything resembling coherent speech.

There it was. For the first time in my life, I was begging a guy to do things to me.

And I wasn't the least bit embarrassed.

The room had darkened to the pale blue of an early spring evening, and the passing cars outside our windows painted streaks of white noise through the air around us. Jordan's gray sheets and his scent all over them - probably just a laundry detergent I wasn't used to plus whatever cologne rubbed off from his skin last night - were foreign enough, combined with the rest of this new-to-me apartment, to completely lose myself. I wasn't Elizabeth Palmer, recent loser grad of the UPenn journalism program who couldn't get a decent job, not even with her dad's connections - I was writhing, nearly naked, beneath the very adept attentions of an incredibly sexy guy I'd hardly thought about for the past six years, feeling things nobody had ever made my body feel before, and enjoying myself very, very much.

All it took was one more whimper for him to slide his fingers all the way down through my folds and back up again, making a very obvious slicking sound and sending a sizzling jolt of lust through me. Instinctively, I tensed, whether chasing the growing warmth at my center or trying to quell it, I couldn't have said. He shifted at that, settling his chest over my thighs, keeping one hand gently brushing against my wetness and sliding the other firmly back up over my stomach. "Relax," he repeated, letting his palm lay heavy on my navel, a reminder of his instructions.

I groaned in surrender to a tension I didn't even know I'd been fighting. I let my muscles loose, allowing the mattress to support my body and the sheets cradle me in a nest I never wanted to leave. The next time Jordan dipped his fingers down, he pressed the tip of one in and out, in and out, each time trailing along one of my walls. I shivered, letting out a breathy moan to let him know just how much I welcomed the invasion.

Once again, his lips traveled over my skin, making me enjoy their journey as much as their final destination. Unlike the way he'd used his fingers, he dove in with his mouth like my pussy was a decadent dessert he couldn't wait a second longer to enjoy. A hot, open-mouthed kiss to my clit was all I needed to go into a full-on frenzy, barely able to keep breathing in and out, let alone keep my hips from jolting off the bed once again. I would have sworn Jordan chuckled then, pressing once again down on my belly, all at once caring and commanding.

"That's okay, then?" he asked, a slight hint of teasing in his tone, even though he clearly had very little intention of teasing me tonight.

"Oh God, yes," I moaned, the words rasping out of my throat in pure supplication. "Don't stop."

His tongue went back between my legs eagerly, and he only half-managed to control my hips, keeping the movement down to a gentle thrust in time with his licks. The wet warmth of his mouth perfectly met the little throbs of need pulsing through my center, and with each movement of his lips, the noises rolling off my tongue became throatier, needier. A coil of desperation for whatever lay at the end of this path wound tighter in me every second and reached a nearly unbearable tension when Jordan's fingers brushed through my folds once more.

Gently, he pushed one, then two fingers inside me, mapping the most secret part of my body with the ridges of his fingerprints. I rocked my hips against his hand, only for him to pull out again. A cry of half-agony, half-indignation broke past my lips, but half a second later, he'd replaced one finger with two, tracing magical patterns inside me, like he could touch and feel the tension there and, instead of relieving it, would be content to sit and memorize its shape and weight for hours.

I would be content with no such thing. Not now that he'd started.

Even though his fingers worked patiently, the rasp of his tongue against my clit became faster, more intense, like he'd been climbing a mountain all this time and now, seeing the peak, was newly encouraged. Every nerve ending seemed to have shown up for this party, and I was sure I could feel individual taste buds collecting the drops of my arousal and drinking them in. Suddenly, the pressure on my clit changed. Jordan stopped reaching his tongue out to taste it and finally went all in, wrapping his lips around the tiny bundle of nerves and flicking it back and forth, letting it scrape against his teeth.

"Oh... oh my Godddd," I keened in surprise as my head flopped to the side, the coolness of the pillowcase against my cheek a welcome oasis in this bubble of heat Jordan had suspended me in. But I didn't have much time to get used to that before his fingers began to move with purpose, too, joining together and hooking upward into my channel. He pressed them both into the small, rough spot of flesh there with a steady, firm pulse.

He'd just lit the fuse on the grand finale of fireworks on the fourth of freaking July.

Every cell of my body, every fiber of my being, turned its attention to that one deep, throbbing heat inside me, pulling in farther and farther, tighter and tighter, until my body just couldn't hold it back any more. A deep, consuming warmth crashed over my whole body in waves, and I let out a heady, keening gasp as my neck bent straight back, my forehead pressing into the pillows as I gasped helplessly.

Slowly, I relaxed, the air in Jordan's room suddenly cool against my sweat-sheened skin. The shattered pieces of my reality slowly gathered themselves back together under Jordan's gentle, rhythmic touch, like iron shavings to a strong magnet. His fingertips skimmed over my belly, down one thigh, then back up again and down the other side. One breath at a time, my chest stopped heaving. The empty spaces between my muscles and bones and skin started to fill with a deep, pleasant weight, and I let Jordan's soft sheets and strong arm cradle me as I recovered.

Finally, I felt that I could open my eyes. He was waiting for me, and his deep brown eyes looked into mine with a look of tenderness and amazement and lust and excitement, all rolled in one. The amazing full feeling I'd felt down low just minutes ago seemed to have migrated to my heart, now so full-up I could swear it would burst.

Jordan scooted up and brushed his talented fingertips along my hairline, tucking a stray, slightly-sweaty strand of hair behind my ear. The delicious smooth weight of his torso half-pressing down on mine was a grounding comfort, and I hummed in approval. He watched me, curious and sweet, and I gazed back for a few moments until I realized he was waiting for me to say something.

"That was..." I breathed, at a total loss for words. "Wow," I finished lamely. "Thank you," I said, watching the crinkle of his eye with his little smile, suddenly wanting very badly to trace the planes and contours of his face with my own fingertips.

He shook his head, and I became focused on his curls. When had they gone from geeky to so completely touchable and sexy? *Probably about the same time he got pecs and a six-pack, idiot.*

"Don't thank me," he said, letting his forehead touch my shoulder for the briefest second. "I enjoyed myself just as much as you did."

My eyebrow arched up, and I raised my head as much as I

could manage. "I find that very hard to believe," I said, sighing at the boneless feeling in all my limbs and letting my head fall back to the pillow once again.

"Yeah?" he grinned. God, that smile was infectious, and I swore I could have stared at it all night, even though I knew it was a clear sign of Jordan's rapidly growing cockiness.

"Don't let your head swell up too much over this, but...yeah," I said, my voice growing softer on the last word as I drew my bottom lip behind my teeth. "It, um...I don't know what you did? But I've never felt anything even close to *that* before."

He propped himself up on one elbow, shaking his head a bit like he couldn't believe what I was saying. "Never? Like...never had an orgasm before?"

"Not one like that? Not even, um...not even one I gave myself. You, my friend, are a total outlier. Completely unique."

The grin that stretched across his face then brought a giggle bubbling out of my throat. "Yeah, yeah. We're both pretty happy about it," I said through a smile of my own. "So, you know. Thank you."

He reached up and tipped the brim of an invisible cowboy hat, winking at me. "Much obliged, ma'am," he said in an exaggerated Southern accent.

Finally regaining some strength in my arms, I giggled and swatted his shoulder. "Okay. Never do that again."

He chuckled, finally flopping to his back beside me. We spent a few seconds gazing at the ceiling. I was just grateful he wasn't staring at me anymore because I could finally let the grin really take over. I'd just had the best orgasm of my entire life, and hell if it didn't make my entire day shift from the realm of Entirely Shitty to the Land of Completely Fantastically Extraordinary.

God, I'd probably needed to come like that more than I imagined.

"Do you need anything?" Jordan asked quietly, turning his head to me again. "Washcloth, a glass of water? More wine?"

He started to inch toward the edge of the bed, and something deep in my chest panged. Before I could even think about it, my hand darted out and grabbed his arm. "Wait, are we—we aren't—I mean, we're not done, are we?"

CHAPTER 7

JORDAN

HER EYES WERE SHOCKED and wide, and I swore up and down that no girl's face had ever made me want to do anything more than Liz's had. Her hazel-swirled-with-green retinas bordered on hypnotic.

I reversed course immediately, sliding back under the covers just in time for my cock to begin its fast re-ascension. It was like Jesus Christ himself, except I was sure in this moment that Liz's body was more heavenly than anything He would have been headed for, and my cock sure as hell wasn't going to take three days to arrive there.

But I did want to be sure. My offer to Liz, my desire to show her what pleasure could be like, had been open and real, no strings attached. Obviously, I'd been damn eager to get my mouth on that delicious body of hers, and the fact that she'd never been treated like a real lady in bed was the travesty that sent me on the give-Lizzie-an-epic-orgasm warpath. I wasn't expecting anything more from her than to let me show her how a nice guy treats a girl like her in bed, but I sure as hell wasn't going to complain if she wanted to return the favor.

Five years at Stanford really had made me a genius, the

most important evidence of which now was the fact that I'd kept the box of condoms from my nightstand in California in the same box as my bedding. Sheets went into the washer, and condoms went right to their new home on the opposite coast.

Not that I was thinking of anyone in particular to use them with when I dropped them in there. Not that I found myself slipping into daydreams about Lizzie and her shiny hair and bright smile and perfectly grabbable ass since I'd spent some mental time with her in the shower the night before.

Okay, I had. Whatever. Now that she was offering, no harm, no foul, right?

"We don't have to be done," I growled, rolling myself over her and propping up on my forearms. She wasn't a tiny little thing that would be crushed by my weight, not by any means, but I still didn't think it would be a good idea to suffocate her after the way I'd just ratcheted her heart rate up five minutes ago.

Just thinking of it put a smug smile on my face. I wondered whether, if I licked my lips, I'd still be able to taste a tiny bit of her juices lingering there.

I'd be lying if I said my heart rate hadn't gone right up with hers. I'd never been with a girl as responsive as she was to every single contact between my fingers and her skin, never been so turned on by the sounds coming out any girl's mouth, never gotten so hard going down on a girl because I was imagining that mouth on my cock while I sucked on her clit.

Every other girl I'd been with had been a little flustered while giving me oral sex instructions - a geeky engineering student had to learn somehow - or only humored me with half-hearted grunts when I wasn't hitting exactly the right spot. But Liz? She loved every second of what I did to her, and it felt damn good. It was enough to get a guy addicted.

"Good," she said, smacking a kiss to my mouth and

following it with a teasing smile. I rocked against her almost instinctively, making sure she could feel just how hard I'd gotten in the last twenty seconds since she'd pulled me back to bed. She sucked in a breath and I could have sworn her eyes rolled back a little, too. She ghosted another kiss against my lips. "Do you...have something?"

I grinned wolfishly at her. This was one of the things other guys didn't realize - if you go down on a girl, it's a near guarantee that when it's time to get to the hips-to-hips portion of the evening, she'll be wet, ready, and dying to have your cock inside her. "Yep."

"Wow, are you like some sexual boy scout now?" she teased. I tilted my head to the side. I didn't want to talk about experience, or ex-girlfriends, or whether I was looking for something more serious - not now. Thankfully, judging by her little laugh after she asked the question, she wasn't either.

"Compared to the last time you saw me? I would hope so." I growled as I kissed away the joke, and stretched an arm to fumble in my drawer, pulling a little foil packet out of it triumphantly.

I was still wearing my pesky pajama pants, but Liz was already shoving her fingers into the waistband, raking her nails over my ass and making my cock even more rigid. I sat back on my heels, pulled them halfway down, rolled the condom on, and kicked them the rest of the way off as I stretched back out over her.

I supported myself on one elbow and brushed the hair from her forehead. "You okay?" I murmured an inch from her lips.

She nodded and reached down, wrapping a warm and steady hand around me. "Very, very okay," she said, and in the next instant, I pushed into her, bit by bit, trying to assess how we'd fit together. How fast I could go.

As I pressed in, she pushed up, and I groaned at the realization that we fit together fucking perfectly. Every centimeter of her was exactly snug enough to stoke a hot fire inside me, and just slick enough to let me bury myself inside her with a single thrust.

Her head tipped back again, mouth dropping open in a silent moan, and I let my eyes flutter closed, giving myself over to the deep, dark pleasure coursing through my veins. It wasn't until Liz squeezed herself around me that I let my head drop to her shoulder and began a slow, steady rhythm, pulling back and giving in, over and over. I could have done this forever.

"Fuck, Liz," I managed to grunt when that light electric current started buzzing through my limbs, signaling the beginning of the end. We couldn't have been doing this for more than a few minutes, and I couldn't help but feel a flash of embarrassment for all I'd talked myself up. Dammit. "I'm so close," I ground out, breathing hot air against her neck.

She grinned at me and flicked an eyebrow upward. Then she unhooked her arms from where she'd settled them along my shoulder blades, cupped my ass in her palms, and squeezed the next time I was completely inside her. "Good," she said. "That's the goal, isn't it?"

"But...are you?" I was panting now, a man fighting ultimate sensation and chasing it at the same time.

She licked her lips and twisted her hips so that her walls squeezed around me in a completely new way. A moan dropped from my lips, and as much as I wanted to hold back, my movements only sped up. "You already took care of me," she said, her soft kiss against my temple standing out in sharp contrast to the way I was snapping my hips against hers.

I shook my head, dragging my forehead back and forth on her collarbone. "The goal," I said, allowing a deep rumble of pleasure to break through my words, "is twice. At least. You don't need... unh... recovery time like I do."

I pulled back to look at her, and her expression was all amusement. "That's really not necessary," she whispered with that teasing little smirk. "I'm enjoying this very much. Whether I come again or not."

Obviously, she had no idea what she was missing. Giving a girl an orgasm with penetration could be difficult, but was certainly not impossible, and I intended to at least try. She was trusting me to take care of her tonight, and I planned to do just that.

I twisted to the right, just enough to hook her leg under my arm and slide it up so that the back of her thigh rested on my shoulder, then thrust in hard. Her eyes squeezed shut and her mouth dropped open in a silent moaning 'o.' I grinned in satisfaction. If I'd had a free hand to pump in the air right in that moment, I would've.

She was pulling in little gasps every time I filled her, exhaling when I pulled out. "Oh my God, Jordan, that's - ahhh! - right there. Jesus, that's - unhh - incredible." Her pitch got higher with every passing second, so I slowed my thrusts, making them harder, more powerful. The deep groan that came rumbling out of her then filled me with satisfaction. Maybe I was going to manage this after all.

I was starting to lose focus, though, the deeper penetration sending me into a frenzy of need. I was crazed, chasing what I could already tell would be one of the most incredible orgasms I'd ever had.

"Unhh, Jordan, I'm gonna -" and then she arched up higher than I thought was possible, bumping our hip bones together and sending me into a frantic crescendo of motion. I quickly lost my rhythm and didn't give a single shit about it.

I slid a hand to the small of her back, holding her hard against me. "Come on babe, I've got you. Come for me, Lizzie," I growled against her earlobe.

That did it. She screamed my name and strings of curses and nonsense as her pussy clenched around my cock, and I drove into her like my life depended on it. Every muscle in my body tensed then, and I let loose an insanely animalistic half-groan, half-growl as my vision blurred at the edges and I gave myself over to the pleasure coursing hot through my veins.

I stayed deep inside her for precious seconds before my limbs began to shake. Reluctantly, I fell to her side, loving the cool air on my skin but hating the fact that I wasn't pressed up against her anymore. I wondered if I'd ever get to touch her like that again.

After all, I was the one who said this could just be a one-time thing if she wanted, that it would be okay with me. But now, after everything she'd made me feel? I wasn't so sure if that was true at all.

Fortunately, Liz's still-breathless voice distracted me. "Holy crap, Jordan. I've never - I mean, that was - I didn't think girls could do that more than once in - you know, I'd *read* that it was possible, but I kind of thought those girls were exaggerating. Just...whoa."

I managed to turn my head to look at her. "Yeah?"

"Yeah," she chuckled. "Definitely." After another few breaths, she murmured, "Thank you."

"Hey. You were amazing," I panted, realizing that I hadn't complimented her fucking incredible performance yet. The truth was, I realized, it was less how she moved and more who she *was* that I found so completely engrossing. The way her smiled made my heart soar, the way her moans spurned me on, the way her pussy perfectly clenched around me, and that look she gave me, like she wanted me desperately and completely trusted me at the same time - it was all irresistible. Addictive.

My heart twisted as the realization swept over me - I didn't know how to tell a girl I'd promised just one roll in the hay, just to relieve some stress, that I kind of wanted to do it again. And maybe again after that. It twisted even more when I realized how badly I wanted her to stay here, next to me, in my bed. Even though that made no sense. We'd both known what this was when we started. Right?

It didn't help when she rolled to her side and slid her arm over my waist. "Kiera did not tell me that you'd gotten so cut," she said drowsily, tracing lazy patterns over my abs. Her eyelids were already drooping, her head pressing heavy into the pillow. I turned my body toward hers just enough to reach up and let my fingers run over her hair. It was so damn soft. Next time I'd have to somehow get her to run it over my skin, just to see what that did to me.

There probably won't even be a next time, you perv. Chill the fuck out.

"Astronaut goals," I murmured, watching her eyelids go all the way shut, stay that way for a full second, then drag open again. "You have to be in perfect shape to even be considered. Have to start years in advance."

"Mmmm," she said, her lips curving into a smile. "Well, I really appreciate the side effects of your career goals, Rocket Man."

That made me laugh, and before I could talk myself out of it, I slid my other arm under her and pulled her close. She didn't miss a beat, snuggling into my side like she'd done it a thousand times, and would do it a thousand times more. Her hair slid over my bicep, and just that contact had my cock halfheartedly trying to twitch back to life.

"I'm just gonna close my eyes for a second..." she managed before her body grew heavy against mine and her breathing slowed.

I kissed the top of her head and pulled the covers over us with a sigh. "Goodnight, Lizzie P."

I snuggled into her, sighing my pleasure into her hair. My last thought before drifting off?

I'd promised her this wouldn't be weird, that we could be just friends. After just once together, I was already enjoying this much more than I anticipated.

I was in a whole hell of a lot of trouble.

When I woke, it was morning, judging by the harsh light slicing through my bedroom window and directly onto my face, much later than I'd woken up in a long time. I rolled, burying my face in the pillow beside me and groaning. A deep breath in filled my nose with a fresh, distinctly feminine, scent.

In a rush, the events of last night came back to me. One drink with my kid sister's best friend and my new roommate. Her seeming nonchalant about never having had good sex in her life, and looking more and more delicious with every word she spoke. Me coming on to her, offering to "help."

I rolled onto my back, letting the sun assault my eyes again, rubbing my palms up and down slowly over my face, muffling the groan that passed my lips. The sex had been incredible, Liz was incredible, but oh my god, we were *roommates*. At least she wasn't lying here now, witnessing my flood of indecision over what it all meant and what the fuck I was supposed to do now.

It was with my next deep breath that I smelled the heavenly aroma of coffee wafting through the air. There was no resisting seeing her now. My successful cramming of five years of engineering school into four had turned coffee from a mere beverage to an elixir of life, and if I didn't get some soon, I'd be dead.

Our apartment let in so much natural light that it made the lone beam sneaking through my windows look puny. I blinked against the brightness, only realizing after I'd stepped out into our common area that I hadn't put a shirt on.

"Morning, dweeb." Liz turned to greet me, coffee cup in hand, and leaned against the counter where stared at me, smirking. Her smooth, shining hair seemed to arc over her shoulder in slow-motion, sending the same scent that was stuck on my pillow right back toward me, and for a split second the only thing I could think was how badly I wanted to touch it again.

She'd already dressed for work, in a crisp white button down, open to show just a little cleavage, black pencil skirt that hugged her ass perfectly, and a little red jacket that flared at the waist. Her outfit was practically a diagram for all the places I most loved grabbing and squeezing her the night before.

I only realized that I hadn't answered when she started talking again. "I made plenty of coffee for the both of us. I don't know how you take it, but if you want to get your own coffee pot that's fine with me. You got stuff to do today?"

It was a completely normal conversation, between two roommates. Not between two people who had engaged in what I thought was pretty incredible sex the night before. But I had to say something, eventually. "Uh, thanks. I'm not picky."

"Good," she said, clearly absorbed in pouring the rest of her coffee into a travel mug and gathering her phone, keys, and bag. "I assume you have UPenn stuff today. Need any help finding anything? University City's pretty straightforward, but..."

"Uh, no," I said, blinking and stretching my neck, hoping that would bring me a more level head for this conversation. "Thanks."

Then she walked right past me, to the door, and placed her palm on the handle. My feet were frozen in place, my face slack, watching her to see what she would do next. She still had one foot in the apartment when she turned around and smiled at me with an adorable flick of her eyebrow. "Thanks for last night. It was really nice."

Then she was gone.

Dammit. Obviously, she had a firm grasp on this whole situation, and I had never felt more lost.

CHAPTER 8

LIZ

WORKING at Philly Illustrated got a tiny bit more bearable every day. The knot of nerves in my stomach that had formed when I'd been bombarded by surprise after unwelcome surprise on that first day began to loosen a bit. Over the next week or so, I made my cube homier, got to know some of the other underlings in the office, and figured out I should use the bathroom on the floor below our office if I wanted to avoid the leer of the creepy dude from HR.

I found out that the dating project would not be my only focus - I'd also be proofing others' articles, and Monica even gave me a little freedom to make editorial suggestions for them. She would decide if they had any merit before passing them on, but, as my father reminded me, learning why I was wrong about something I was still learning. This was an internship, and I was here to learn.

I tried to tamp down the creeping horror over the fact that I'd spent four years learning about journalism to get this internship, where I was just supposed to do more learning. When would it end? Would anyone ever believe in me as a journalist? I hated the feeling that not only did I not know where that road was, but I didn't even know where it started.

As much as I hated to admit it, the path might have to start with dating several random guys and writing about the experience.

I sighed as I read over Monica's response to my latest email - she thought including reviews of local restaurants and venues would be a good choice, as long as they agreed to pitch in to sponsor us, and as long as I could convince them to do so. Great. So now I was supposed to be a ad sales girl.

Chin up, Elizabeth. She liked one of your suggestions out of the dozen you gave - that's better than nothing.

I almost closed out the email before catching the last line above her standard signature.

"Now, for something entirely different - we've got your first three date candidates, and we're putting them on the site for a vote tomorrow. Want to check over the copy?"

I bit back a groan of frustration, lowered my forehead to the single empty space on my pitifully small desk, and softly banged it there several times. Then I pulled myself together, sat up, brushed my hair off my forehead, and blew out a long breath.

Then I pasted a smile on my face - they said that just forcing yourself to smile could make your emails sound more positive - and started to type.

Thanks for the suggestions! I'm learning tons from you. :)

I'd love to see the guys' write ups. This is so much better than Cupid's Arrow!

. . .

EHP

I sighed and clicked send. It was *not* better than Cupid's Arrow, the dating site my mom and sister had bugged me to sign up for as soon as Josh dumped my ass, and only slightly better than Sparkplug, the dating app where guys seemed to feel widely at liberty to send nasty private messages and, occasionally, dick pics, at all hours.

The email came back from Monica almost immediately.

Cool. Alphonso put these together and we're about to send them to a little focus group at UPenn. Let us know what you think.

I groaned again. That focus group was probably made of students I'd been walking past on campus just weeks ago. Hopefully they didn't recognize my name.

1. "Prince Charming"

I love nothing more than treating my date like a Princess. Nothing is too good for the beautiful women I choose to take out. You'll feel like a queen by the end of our night together.

. . .

~ Sam, accountant, 32

I tilted my head at that one. Maybe this guy had some obsession with royalty, but that couldn't be all bad, could it? Though, he was an accountant. Stereotypically boring. Maybe his job gave him such an inferiority complex that he had to style himself as royalty just to keep things interesting.

2. "Dance the night away"

I believe if a guy can't shake it, he doesn't deserve to make it. Why walk through life when you can dance through it instead? I know the ins and outs of all the Philly clubs and I'd love to show you, too.

~ Brad, print model, 28

My left eyebrow curved up. This one might not be so bad. I didn't love clubbing - too much alcohol, too many people grinding against each other with too little fabric separating their bodies - but I didn't mind it, either. Carl sounded fun. Maybe it was about time I toured the trendier side of Philly - Josh's social life had been all frat bullshit and law school seriousness.

3. "Hear me roar."

. . .

I'm just a little shorter and much smarter than your average bear. Also, a total bear in the sack. If we get along, I'd love to take you back to my den.

~Alex, outdoor enthusiast, 25

I wrinkled my nose. There were very few things that attracted me to bears. Also, was "outdoor enthusiast" considered an actual job?

I jotted off one last email to Monica, approving the choices and amping up my chipper factor about the entire project, before getting on the train back home.

I had no idea how it was possible to feel as exhausted as I did once I finally got settled. The trudge from my stop to the apartment felt interminable, and in the last half a block, I was practically fantasizing about taking off my heels.

And then I walked in the door and started fantasizing about something completely different.

Jordan, who I hadn't spoken more than two words in passing to since that incredible night we'd spent together, was standing in the kitchen, wearing a white undershirt and blue and white striped cotton pajama bottoms, shimmying along to salsa music piping from his phone, arm-deep in a sink full of soapy water.

And his ass certainly looked good doing it.

I couldn't even begin to suppress my giggle, and when he froze, I just dropped my bag at the door.

He turned around, his smile gleaming at me. I scolded myself for avoiding him as much as I had this week. The lingering embarrassment from that night - he'd been licking my labia, for God's sake, and I hadn't known what in the hell to say to him ever since - washed over me, tinging my cheeks red.

Say something, bitch. Say. Something.

"Sorry I left those dishes," I managed to stutter out.

"No problem," he said smoothly, while still managing to keep that smile teasing at the corners of his mouth, making me want to kiss them again. "My college roommates and I had a schedule and everything, but I thought we'd see if we could maybe fall into a rhythm on our own. Gave me the opportunity to throw something in the oven."

God, just the way he said 'fall into a rhythm' reminded me of the rhythm he'd set between us all those days ago. During the amazing night that we still hadn't talked about.

What was the point of talking about it, really? We had had sex. Amazing sex. It was pretty clear from his offer that it was one night only, and he had kept out of my sight since then.

I'd tried to keep myself from wondering whether it was intentional or not, as I'd settled into a depressing habit of frozen dinners and West Wing every night. In the mornings, I'd been staying in my room until he was in the bathroom, then slinking out the door, doing my makeup on the SEPTA train. I assumed he'd been pulling the same kind of stuff with me in the evenings. It was ridiculous, I knew - we lived together, and would be for at least another eleven months - but the prospect of hanging out with him and not touching him, kissing him, begging him for a repeat of that night, just felt like too much to handle and not enough to satisfy me, all at the same time.

I was too chicken to ask if it had been on purpose.

"Dinner?" I asked, remembering the last time I'd seen him in the kitchen, realizing what an idiotic question it was all too soon. Something smelled incredible in here. I sniffed the air to show him that I noticed.

"One of my famous dishes," he said. "Could be dinner, if you want it to be."

A growl from my stomach punctuated the silenced. I laughed, nervously trying to gauge the temperature of everything left unsaid between us. Whether there was really anything unsaid at all. "Obviously I'm starved. Did you make enough to share?"

"With you? Of course." Everything about Jordan, from his smile to his voice, was so warm. "There's no point in playing around with delivery in this town when you've got something waiting for you at home." There it was again. Just another turn of phrase that sent blood rushing through the capillaries of my cheeks and the swells of my breasts. "I mean, it's just nachos," he continued. "But they're serious nachos."

"Oh, that's what smells so amazing."

I watched as he poured us glasses of water, his eyes flicking to mine between steps. Each glance ratcheted the temperature up a little higher. I didn't want to be the one to walk away from him but hell, if I didn't, I'd combust on the spot.

He sat down beside me, silent.

I wasn't sure when the spark had been ignited between us the other night, and I wasn't sure I wanted to rekindle it. Too many complications, most obviously the fact that I was contractually obligated to date a bunch of different guys in the coming week. Then again, those orgasms he'd given me had been too good to completely forget.

"What have you been up to the past few days?" I asked, not even daring to look him in the eye.

I pulled in a slow breath, admonishing myself. This was *so* not the time, when I was exhausted and starving and confused over what the hell to do about...well, him. TV. TV would be a decent distraction. With a few clicks, Josh and Donna were engaging in some witty banter on the screen, and I pretended to be interested.

God, my feet hurt. I pulled my feet up to my side on the couch, pressing my thumb into the ball of each one. I moaned again. Jordan pulled a pillow onto his lap. I smirked.

He cleared his throat. "Oh, you know, just getting some stuff taken care of for starting classes. Student I.D., reading lists..." His voice trailed off as his eyes raked down over my body, so quickly I might have missed it. But I didn't.

I grinned and turned to look at Jordan, full-on. It hit me all at once, then, that I hadn't really looked into his eyes since the moment before he'd pushed inside me. A fuzzy feeling took my head over then, and my hand flew to my neck as I instinctively tried to smother the heat that arose there.

He was beautiful. Growing from a boy into the model-caliber man he was now may have been the most impressive thing he'd ever done. Besides, you know, getting into one of the most prestigious aerospace engineering PhD programs in the country. It was overwhelming, actually, because thinking about him as a bona fide man made me realize that maybe I was a woman. No, I *definitely* was a woman, one that Jordan said deserved to be taken care of.

Nothing had made me feel so grown up, so suddenly, until just now, when I remembered that.

After a week of careful avoidance, I was right back here in his maddeningly strong orbit. All I would have to do to kiss him again would be to move a few feet. The fact that I really, really wanted to do just that didn't change the fact that he was my roommate, and my best friend's brother, and especially that my job for the foreseeable future would be to date anyone in Philly but him.

The heat creeping over my skin spread, and I didn't know whether I wanted it to stay or go.

The high-pitched drone of the oven timer pulled me out of my thoughts, and up from my seat snuggled on the couch. "I'll get them!" I called on the short trip to the kitchen, quickly finding an oven mitt and pulling the nachos out of the oven. "I am a *woman*," I muttered to myself as I set the pan on the countertop, unsure of exactly what reassurance I was hoping to give myself. I pulled two plates out of the cupboard and started to pile nachos on each one.

"I already chopped up some toppings," Jordan called from the couch.

"M'kay," I said, wrenching open the door and locating half a dozen bowls filled with cheese, tomatoes, guac, and other goodies. "You want everything?"

"Absolutely," he said, and I told myself that he probably didn't intend for that word to sound dirty. Even though it totally did.

I set to work layering the cold toppings on each of our plates and shoved a bunch of finely chopped green peppers in my mouth as I did. Only, one and a half chews after my fingers touched my lips, I knew those were no green peppers.

"Jordan?" I said, the pitch of my voice rising as heat raced over my tongue. "What the hell kind of peppers are these?"

That was all it took to get him scrambling to his feet and quick-stepping to the kitchen. "Jalapenos," he said as he rounded the corner. I groaned and clapped a hand over my lips, only realizing as I did that I'd be spreading the peppers' spiciness there, too.

"Oh, sweetie," he said, his eyebrows pulling together as he wrenched open the freezer and rooted around frantically, several long seconds later pulling out half a pint of Haagen-Dazs chocolate I'd stashed there. A deep whine came from the back of my throat as the heat crept toward along my tongue. Jordan plunged his other arm in the space between my hip and the utensil drawer and nudged me to the side, pulling out a spoon. He yanked the top of the ice cream off with his teeth, carved out a spoonful, and wedged it between my lips.

The frozen spoon stuck to my tongue, stiff and dry and a blessed, perfect relief. "Hold it in there," Jordan murmured. A tear escaped the corner of my eye, probably a side effect of the shock of my mouth nearly catching on fire, and he reached up to wipe it away with his thumb. The ice cream started to melt, coating the sides of my tongue and pooling beneath it. For the second time that night, I moaned good and loud, and this time, I got a prime view of Jordan's face when I did.

I would have bet twenty bucks that his eyelids fluttered just a little when he heard me.

He swallowed hard, letting his fingers slide under my jaw and brush the top of my neck before dropping his hand. "Better?"

I nodded, even though I knew my face was still contorted in pain. The horrific burning had subsided to a mere stinging heat.

"Swallow," he instructed, his voice just a bit hoarser, and that totally-unrelated-to-jalapeno warmth was back to spreading over my skin. I obeyed, filing away the sound of that word on his tongue for my alone time later. He didn't break eye contact with me as he dropped the spoon into the ice cream again, digging out another spoonful. "More," he said. God, I could get used to him speaking one-word commands to me. I opened my mouth and wondered if it looked sexy.

"Better?" he asked when I swallowed again. I nodded. "Your lips?" he asked, leaning in and peering at them and hell if my lids didn't flutter a little then. "Do they sting?" he clarified.

"I...um..."

But he wasn't waiting for my answer, not really. He'd already run a finger around the inside edge of the pint and lifted it to my lips, painting chocolate ice cream over them like lipstick. A rough noise came from the back of my throat, and a breath later, he was back to cupping my jaw with one hand while tilting his face toward mine. I let my eyes close, but instead of the pressure of lips I expected, it was the careful attention of his tongue tracing my mouth, licking the ice cream from every dip and curve.

I melted into him faster than the ice cream had on my pepper-ravaged tongue. I swept it past his lips, relieved that the burn had quickly faded to an annoying tingle, idly wondering if stroking it along his tongue would scrape away the last traces of heat.

Either way, the ache of need between my legs was quickly claiming my attention over any jalapeno burn.

Several scorching seconds later, Jordan pulled away, tangling strands of my hair in his fingers. We both sucked in air, staring at each other, lips parted.

"Tell me that last week, when we were together. Tell me it was more than nice." His voice was low and smooth, stoking the spark that had lit deep inside me into a healthy flame.

"What?" I gasped as he pulled away just enough to say the words.

"The morning after. Last time. You said it was *nice* and then you left for work."

At the time, it had been the only thing I felt I could do without jumping on him again and tearing off all his clothes. But I warred in my head over whether I should come out and say that.

"We didn't exactly have time to talk about it very much before we...you know," I managed, dimly aware of my fingers instinctively twist themselves in his shirt. My body was pulling him closer even though my head wanted to put space between us, to figure out what the hell he wanted from me other than this.

"I thought it was more than nice. Did you?" He leaned into me, just enough to brush his lips against mine, then pulled back again. Not a kiss. A tease. And it was working.

I moaned into his mouth, and he huffed a small breath back into mine. Still, he wouldn't kiss me, even though my entire body was practically singing for him and I was sure he could hear it. Hell, the whole city could probably hear it. I should have feigned ignorance, tried to keep some degree of control and dignity over this whole exchange, but I was powerless already. His touch was gentle, his fingertips holding me lightly to him, but the pull of him was so strong that I couldn't walk away, didn't even want to.

By the way he smirked, it was like he knew.

Dammit, he was still waiting for an answer. "Yes," I managed breathlessly.

He slid a hand up the back of my neck, twisting my hair gently through his fingers. He bent my head back and sucked at my pulse point, and I whimpered. "Say it," he said, his words barely audible as they muffled against my skin.

"It was more than nice. Incredible," I managed. "I told you that. When we were..."

"Right after you came, yeah," he said, his eyes trained to the floor all of a sudden. "But then the next morning..."

Was Jordan Jacobs nursing some weird sort of inferiority complex? Did he have trust issues? What the hell was going on? "Listen," I started. "It's not you. I just...I don't know what this is. What this can even be. You know it's complicated."

"Yeah," he said, nodding and looking back at me. "Yeah, it is. Your job, and—"

"Roommates," we said together.

We both grinned at that, like we'd reached some one-word brilliant conclusion. I wondered for a fleeting moment if that was the same look he got when he figured out the answer to some particularly difficult problem for one of his rocket science classes.

And then I remembered that, if I didn't want to get attached to him, I really shouldn't be thinking about those things outside this very moment. Unless I wanted the moment to stop.

He must have had the exact same thought, because he dropped his hands from my face. One of his feet slid back, then another.

"Right," he said, clearing his throat. My heart twisted and started dropping, further down with of his steps backward. He turned to walk out of the kitchen and I had to press my lips together to keep from whimpering. "Help yourself to the... y'know..." He clipped his knee against the wall and swore, pulling in a hissing breath. "I'm just gonna...um. Shower."

A few seconds later, the door to the bathroom shut and the shower cranked on with a squeak of the handle.

I don't know what I was thinking—maybe I wasn't thinking at all. We'd just said we shouldn't be doing this, for so many reasons, and I supposed they were valid. No, I *knew* they were valid. But my body was already moving toward the bathroom, propelled by the memory of that kiss and Jordan's clever tongue and strong hands touching every inch of me.

I'd been doing what I was supposed to do, what people expected of me, for long enough. Now that I could identify one thing I wanted, deep down in my gut, I was going to go after it.

I laid a trembling hand on the bathroom doorknob. It wasn't fear, though, that was making me shake now. No, it was imagining how incredibly hot Jordan would look under a spray of hot water, surrounded by steam.

I held my breath, twisted the knob, and stepped in.

CHAPTER 9

JORDAN

I HADN'T WANTED to spend the last week avoiding Liz, but I knew in my gut it was the only choice. Either that, or I'd desperately want to do something that we had both just clearly said we shouldn't be doing.

Sure, I could have turned up the heat until I made her want me just as badly as I wanted her. I had no problem acting gruff and alpha when a girl wanted it, but I just didn't have that great of a read on my new roommate yet. If I turned up the heat between us now, it might reach a point of explosion before our lease was up. I wasn't sure I wanted to know what that would look like.

Even though I'd last seen Liz when she was a squeaky sixteen-year-old, she was practically a whole new creature now. A creature that I kept fantasizing about throwing on the kitchen floor, stripping naked, and tasting from head to toe. I'd stop and spend lots of time in the most important locations, of course. Like her nipples, reminding me of little bits of hard candy, begging to be licked. Or the more complex sticky sweetness between her legs.

My cock twitched as I wrenched the shower on and stepped in before it even had a chance to get hot. *Calm down, bucko. This is gonna be a long year if you can't learn to rein it in.*

That was when the bathroom door swung open, displacing the steam with a cool gust of air. Liz was standing there, pulling her bottom lip between her teeth and making me wish I was the one manipulating her mouth. As if I wasn't having enough trouble getting my cock to calm down.

When she grabbed at the hem of her shirt and raised her eyes to mine, I practically growled. "Liz, if you don't want—"

"But I *do* want," she said, her voice barely loud enough to hear over the insistent patter of the water on the floor of the shower. I should have stopped it, so I could really talk to her, should have grabbed a towel and covered myself. But I knew even as I thought that, neither of those things would help this situation, and both of them would suggest that the most basic truth in this whole ridiculous scenario didn't exist.

I wanted Liz, naked and slick against me, and I wanted her to want the same thing and I didn't want to talk about it. Not now.

"Can I?" she asked. I couldn't find any more words - couldn't imagine any that would sound better than her skin would feel against mine. So I just licked my lips and nodded. A week ago, she'd been thirsty for attention from me, but now, I was starved for her. All of her.

Hell, I'd even go down on her again and stop right there, no dick involved, just to feel her tremble against my mouth.

Within seconds, she'd kicked her shoes to the side and stripped out of her clothes, leaving just a bra. Holy fucking hell. She hadn't been wearing panties. Did she *ever* wear panties? From the moment I said a casual hello to her when she walked in this evening until I'd personally shoved a spoonful of chocolate ice cream into her mouth and licked the extra off her lips, there hadn't been anything between that delicious pussy of hers and her skin-tight pants. In the next breath, she shouldered out of her bra, and now she stood before me completely naked. Not bashful. Not ashamed. Just looking right into my eyes.

Christ almighty.

She ducked past the shower curtain and into the steam-filled space, standing there with arms crossed, like she was suddenly shy after barging in on a naked guy's shower and asking to join him. The sight of her was too damn beautiful to ruin and too tempting to keep from touching, all at once.

Temptation quickly won.

My hands moved like magnets to her hips. God, it was like they were made for my fingers to rest on them. My palms fit right in spot where they flared out, and her hipbones made the most subtle convex pinpoints at the exact distance the pads of my thumbs could reach. I dug the rest of my fingers into the upper curve of her ass, and she responded with a little grunt and a smirk.

Being with her while standing let me map her body with my hands in a completely different way than I had a week ago, and I let them skim worshipfully over her front, memorizing the exact curve of her ample breasts over her ribs, weighing them, making myself even more desperate to suck them inside my mouth.

She was half a foot shorter than me without her work heels on - an unexpectedly huge turn-on. Her height let me control the angle of her jaw and guide her lips to exactly how I wanted them against mine. The water poured over my shoulders and pooled between us in the valley of her breasts; watching each drop plop into that tiny pond made me want to drink from it. I had to get even closer. After all, it was a damn shame that I hadn't paid those perfect nipples nearly enough attention the first time we'd been together.

"C'mere, sweetheart," I said as I moved my hands all the way around to her ass, squeezing and lifting her up in one smooth motion. Liz was not a thin woman, meaning lifting and securing her that fast required a little skill and a lot of strength. Luckily, I'd spent the last few years working out, benching well into the two hundreds, and deadlifting about the same. With her enthusiastic cooperation, Liz's one hundred and sixty pounds or so was just challenging enough to show off my biceps and pecs, and just easy enough to...well...show off my biceps and pecs.

Her back hit the wet tile with a slap, and now I was the one tilting my chin up to kiss her. This may have been the perfect position for us - my mouth was in easy reach of her lips, neck, collarbone, and stunningly perfect tits.

Yeah. This was heaven.

The shower water hit the back of my calves now, safely out of the way of where my mouth wanted to be to be but in the right spot to keep me warm and the room steamy. Perfect.

I got to work licking and biting along her shoulder, then retraced the path an inch lower along her collarbone. Then, the only uncharted territory left (at least, for today) was her chest. Levering her weight between my hips and the wall notched my dick in the perfect space between her ass cheeks, and gave me a free hand to admire, touch, and play with those perfect tits of hers.

I took my time, tracing my tongue around the outer curve of one and sucking a series of love bites there. She panted every time my tongue laved her skin, like this one little flick of my tongue might be her undoing. I grinned as I nipped at the underside of her right breast and she groaned. Any time she looked in the mirror or twisted around while she was getting dressed in the next couple days, she'd see evidence that we'd been together. Hopefully she'd remember how much she loved it.

If I was lucky, she'd want more.

I paused for a second at the thought, letting the tip of my tongue idly swish against her skin. Where the hell was that desire coming from? I'd never felt like I wanted to mark a girl as mine before, to make her feel weird about being with anyone else in the near future. Liz was making my head go places it had never gone before - part of me even wished I could say I was sorry about it.

My thoughts broke when one of her hands snaked behind her back and under her ass, gently circling the head my cock, which was hard as steel and felt five degrees hotter than the water. I moaned at the contact. Something about the delicate attention of her fingers combined with slight scrape of her nails with every pump was already driving me absolutely wild. I growled and switched to her other breast, no teasing this time. I sucked her nipple into my mouth hungrily, stroking the underside of her breast with my tongue with every pull. She moaned and arched into me, pumping me harder, now fanning her fingers out every time she reached the base to caress my balls, then pulling away.

It was an exquisite torture, and soon one of us would break. We both knew it.

Reluctantly, I pulled back, taking the time to lightly scrape the perfect hard bud of her nipple with my teeth before completely letting go. I tilted my head back one more time and plundered her mouth with a bruising kiss, which she returned measure for measure. When I forced my lips away from hers and licked my bottom one, I could swear I tasted a trace of blood.

"If we're not careful, I'll come before you do."

She shrugged and grinned down at me like she was Huck Finn and I was blueberry pie. Like she was getting to taste something she never thought she'd have. "I wouldn't mind that much, except that's not what I came for."

"Tell me what you want," I murmured against her ear before sucking the lobe into my mouth. She moaned, even louder than she had when I was doing my worst to her tits. Who knew she'd love attention to her ear so much? I grinned. She wasn't the only one winning here.

"You. Inside me. Please."

She didn't have to beg, but hell if I wasn't glad she did.

"You okay if we don't have a condom?"

"I'm clean, if you are."

I sucked a line of wet kisses down her neck, and she let loose a rhythmic whimper. "And—ahh—I'm on the pill."

"Music to my ears," I grunted, already imagining how amazing it would feel to have her surrounding me again, this time with no barriers.

With the angle I was bracing her against the wall, I didn't even have to reach down to line myself up. I just pulled my hands back up to their perfect resting places on her hips, notched my thumbs under her hip bones one more time, centered her over me, and tugged her down as I thrust up.

Her quick gasp followed by a throaty scream made me pause for a second, worried I'd hurt her. But when I checked her face, there was only a breathless smile.

She tilted her eyes to mine. "More," she said, and I got the feeling that if I didn't give it to her, there would be hell to pay. Not that I minded one bit.

I gripped her hips even tighter and redoubled my efforts, answering every moan and sigh with a kiss and every demand for "harder" or "right there, again!" with exactly what she asked for. As the seconds ticked by, my legs started to burn with exertion. Quickly, though, the burning turned to a steady, electric pleasure racing through every muscle and nerve. It drove me to get closer to her, faster, just as she was begging me to do the same.

Liz's head lolled to the side, her cheek pressing against the cool tile. "Jordan," she panted. "I'm so—" and then she arched her back and let loose a delicious scream of ecstasy, pulling the most intense wave of pleasure I'd ever felt from every cell of my body.

I instinctively stepped into her as we both came, chasing the closeness I craved as my orgasm faded, There was something so incredible about the feeling of her against the wall securely as her body shuddered and she drew deep, desperate open-mouthed breaths. My forehead seemed drawn to hers by some pull I had no hope of controlling, and I smiled as my breath swirled against her neck through the steam. It felt so safe here, with her, in our own little word.

It also felt dangerously addictive.

Finally, Liz's eyes floated open and she turned so that our foreheads tented together. She breathed a feather-light, lingering kiss against my lips, and then groaned as she tightened her arms' circle around my neck, pulling herself up.

I chuckled. "Okay, sweetheart. I've gotcha. Easy does it." I pressed her body to mine, and I swear my eyes rolled back in my head at the feel of her breasts pressing into my chest. She kissed my shoulder one more time as she let one leg drop, then the other, which brought her torso sliding down against mine, just a few inches.

She could have backed away, could have claimed her own space and cleaned up and gone to bed. We didn't owe each other anything more than that. But, without pulling away from me, she reached one arm out to grab a sponge, then pumped soap onto it from a shelf hung over the shower head. She took her time working it into a lather and then lowering it to my still half-hard cock, washing it gently and slowly, like she wanted me to feel safe. Like she wanted to make me feel loved.

I leaned my cheek against the top of her head and allowed myself a low hum of approval. When she'd covered my whole body, knees to neck, with suds, she relinquished the sponge and I did the same for her. She was still slick and hot between her thighs, and I didn't miss the stuttered whimper that snuck out when my fingertips lightly traced the sponge's path.

When the water started to cool, I reached over and turned it off. Suddenly, without constant bombardment of droplets, it felt like a spell had been broken. My heart stuttered with fear of what would happen if I broke the spell by speaking out loud. The intimacy of what had just happened felt heavy to me, but in a good way - like a thick blanket cocooning me against the scary unknown. Maybe it was because I'd known Liz for so long, but it was different from what I'd felt with any other girl, ever.

I didn't say a word as I reached for a towel and handed it to Liz, then got one for myself. I opened the door to the hallway, which felt blustery in comparison to the steamy bathroom, and stepped out, ready to head to my bed. But Liz was right behind me, and before I could even take a single step away from her, the pads of her fingers brushed my palm.

"Stay with me?" she asked in a hopeful, yet confident, whisper. I just grinned and caught her around the waist, playfully tugging her in front of me.

"As long as I get to be the big spoon," I said in her ear. She let her head fall back to my shoulder and laughed out loud, and a thrill ran through me as the firm pillow of her stomach shook against my forearm.

"I wouldn't have it any other way."

Somewhere along the way back to her bed, our towels fell on the floor, and we slid under her covers hastily, with little space between us, like the air outside those blankets would freeze our skin on contact. Liz pulled my arm back around her so my fingers were free to trace patterns around her navel. When I pressed every part of my front against her back, she sighed.

"You called me sweetheart," Lizzie murmured into the air, when we'd finally stopped squirming for the perfect arrangement.

I raised my eyebrows. "Did I?" I'd call her "Princess Liz" if that's what would make her smile. "Is that...is that okay?"

"Just not what you would normally call someone when she's riding you like the Cavalry."

I chuckled. "I guess not. But, you know. You're more than just a rider for this stallion."

She laughed, a full-on, deep-from-her-belly laugh. "Is that so? What else am I? The hot stable hand?"

"Something like that," I said, not able to stop myself from pulling her even closer and nuzzling into her neck.

"You know, stallions only nuzzle into people like that when they want some more sugar."

I pulled away from her a little, checking her expression to see if she really did want to go another round. I knew that this might be our last time doing this, and I was certainly not opposed to stretching it out further. But Liz's eyelids were very clearly growing heavy, just like her body as it leaned into my shoulder. She let a soft laugh tumble out from the back of her throat. "Oh, I don't know. I never rode horses, you know. Too busy playing tennis and doing summer internships and whatever other bullshit my parents decided a girl like me should be doing."

She had to be sleepy if she was discussing her childhood with me. She hadn't given me very specific objections to us being together like this, but I knew one of them was that she didn't want things to get weird between us. Her friendship with my sister was important to her, and I knew she didn't want to bring it into whatever this thing was between us. Just as I was about to say something, though, her head grew heavy where it lay on my arm, and her breathing picked up a light snore.

I swept her hair over her shoulder and pressed a soft kiss to the nape of her neck. I felt my eyes drift shut and sighed into the feeling of finally letting them stay that way.

CHAPTER 10

LIZ

"I HAVE TO GO TO WORK."

I spoke even before the streaming sunlight nudged my eyes open the next morning. I stretched my legs, wincing a little at the soreness between my thighs. Beside me, Jordan lay on his stomach, arms crossed under his head, his curls framing his brow over fluttering eyelids.

He took a deep wakening breath, then hauled his eyes open. "Hmmm?"

God, that voice alone could start up my libido all over again. Any other day I would have considered straddling him and going for another round, but if the sun shining through my windows, it meant I was very nearly late for work. And today, of all days, I couldn't be late.

It was Friday. The day the poll results would be in. The day I would spend trying to get as much information as possible on whatever Mr. Rando Philadelphia had chosen as my date before I went out with him.

I kept trying, and failing, to stop thinking about the fact that exactly zero of the guys I'd be dating for this little journalistic romp would be the guy lying naked in bed beside me. The guy who made my heart swell and flutter whenever I thought of the gentle way he touched me, or the way his voice seemed to curl into my ear and stay until it warmed me to my toes. The guy who seemed uniquely capable of making my body feel like it could explode and melt at the same time, and like I'd love every second of it, to boot.

"I have to go to work," I repeated with a whine, forcing myself to shimmy out from under the covers. I snagged the flat sheet and wrapped it around my body, just under my armpits. The more tangled up I made myself in his presence, the less tempting it would be to unwind myself and drape my body over his again.

Jordan just groaned, rolling over onto his back while shielding his eyes with crossed forearms. Unlike me, he gave absolutely zero thought to covering himself, and the comforter slid to the side just enough to give me a glimpse of his abs, the little muscle above one of his hipbones, and the edge of the thatch of hair above his cock.

God, I loved that thing. Like, really loved it. I loved it more than I had after the last time we'd done this. I may have been becoming obsessed with it. Even addicted.

"I only have one meeting today," Jordan said, but then quickly groaned, covering his eyes with his hands. "And I have a thesis proposal review. Almost forgot." He rolled onto his front, making the sheets curve over his beautiful, muscular butt. I wanted to bite it.

"Is it a humungous paper for you, like it is for journalism?"

"Nuh uh," he mumbled as he lifted his face off the pillow. "I have to build something, *and* write a moderately-sized paper explaining how and why it works. I think."

"So, like, a really grownup science fair project."

He chuckled. "Sure, but without the trifold display. "The

morning scratchiness made his voice even sexier. "You could help me with my paper, maybe. Writing's not my strong suit."

My heart swelled in my chest at his trust in my abilities. "That means a lot, Jordan."

He gave me a soft, sleepy smile. "I'd be stupid not to ask an expert." We shared a few seconds of eye-gazing in which I seriously considered ignoring work completely to burrow back under the covers with him. In those same seconds, though, Jordan had resigned himself to being a grownup.

"Want me to pick up dinner for tonight? I could try cooking again, but I'd rather cut my losses and blame someone else if you accidentally ingest flaming peppers. At least for this one night."

I took a deep breath. Had I even told him the whole "Date an audience-selected Philly bachelor!" thing was starting this week? *No time like the present, I guess.* "Well, I, um...I sort of have a date tonight."

Slowly, Jordan let his other arm drop, pulled himself to sitting, and blinked exaggeratedly at me. Several long seconds ticked by before he said, "A date? You? Tonight?"

"Jordan, I told you about this. The work thing, remember? Liz Dates Philly? The feature series I'm so super lucky that I get to write?" I hoped the sarcasm in my tone was evident, hoped that it hid the nervousness. I couldn't have blurted out what I wanted to happen between us if I'd tried, but I knew one thing for sure—I didn't want it to end.

"Oh, my God. Yeah. I just didn't realize it was so...soon." He took in another deep, just-waking-up breath, and dragged his palm down over his face. "Okay. Do you—um, do you know who your date is?"

"No," I said, giving in to the urge to be a little closer to him, even for a few more seconds before I had to get ready. I flopped back down onto the bed and rolled on one side to face him. "The voting closes at four today. Date's at seven."

"Are you okay with it?" His eyebrows drew together as he searched my expression.

I shrugged and let out a rueful laugh. "I mean, I guess I have to be, right?"

He shook his head. "Not really. No. Like, in the dating world, I'm pretty sure it's protocol that nobody has to do anything they're not okay with."

"But this isn't dating," I said, suddenly feeling defensive. "This is journalism. If I don't ever leave my comfort zone, I'll never get anywhere. Definitely not in my career."

He sighed again. "I'm not gonna argue with you. Obviously, you're a grown woman, you can make your own decisions."

I smiled a little at hearing him say that. A woman. I was a *grown woman*. Nobody else had ever pointed that out, and he'd done it twice now, in two different contexts. Nobody else had ever even said the words, let alone treated me that way.

Then again, nobody had ever fucked me 'til I couldn't see straight and then made me feel like the most cherished human being on the planet mere minutes later.

"Anyway, I won't be here for dinner tonight. But I won't be late, either." I looked down at my comforter while I asked him, "Do, um...do you have any plans for tonight?"

His eyes were still trained right on me, I could feel it. "Haven't really met anyone yet. I mean, any friends. I'll probably just hang out here. Watch a movie or something."

"Okay, um...well...maybe..." I'd twisted a handful of blanket between my fingers, and released it, leaving a three-inch sweaty circle on the bed. "Maybe I'll join you?"

"Sounds good," Jordan said. "Listen, Lizzie."

"Liz," I said. "Everyone calls me Liz now."

Lizzie was a little girl.

He nodded. "Okay. Liz. My friends call me JJ. Guess we're grownups now, we should probably use our grownup names."

If I didn't know better, I would swear I heard sadness in his voice.

"So, um, listen," he continued. "I don't know what this is, between you and me."

My heart thumped wildly. "Well...um...we're roommates?"

Thank God, he just laughed. "Yeah, but a couple of times we've also been the stallion and the stable hand."

My deep laugh at that took me by surprise. I beamed at him. "Okay, we're gonna have to banish those terms from being used in reference to us. Never, ever again."

"Agreed," he said, grinning back at me, then sticking his hand out. "Let's shake on it."

My mistake was in reaching my hand out to touch his. As soon we made contact, a warmth spread through me, making my stomach swoop. "But, um," I chanced, "you want to know what this is?"

"Yes," he said. "And, to be clear, by 'this' I mean the two times we've had sex in the past week."

Had sex and then clung to each other all night long like we were desperately in love.

"I don't see why we can't enjoy this, do you? It's almost better that we're roommates. I mean, since I'm dating whoever Philadelphia wants me to date for the future..."

"Yeah, I guess you couldn't really have a boyfriend, huh?"

My gaze flashed to his.

"Not that I'm saying that's what I want. I mean, not that I *don't* want that, but I don't want to, like, claim you or anything... not that boyfriends own their girlfriends..." He looked up at me with widening eyes full of panic.. "Help," he begged.

I stifled a giggle. He was adorable, all rumpled and searching for the right words.

"Well, since you couldn't be my boyfriend, even if you wanted to, or even if I wanted to be your girlfriend, which neither of us is saying we want," I supplied, checking his expression for confirmation.

He nodded.

"And since we want to continue the...you know...*this*," I said, motioning between us again.

He nodded enthusiastically, eyes wide, which made me laugh again. God, I loved—and hated—how easy everything seemed between us.

"Under those circumstances, then, everything stays in these four walls," I said. "Our apartment can be like another world where we get to have really mind-blowing sex, and we still have our own bedrooms."

"Even if we don't use them," he rushed in. I couldn't identify his tone—was it disappointed? Hopeful? I may have known Jordan a long time, but I wasn't used to his face being this mesmerizing, let alone caring what his expressions meant. "Like, I don't want you to think you have to go to another bed or anything," he finished. This time it was Jordan - *JJ* - who played nervously with the blanket.

He looked back up at me steadily. "So this is friends with benefits?"

"Old friends with benefits. Roommates with benefits. Roommates who are perfectly free to date other people," I said.

"Even if by 'free' you mean 'contractually obligated to,'" he said.

I sighed. "It's not that. I did agree to it. And we're not—I mean, this isn't... this is good, but... yeah." I waved my hand helplessly and tried to sound like I knew what I meant.

"Yeah," he said. "Good." I couldn't help but think his voice was a little softer than usual. Disappointed, maybe. Or maybe that was just wishful thinking.

"You wanna shake on that, too?" I said, standing up and circling around to him. God, he looked good enough to eat. I seriously could have spent an hour just licking his smooth, taut, caramel skin. Every freaking inch of it.

I sighed when I reached his side of the bed. Maybe later.

"Why not?" he said with a tight smile, sticking his hand out one more time. "Old friend roommates with benefits?"

"Yeah," I said, clasping my palm against his. "That."

Then I ducked in the bathroom to get ready for the day. When I breezed out into the living room, dressed in my go-to pencil-skirt-and-blouse getup, Jordan—JJ, I harshly reminded myself—handed me a travel mug of coffee. I couldn't help flashing him my biggest grin. "Thanks."

"You got it, friend." He grinned back. "Good luck today. And, you know. Tonight."

"Thanks," I said, trying to ignore the pang in my chest. "Friend," I echoed before ducking out.

Five minutes later, I slumped against the wall at the train station and sighed. I sipped the coffee and pulled a face. It was way too sweet and creamy.

The fact that JJ didn't know how I took my coffee only made me feel a little better about being his friend. His old friend. Old friend turned roommate. With benefits. Nothing more.

The train pulled up and I growled, frustrated at everything and nothing all at once. On the way to the boarding platform, I dumped my coffee in the trash.

CHAPTER 11

JORDAN

WHEN THE DOOR shut behind Liz, I immediately let out a long breath. I felt my chest deflate and my shoulders slump. What a difference twelve hours could make.

It was easy enough to dismiss that first night as a fluke. I'd just moved, and maybe I was feeling a little unmoored, and there Liz was. Someone from home, now so attractive I could hardly stand it, welcoming me to Philadelphia and looking at me with those kaleidoscope hazel eyes. How could I have resisted?

Yeah, the sex was incredible, but we'd been drinking. Maybe that had clouded up the memory a little.

But that second time? She'd been a mess. Exhausted from work, mouth flaming from the jalapeno. I was a disaster too - My fingers were sticky from the ice cream I'd shoved in her mouth, and I'd been sweating all day while I walked around campus. It would have made more sense for to get her a wet paper towel and help her clean up, than to seductively feed her ice cream and excuse myself for a shower. Alone.

If we were really just friends, who wanted nothing more from each other than sex, kissing her senseless would not be the most logical thing for me to do in that moment.

But it had been the only thing I'd *wanted* to do. In fact, it was the only thing I'd been able to think about that day as I wandered around UPenn's campus, familiarizing myself with the buildings that would hold my classes, dropping a few things in my cubicle in the Engineering offices, picking up the last few papers I needed to fill out to officially start classes next week. I'd found myself wandering around dreamily, wondering what Liz would have to tell me about this campus that had been her home for the last four years.

Sex between two friends didn't "just happen" unless there was something more there. I knew that. At least I thought I did. She hadn't seemed very torn up at all over the idea this morning —in fact, it seemed like she had been ready with the solution. She'd handed it to me on a platter and offered it up like it had a foregone conclusion, to her. Like the only missing part of the agreement was me actually being awake so I could nod dumbly while trying to blink the sleep out of my eyes.

By the time she'd finished her, "Let's be friends with bene-fits. We can still be roommates without it being awkward at all, I promise!" diatribe, I knew that the only way I'd have a chance of spending any more time doing what we'd done the night before would be to agree.

Even though she was going out with someone else tonight.

Even though I didn't have to give it a single second more thought to know that, from Liz, I wanted more than that.

I sighed and slid into one of the chairs at the tiny four-person dining table I'd found at a secondhand shop and managed to situate comfortably right inside the entrance. I'd spent half of yesterday setting up the UPenn-issued laptop that every Engineering grad student got, and now I was glad I did. I had to focus on polishing up my thesis proposal before I did anything else. I'd managed to narrow it down to "The Develop-ment of Multi-Functional Structures for Small Satellites," which reminded me of fancy James Bond tech, and "Development and validation of 3-D cloud fields using data fusion and machine learning techniques," which would help me learn a skill that might make me indispensable on actual missions.

After doing a few more things to get ready for summer term to start on Monday, I fixed myself a sandwich and salad and finally gave myself over to what I hadn't been able to truly keep off my mind all morning – Liz, and who she'd be going out with today.

I navigated to Philly Illustrated's main page and raised my eyebrows at what I saw there.

Liz had made this "Liz dates Philly" feature sound like kind of a small deal, but it was right there on the opening screen, dominating the right column with title letters in a marquee font you just couldn't miss. There was a photo of her looking absolutely fucking adorable, standing on one of the busy downtown streets, the city buzzing behind her like it was just waiting for her to explore it.

She wore a bright green sleeveless dress that flared out at the waist and ended just above her knees, and hot pink heels that accentuated every contour of her gorgeous legs, which looked particularly fetching when she stood on one tiptoe with one heel kicked up behind her. She clutched the strap of a little pink handbag with both hands, which squeezed her chest together just enough to show a little line of cleavage.

I knew what the rest of that cleavage looked like. I'd seen it a precious few times, but I already felt like every detail of her body was burned on my brain. A strange caveman possessive urge came over me. This was the girl I'd practically grown up with, then had the privilege of stripping down and licking every inch of, on the front page of the Philly Illustrated website, asking its readers to vote on her date for tonight.

I was just about to click on the first undeniably handsome

asshole's profile when my phone vibrated, skittering against the table and scaring the shit out of me. Who in the hell could be calling me now? I glanced over to hit the 'decline call' button when my sister's bright white grin and wild curly hair filled the screen.

I let out a short laugh and clicked 'accept,' propping up the phone on a salt shaker right next to my computer.

"Why didn't you just text?" I asked, shoving my fingertips into my hair when I wondered if mine looked as crazy as hers did. Probably.

"I missed your face, brother," she said. "You were home for like two weeks and I talked to you every damn day, and then you're in Philly for one week and I barely hear a word from you! What gives?"

Oh. She had a point there. Between getting settled with school and... getting settled with Liz, I'd been kind of pre-occupied.

"Just school stuff. It's a little crazy here."

"But classes don't start 'til Monday, right?" She leaned in even closer, her one visible eye squinting into the camera, like she could pull information out of me with some magic little-sister glare from all the way across the state.

"Right, but I have a thesis topic meeting this afternoon already. Syllabus to go through and then the rest is getting my IDs and stuff. Registration. Moving into my office."

She continued to stare at me with her eyebrows raised.

I sighed. "I don't know, Kiera. What do you really want to know?"

"I want to know how you and Liz are getting along."

I twisted my lips. I should have known. Even with her own brother and best friend, Kiera was meddling in love lives. It's what she did best. In her head, all of life played out like a romantic comedy movie, one couple at a time - all you had to do was watch long enough.

KiKi been hoping I'd be the star of one of one of her little fantasy rom-coms at some point, so she could watch up close. But any girl I'd even come close to bringing home just hadn't stuck around long enough. Or maybe I'd made sure that they weren't around whenever I got ready to take one of those trips home in the first place.

I was picky about which girls I brought home, but with good reason. When Kiera got attached to a girlfriend of mine, I wanted to feel attached to her as well. I loved my sister, and I wanted to make her happy. I wanted to be able to see a future with whoever I let past my Stanford firewall and into my family.

"She's great," I said. "Very sweet. Very driven. She's grown up a lot." As soon as I said the last thing, I winced internally. I knew Kiera would be ready to pounce on that one, for sure.

"She sure has grown up, hasn't she? Absolutely gorgeous, right? Stunning. Like, you know all my friends are pretty, but Liz is..."

I waved my hand in front of the camera. "Okay, okay. Whoa there. I know what you're trying to do."

Kiera sat up with wide eyes and swiveling neck, like a mama meerkat on high alert. "Me? Trying to do something? I can't imagine what you mean!"

"And I can't believe you don't realize you only sound exactly like Scarlett O'Hara when you're meddling." I took a deep breath, hoping the exhale would push the sound of deception out my next words. "Liz is very nice. Nowhere near as annoying as she was as a kid. A great roommate so far. The end."

"Mmm-hmm." Kiera crossed her arms and finally sat back in her chair, letting up on her assault. I tried to subtly let out a relieved breath.

Instinct told me to add something about how I wasn't even attracted to her, but my gut feeling rebelled against it. Finally I realized there was something true I could tell Kiera that would absolve me. "She's dating someone else," I blurted out, feeling an unexpected sadness settle in my chest at the words. "So, you know. It's not a thing. And it's not gonna be, because we're *roommates*."

Kiera sat back and that unmistakably pissed-off glint flared in her eyes. "She didn't tell me she was dating someone."

Dammit.

"Well...it's complicated. You know what, KiKi? I gotta go. A bunch of the STEM guys are getting together for drinks tonight and I have some stuff to finish up before we do." It was true. I'd seen it in one of the dozens of Engineering department emails that had already gone out since I arrived. I hadn't planned on going, exactly, but the more I thought about it, I could use a social distraction. "Call if you need anything, okay?"

"What I *need*, Jordan, is for you to tell me what the hell is going on with—"

"Love you sis! Bye!"

I let my forehead thunk on the table. What the hell had I been thinking, letting her suck me into talking about Liz at all? I should have known Kiera would figure out that I had a thing for her in a split second. More importantly, I should have thought about the fact that maybe Liz didn't want her friends to know about her highly unorthodox, sort of ridiculous dating journalism adventure. Then again, in the internet age, Kiera would have found out about it anyway...

The link to Liz's dating poll was easy enough to find. I copied it, then pulled open the text window and typed a quick message. **Sorry. Had to run. This is what I was talking about.**

The three little reply dots popped up, then disappeared, then popped up again. I chuckled. I could just imagine Kiera reading the intro article to "Liz dates Philly," her mouth dropping open a little farther with each line. I clicked on the link myself, remembering how hard I'd laughed at what Liz had written about it. "And to think I thought online dating was the laziest way to find that special someone. Leave it to a slacker like me to find an even lazier way to find the most eligible bachelors in Philly!" when I'd first read it. Poring over her words almost felt like talking to her. I couldn't tell if that made me feel better or worse—closer to her or even farther away.

Dammit. I was pining, wasn't I? How did this girl who meant next to nothing to me two weeks ago now consume this space in my head that I didn't even know was empty?

Finally, Kiera replied: **Daaaaaamn. #2**

I sighed and clicked on the link, still unsure if I even gave a damn that Liz had managed to turn me into a pathetic mess. Kiera was right.

I shoved my hand back through my curls, wincing when my fingers snagged in the tangled mess. The short flash of pain snapped me back into focus.

Each choice of guy on the "Liz Dates Philly" poll had a little paragraph description, complete with cheesy personal-ad style headlines. "Dance the night away?" "Hear me roar?" What the hell? I groaned and covered my face with my hands, pulling my fingers apart to keep reading through them. The three pictures, all in a row right above the poll made matters ten times worse. They were all decent looking guys, even if #2 was balding and wearing a suit that didn't fit him too well, #3 was trying way to hard to flex each one of his naked muscles (oh, yeah, he was only wearing underwear, for fuck's sake) and #1 looked like a goddamn lumberjack.

Not that there was anything wrong with lumberjacks.

Maybe Liz liked lumberjacks. How would I know? I barely

knew *her*. Our lips had been smashed together for more total minutes than they'd been talking to each other.

Maybe a slender engineer with crazy hair and bordering-on-hipster glasses wasn't her type. Maybe even though she thought I was good in bed (and I knew she did, no girl could fake an orgasm like the ones she'd had) that was all she wanted me for.

Maybe I could use this whole "Liz dates Philly" thing to find out.

Each of these guys had a very distinctive type. Business man, flamboyant egomaniac, burly mountain man. I swore when I checked the voting count so far - of course the guy in the underwear ad was up four to one. With one easy tap of my thumb, I voted for Liz to go on a date with Baldy. Then, just for good measure, I did the same on my laptop. And opened up a second browser and voted for him there. Wasn't a bad time to see if I could raise Internet Explorer from the dead, so I voted there, too.

Four votes toward steering Liz away from Mr. Tighty-Whities. I sat back in my chair and felt my lips twist. Four votes were nothing against the hundreds that were only multiplying by the hour.

I sighed and sent another text to Kiera.

Me: Vote for #3.

Kiera: Already done x20. There's no way Liz is psyched about going out with any of these dudes so I decided to vote for the one who would be funniest.

Me: You're so smart. Does she know?

Kiera: I don't think she'd be pissed. It's not like she's looking for her soul mate.

Me: Did she say that?

Kiera: No. But I know her well enough to know she's not relying on a magazine gimmick to find Mr. Right.

My thumb hovered over the keypad. Just because Liz wasn't trying to find the right guy through these stupid dates didn't mean that she wouldn't. God, if that happened I'd just be the pathetic pining roommate. I'd rather be the roommate she was fucking thrilled to come home to after a string of horrible dates. Wouldn't I?

Then something occurred to me. I scrolled back up to re-read Kiera's texts.

Me: Wait. It let you vote for him 20 times?
Kiera: Yep. Well, 25 now.
Me: What do you have to gain by making her go out with this middle-aged guy?
Kiera: What do *you* have to gain by talking to me so long about this?

I sighed and shook my head. She had me there. I turned my attention to voting for guy #1 and guy #3 a few more times. My phone buzzed again.

Kiera: You could give any of these pasty-ass Philly bros a run for their money.

I sighed. She knew I had a thing for Liz. Of course. There was no point in trying to outsmart my sister, I supposed. It was just a matter of how long I could hold off her nosy badgering questions before admitting to her completely correct suspicions. I had a crush on Liz.

Me: Love you KiKi.
Kiera: Love you back.

I knew I should have been thankful for my thesis meeting, and by the time it ended, I was. For an hour and a half, my mind had been busy with sensors and rare metals and circuitry and not with my new roommate. My advisor praised my satellite research concept as original and exciting, and as I walked out of her office, I was on top of the world. A few minutes later, though, my stomach rumbled, which made me think of dinner, which made me think of Liz, which then made me think about how I would not be having dinner with Liz.

Maybe I could distract myself with cooking something nice, anyway. Maybe I'd offer her leftovers when she got home. I ran to the market and made it to checkout with half the ingredients for the meal I'd thought about making, but with a slice of cheesecake I barely remembered even seeing. I took the train to check out a running trail that was on the train line but far enough away from downtown to feel peaceful, even though I hardly ever ran outside. The whole time, I was refreshing the Philly Illustrated poll site, watching the votes roll in and putting in more of my own.

Damn it all to hell if Philly didn't really, really like underwear models. When my phone died a few minutes before 3:00 PM and I was still an hour away from home, my stomach dipped and rolled like I was on a ferry on choppy water. The poll closed at four. Liz would be meeting whatever guy the rest of Philly chose at seven.

And I would have to figure out what the hell to do with myself between now and whenever she came home - *if* she came home. After all, she'd never said she wouldn't sleep with the guy, and, well...he was a *model*.

It was going to be a long night.

CHAPTER 12

LIZ

I SLEPT WITH JORDAN JACOBS. I slept with him, and he was gorgeous, and it was amazing. Then, six and a half days later, I did it again.

And now I was going to work to see who the city of Philadelphia picked for me to date tonight. Or at least the few thousand people who actually read Philly Illustrated on a regular basis.

And then, after the date, I was going to go home, and Jordan Jacobs, the guy who'd given me no less than three mind-blowing orgasms in seven days, would be waiting for me there. Because he was my roommate.

Yeah. This was going to be totally fine. No, it was going to be fabulous, and I'd have a great time, and my articles about dating random Philly guys would be nothing short of revolutionary masterpieces filled with feminism and snark and wit.

Because it had to be fine. I didn't really have any other option.

I hopped off the train and headed down the street toward the Philly Illustrated offices, wincing as I passed the spot where I'd posed for a photographer a couple days ago. The photo was supposed to attract eligible bachelors to me and serve as a thumbnail for every article I wrote. I thought it made me look like a manic cross between Mary Tyler Moore, a Kardashian sister, and June Cleaver.

Plus those heels were not practical for any human to wear, ever. The balls of my feet had ached so badly after that shoot I thought they'd bruised.

"Here's our doll baby Philly Princess!" Monica crowed as I walked into the office. "Most eligible bachelorette in the city!" she crowed, coming up to me and brushing her fingertips along my jaw. My eyebrows pulled together and I managed a small smile. This was not characteristic of Monica.

Maybe she'd gotten laid last night, too.

"What's got you so happy? Just excited it's Friday?" I asked as I made my way over to my cube and set my bag down. I thought about changing from my flats into the heels I'd packed, but surveyed the office and decided there was no need. In fact, most of the women who worked at Philly Illustrated were dressed much more casually than I was.

Honestly, I hated that I had to think about it at all. I was pretty sure Alphonso never had to think too hard about his outfit. I could just imagine him standing in front of his closet. Hmmm, would it be pants, or...pants? A button down, or a button down with a sweater? Flat-soled dress shoes or flat-soled casual dress shoes?

I sighed. Maybe I should have tried my hand at being a full-time novelist instead of working in journalism. I'd heard that fiction writers wore yoga pants literally all the time. Seemed like a good enough reason to write pulp fiction for a living to me.

"Well," Monica said, motioning for Alphonso, who set a steaming hot cup of coffee on my desk, "You, my little star. You are what's got me so happy. Or rather, my idea of a feature that you agreed to be the star of."

I blinked.

"We are such a great team already," she said, leaning in and waggling her eyebrows conspiratorially.

I looked over to Alphonso, silently pleading for an explanation.

"Last night, a local business called in asking if they could sponsor your first date. It comes with enough advertising money to make up like ten percent of Monica's annual quota, so, you know. She's pretty happy."

"Ten percent *in one call!* And this is only the beginning, baby! It's all downhill from here. That is, if we play our cards right with this date."

"What do *I* have to do to play *my* cards right on *my* date?" Geez. I knew this was for work, but I deserved to at least treat it like something approaching normal.

"Oh, you know. Just act like it's a great place for a first date. Doesn't take much to put a positive spin on something, and it's important learning for every area of journalism, so..."

Over Monica's shoulder, Alphonso winced and then mouthed 'sorry in advance' to me.

"Oh God," I said in a moment of realization. What establishment is this that so badly wanted to sponsor my date tonight?

"Uncle Phil's Philly Phun Zone!" Monica crowed, this time with an obviously fake smile that only attempted to hid her worry. After a couple seconds of dead silence from me and Alphonso, she rolled her eyes, still managing to keep that smile. "Come on, Lizzie. It'll be fun! With a 'P-H!'"

"Liz," I said, my heart sinking at the unbidden memory that flooded my mind - Jordan moaning 'Lizzie' in my ear as his fingers traveled to the one place I desperately wanted them.

"...I mean, there *is* a salad bar, I think, even if there's no alcohol—we wouldn't really want you to get very drunk on one of these dates anyway, would we—and skee-ball! Who doesn't like skee-ball!" She finished her sentence with a flourish, like she just announced that I'd won a Grammy or something.

I sighed resignedly. She was right. There were worse things than skee-ball. And even though I'd never imagined my first byline being sponsored by Uncle Phil's Philly Phun Zone, I did have a job. I was getting paid to write words about the city I lived in.

And I could always have a drink once I got home.

"Alright," I said, sliding into my desk chair and doing a little spin. "Who's the lucky bachelor?"

"Well, let's take a look at how voting's going," Alphonso said, striding over to his desktop. Monica and I followed.

In the end, the voting between the three guys was a lot closer than I ever anticipated it being. Guy #1, Mr. Accountant with thinning hair, got 183 votes. #2, Underwear Model Man, got 231. And #3, the Lumberjack, got...72? Really?

"I just think it's weird that #3 didn't get that many votes. Right? Clearly, he was way more suited to me than #1," I said to Monica over a 4:00 cup of coffee. I worried at my thumbnail with my teeth. I was supposed to meet #2 at Uncle Phil's in just under 3 hours, and my stomach had started to do flips. Coffee probably wasn't the best decision at this juncture, but I needed to find some energy to put on a smiley face tonight. Caffeine was one of my best bets for achieving that.

"Are you nervous? You look nervous. Don't be nervous," Monica muttered, her eyes flicking up at me over the rim of her mug.

"The more you say 'nervous,' the more nervous I get," I grumbled.

"Listen, just because he's like a human sculpture of hotness doesn't mean you have to stress," she said, waving her stir stick at me vaguely. "What you *do* have to do is write an article about the date that's smart and funny and entertaining."

"And really positive about Phil's Philly Phun Zone," Alphonso interjected from his cube.

"Anything else?" I asked. "Maybe...honest? Feminist? Introspective?"

"Uh...sure," Monica said absently. "Just...try to have fun. Okay?"

After a quick exploration of the Uncle Phil's Philly Phun Zone website, I realized my outfit was seriously not going to fly for a date there. I'd tucked a silk tank, some makeup, and a curling iron into my bag, assuming we'd be going to a restaurant or bar or some other normal, adult first date. These high heels were just not going to cut it for an evening of on-my-feet arcade-playing, and, obviously, my cross-trainers wouldn't be okay for a first date. Then there was the whole matter of trying to drive a go-kart or play laser tag in a pencil skirt.

Monica was about my height, but at least a couple sizes larger than me. After a quick assessment of her frame, I asked, "Do you happen to have any leggings lying around here? And maybe a pair of flats? These heels are killing me," I said, wincing as I showed her. "I'm afraid this isn't going to work for the Phun Zone."

Monica twisted her lips, assessing me. "I have leggings, but they'd just sag off that pert little ass of yours. And we can't have you looking like a mess on your first date. Why don't you go home and change?"

I turned my phone's screen on and flipped it toward her. "Date's in like an hour and a half. No way I'll get back home, get ready, and get to the date in time."

"And I don't suppose you want to just have him pick you up?"

I rolled my eyes. "Do I look like I want to set myself up for sexual assault? Besides, Deanna's going to tag along with me." The photography intern, two years out of college and just returned from a backpacking trip in Europe, had been assigned to photograph each of my date experiences. "I don't want to have to drag her back to my place."

Monica sighed, then pulled open her desk drawer and fumbled with some keys at a metal box inside it. She pulled out a Philly Mag American Express card and tossed it to me. I almost tripped over my own heels trying to catch it. "Get some cute jeans and a pair of flats. Box of band-aids, too, for your heels." I smiled at the sweetness of Monica's concern. She could be a crazy bitch sometimes, yeah, but I could tell she cared about me even after the sole week I'd been working there. "No more than $150. Got it?"

I quick-stepped over to her and gave her a one-armed squeeze around the shoulders, pressing my cheek to hers. I giggled at her squeak of surprise. "Thank you, Monica. You're the greatest."

"Tell any of the other staff writers this happened, and you're toast. Got it?"

"Never bought *me* any jeans," Alphonso grumbled.

"Shut it. I never bought *her* any vodka."

My smile turned into a full grin as I dashed out of the office. I still kind of hated the assignment, but the people here weren't turning out to be so bad.

An hour later, I was walking out of H&M, ridiculously pleased with the way my new jeans hugged my butt and skimmed past my knees into a perfect straight silhouette. I wondered if emergency clothes shopping was good luck or something, or maybe jean matchmaking just happened like magic when you were shopping with someone else's credit card.

Either way, with my new jeans, adorable turquoise flats, and swingy new earrings to match, I looked good - really good. Just the right mix of cute and flirty with the option of sexy if I decided to turn it on.

I swung by the office to meet Deanna, dropping my work clothes and the credit card off while I was there. After doing a little spin and wiggle to show off my outfit at Monica's request, I was out the door.

Deanna spent the entire train ride to the outskirts of Philly taking pictures of weird shit like a wad of gum on the underside of a passenger seat, or the scuff marks along the sliding doors. Since she was half-lying on the petri dish of a floor to line up her shots, I pretended not to know her and spent the time gazing out the window, trying to ignore the twisting in my stomach.

The truth was that it had been a very long time since I'd gone on a real first date. Josh had taken me out on one, almost two years ago now, but only after we had made out at a frat party, shortly after which my friend had to help me get home after I puked on the front lawn. A certain amount of first-date mystique was lost when a guy had had already felt you up in a drunken stupor, not to mention watched you puke up Applebee's mozzarella sticks and vodka.

My experiences with other guys in college weren't real grown-up dates - more like hanging out with guys I'd known for a while and, a couple times, falling into bed with them.

Then again, it wasn't like any of my college experiences had worked out amazingly well. Maybe I should keep an open mind about Mr. Model. If I knew nothing else about him, at least I knew he had nice abs.

I glanced at his profile on my phone one more time. *Brad.* My nose wrinkled when I saw the smirk on his face paired with his overly confident words. I could say for sure that, besides the abs, this guy had an enormous ego.

The packet we'd received from Uncle Phil's Philly Phun Zone instructed me to meet at the front desk at exactly 7:00. Deanna and I got there at 6:55, after a minor freak-out when a big whooping noise and red flashing scared the crap out of us as we walked in. "Just the Alarm of Awesome," a squeaky-voiced skinny teen boy said when we arrived at the desk. Deanna and I shared a rare moment of connection as she rolled her eyes at the ridiculousness of this whole thing and I shrugged with an apologetic smile. I strongly suggested that she use the restroom before the date began so she wouldn't miss a single second of this special, special evening, and she nodded, seeming relieved.

I was nervous, if I was being honest with myself. Plenty of people told me I was pretty, and I believed them, knowing it was true in a girl-next-door sort of way. My hair, though a dull dirty blond, shone after a little product and a rigorous ironing, and I'd gotten particularly good at making my eyes look wide and sparkly with the right makeup. I had a cute butt, nice calves, and a respectable bra size. But this guy - Brad - he was an *actual model*. What if the Philly Illustrated readers had picked him for me just to see what would happen when a ten went out with a seven? Or was 'seven' even too generous for me? Dating an underwear model was one thing - dating one while all of Philly watched was another.

Just as I was considering running and hiding in the bathroom, the track lights around the door started racing and flashing right as the big, whooping alarm went off again. Brad strolled in through the flashing lights like it was something he did every freaking day, and only barely glanced up at the noise. I couldn't help but think that he was imagining himself on a runway, with a relaxed and confident smile and his smooth stride.

When he reached me, he extended a hand like the knights did for princesses in fairy tales, and I slid my fingers into his grip, half expecting him to bring my hand to his lips.

"You must be Elizabeth," he said with a self-congratulatory smirk, like he should be given a prize for remembering my name. I opened my mouth to tell him it was just "Liz," but right before I did, a memory of the night before flashed through my mind - Jordan's lips against my skin, breath steaming hot behind the shell of my ear, groaning, "Liz."

Suddenly, the idea of any other guy calling me that in any sort of romantic context made my skin crawl. So, I forced a smile, squeezed his hand, and said, "And you must be Brad."

"The one and only," he replied with a bleach-white grin. He stepped back and made a show out of looking me up and down and wolf whistling, which was super misogynistic but also made me feel awesome. But when his gaze reached the floor, his face unmistakably fell. He recovered quickly, looking back up into my eyes, but I couldn't stop myself from asking him.

"Is something wrong? With...the floor?"

"No, it's...nothing. I...um...I was just worried I'd forgotten my wallet. But it's there," he said, patting his back pocket.

"Well," a high-pitched voice squeaked from behind the counter, "it wouldn't have been a problem anyway. Uncle Phil's Philly Phun Zone is so pleased to be sponsoring your first 'Liz Dates Philly' date! Everything's on the house for you two love-birds tonight!"

We both turned to see a woman who couldn't have been more than five feet tall and ninety pounds soaking wet wearing a Phun Zone Polo and huge diamond earrings grinning at us. "My name's Jen, and I'm the manager. Welcome to the Phun Zone! I can't wait for Philly to hear all about what a great time you had with us. Let's get you guys started!"

Seriously, if her manic smile had been taken down a notch it would have been contagious, but this was just scary. I had a feeling that if we didn't have enough Phun at the Phun Zone, she'd start chasing us around the pinball machines with a skee-ball, trying to bludgeon us.

I shot a glance at Deanna, who had returned with her camera halfheartedly gripped in one hand.

Jen the Phun Zone Manager started walking backwards through the huge open room full of flashing, screaming machines, giving us what she called "the grand tour." A few dead-eyed teenagers were staring at the screens, robotically moving joysticks or tapping buttons. A couple girls who couldn't have been older than freshmen or sophomores in high school frantically stepped across the stairs on a dancing game, looking over a group of boys crowded around a different game ten feet away every few seconds and giggling their heads off.

Finally, Jen had led us in a loop around the game floor and handed us each a cup of tokens. I turned to Brad, remembering my conversation with Monica. "So...skee-ball?"

"Sounds good," he said, stretching his arm out just a bit and brushing his fingertips at the small of my back to guide me that way. As soon as he made contact, I shivered, but not in a good way, and walked half a step quicker to put some more distance between us.

We started to play, and Brad had amazing skee-ball form. Really. I watched him take a perfect stance and roll the highest score three shots in a row. It was like some crazy cross between bowling and pitching, with a windup and foot positioning that seemed calculated every time. Every time his ball landed in that middle spot, he stepped back, pumped his fist, and let out a rough. "Yeah!" like he'd just speared a wild boar or something.

I decided to ignore the weird yelling. Josh had been a more academic and less sports-centered guy, and I rarely saw displays of overtly masculine anything from him. Maybe some girls found that sort of thing attractive. Maybe I should ask my readers.

When he started winding up a fourth time, I started to feel a little ridiculous, just watching him. Plus, we'd barely said a word to each other. "Okay," I laughed, putting my fingertips on his forearm to stop him. "You've gotta show me what exactly you're doing."

"What do you mean?" he asked, looking truly puzzled. "This is how you play skee-ball. I mean, everyone knows how to play skee-ball."

I laughed again, this time feeling much more uneasy. "I...um...okay." I pulled my arm back to roll the ball up the ramp, but before I could, he gripped my elbow.

"No, no. Here. Let me help."

Smooth. He was pulling the classic first date move from time immemorial, where the guy positions the girl at the mini-golf course or the batting range or, I guess, Uncle Phil's Philly Phun Zone. He let his hands float on either side of my waist as he moved closer, leaning his lips toward my ear. I smiled. If nothing else, this was good material for the column, and it felt kind of nice to be doted on.

"When you work as a model, you get to be really aware of how exactly you're holding every part of your body at all times. I've been watching you move since I walked in."

"Really?" I asked, giving him a little smile and arching up one eyebrow. "Have you noticed anything in particular?"

"Well, for starters? You have really bad posture."

What. The. Hell.

Without missing a beat, he went right back to putting my body into optimal skee-ball position. But instead of being romantic, slow and gentle with his touches, Brad moved me stiffly, almost impatiently. He even punctuated my inability to twist my hips the way he wanted them with a frustrated sigh, then stepped back.

"Maybe you'd be better off if you had heels on."

I let my brows crinkle down for a split second before checking myself. "I don't know. I thought, skee-ball, Phun Zone...casual. Flats." Was I really talking about my choice of outfit - which, by the way, I'd felt really confident about - with this random skee-ball expert that Philadelphia had chosen for me?

He shrugged. "Sure, yeah. Right." He looked me up and down again, just like he'd done when he'd arrived, but this time instead of feeling admired, I only felt more self-conscious.

"How about another game?" I asked, bouncing on the balls of my feet a little and trying to seem much more chipper than I actually felt. If Deanna was going to be taking pictures of us, and if I was going to have any decent material to write about, I would have to at least try to have fun on this date. "Race cars?"

Half his mouth quirked into a smile and he nodded. "Sure." I didn't miss the look of longing he shot the skee-ball ramps as we walked away.

We agreed to play for best two out of three on the racing game, and when I completely crushed him the second time, he immediately left the little booth, watching me expectantly. "Aw, come on," I said with a teasing lilt. "Play a third game with me."

"No point," he said, looking around the place like he couldn't wait to get the hell out of there. "I mean, you already won the two, right? That's what we were going for?" Once again, I decided to just go along with it. I knew that reviewing the dinner options at the Phun Zone was part of the deal, so I glanced furtively over at the snack bar. I thanked God and all the saints when I caught Jen's eye from where she watched us behind the counter. She mouthed, "Ready?" and I nodded frantically.

"I think she has something for us to eat," I said, grinning. "Wanna pick a table?" Josh had always liked to do things like choose a table, let me take his arm, pull out my chair. Since there were no chairs here - only plastic-molded booths - I figured I might as well try to inject some enthusiasm into the situation.

Brad slid into the booth first, and I sat opposite him. Jen came dancing along just a few moments later with a steaming hot pepperoni pizza in hand. I'd been so nervous earlier in the day that I hadn't had anything besides a cup of coffee since noon, and my stomach grumbled. I laughed. "You must have read my stomach's mind."

"Can I get you guys anything else?" Jen asked, as she set a couple glasses of ice water down in front of us.

"Yeah, um...do you have a menu?" Brad asked.

"Well, it's just what you see up there on the board," Jen said, looking slightly confused.

Brad squinted up at the backlit neon-framed menu which outlined the prices for hot dogs, pizza, French fries, fountain sodas, popcorn, cotton candy, and fresh-baked cookies. Pretty standard fare for a game arcade, but his eyes scanned the list of offerings like it was in a foreign language. I caught a glimpse of Deanna shooting photos from a booth across the room, and only hoped she was capturing the hilariously bewildered expression on Brad's face.

"It's just...I'm on a cleanse. I've got a big shoot this weekend and...well, you get it."

I looked up at Jen, who, for once, looked speechless.

"Water's fine," Brad said, rushing to fill the silence. "I ate before I came, anyway."

That was nice of him. If he wasn't going to eat the pizza Jen was clearly so proud of, at least he wasn't making her feel *too* bad about it.

"Do you mind if I dig in?" I asked, unable to ignore the

grinding in my stomach any longer.

"Suit yourself," he said with the wave of his hand, leaning back in against the hard plastic and raking his eyes up and down, appraising me once again. What the hell was he *looking* for? "I mean, a cheat day's a cheat day, right?"

I crinkled my nose. "I pretty much just eat what I want."

"Seriously?" he asked, his eyebrows arching up. "I have literally never dated a girl who wasn't on some kind of diet. Must be nice not to stress about having to look flawless all the time. Just... what do you do when that makes you bloat? Because you know it will."

Suddenly, the pizza was dry in my mouth. Of course I didn't look perfect, but I'd put a lot of effort into looking pretty freaking good. "Well," I laughed, trying to cover my shock, "I guess I just...look bloated."

Brad's eyes trailed down to my belly and I was suddenly self-conscious of every little roll and bump that formed between the waistband of my jeans and my bra, even though the blouse hid them all. Then he eyed the pizza again, and then, like he wasn't even trying to hide it, his eyes flicked toward the door.

All of a sudden, all the times he'd not-so-discreetly evaluated my physical presence that evening added up. And all together, they really, really pissed me off. I wiped my greasy fingers on a napkin, balled it up, and set it on the table, leaning forward and resting on my forearms. I leveled a serious look at him. "Is everything okay, Brad?"

"Totally, I just...I didn't expect this sort of date. You know?"

"No, I *don't* know. Tell me."

"Well, when I signed up, I just thought it would be...you know...classy. A nice place."

I shrugged. "Yeah, but this is kind of fun, right?"

He snorted. "For kids." He looked up at me, maybe for searching for some type of understanding, but I wasn't about to give it to him. "Just...from your picture, I expected...something different."

"So let me get this straight. Based on some outfit the Philly Illustrated fashion editor put together and a professional photo of me in a tight-waisted skirt and impossible-to-walk-in heels, you had a vision of our date? And now you're in some kind of a mood because it didn't turn out to be like that?"

He shrugged. "I guess. I just...I thought this might be good for my career, you know? No offense, but you looked gorgeous in that shot. I thought I'd get some great photos and some exposure from the experience. You know?"

"Oh, yeah," I said, trying to keep my tone even and low. It was a trick my mom had always used when she wanted me to know she was seething mad. It always worked—scared the living daylights out of me. I felt the smallest bit of satisfaction when Brad's widened eyes told me it was having the same effect on him. "I get it. You wanted to be a perfect guy in a magazine, just like you are the rest of the time, and you wanted me to be as perfect as I was in that ridiculous picture, and then you wanted us to be in a magazine together looking perfect, like a freaking Philadelphia Mary Poppins and Burt for the 21st century. Is that right?"

"I mean...sort of?"

"Well, let me tell you something, *Brad*," I said, gathering my purse straps in my hand. "Mary Poppins was practically perfect in every way. She was also not real. So maybe before you agree to go on any more blind dates, you should make sure to ask the girl if she's an actual fictional character. Because if she's not, then you can decide to stay home and focus on your abs and your stupid kale shakes instead of wasting your time with a bloaty, pizza-eating girl like me."

I stood up and whipped my head around, searching for Deanna so we could get the hell out of here. She was already halfway to me. Without looking back, we strode to the door. When my hand grasped the handle, I remembered my manners. I turned halfway and called "Thank you so much!" to Jen with a plastered-on smile. She stood at her post behind the counter, looking completely dumbfounded.

As I held the door for Deanna to walk out ahead of me, I heard Brad calling for me. "Elizabeth!"

What the hell? I decided to humor him. "Yeah?"

"Just...um...the cleanse isn't kale-based? It's probiotic. And pizza is still disgusting."

"You're disgusting," I muttered, stepping out into the warm, humid twilight.

Of course my first date would be a total disaster. Not to mention slightly embarrassing.

Luckily, the train station was only a couple minutes away. As we sat waiting, Deanna turned to me. 'You know, I didn't know what to make of you at the beginning of all this."

I chuckled. "And now?"

"Just...that was pretty fucking awesome. It was a privilege to photograph. That's all."

That was the first thing that had made me really smile in a hours. I ducked my head and watched my fingers weave together, then apart. "Thanks. Really. Thanks."

"Yeah. And you know what? The date sucked, but at least it'll be one hell of a fun article to write."

She was right. I beamed and held out a hand, which she rolled her eyes at before returning my high-five. "To journalism," I said as we settled into our seats on the train.

"To journalism."

CHAPTER 13

JORDAN

"SO THEN THIS girl tells me she's planning a trip to Pamplona next summer, and she didn't even realize it was during the running of the bulls."

I stared at Ethan, who looked like he had just walked off the floor of the stock exchange, in a perfectly pressed white shirt, his tie only slightly loosened, five-o-clock shadow barely allowed to grow in. He was an actuarial science PhD student, one of the suits who determined exactly how much of an insurance risk each and every human on the planet was. And he'd come in freaking out about some girl.

He was also the only other STEM guy who had come to the gathering the departments had supposedly planned. Some effort.

"So?"

"So?" He laughed incredulously. "There are fucking raging bulls running through the streets! She could be gored! She'll probably die!"

"And this is related to you going on a date with her...how?" I raised my eyebrow, daring him to make a connection between the two things that made sense in any universe.

"Obviously I cannot date a girl who thinks stuff like that is fun. Especially after she runs into me in Fairmount Park. With her bike."

I kept my eyebrow up.

Ethan flung his arms out to the sides. "Not even wearing a helmet! Come on, man! I can't fall in love with a girl like that. Especially not if she's just gonna die this summer."

"Going on a date is not falling in love," I pointed out. Even though I wasn't sure I could speak with any authority on that, given the mooning I'd been doing over Liz after one roll in the hay. "Definitely doesn't mean you're going to even care about when she goes to Pimploni. Or wherever."

Ethan took a long pull of his beer. "Pamplona, friend. Remember that, and stay away if you don't want to get gored by a bull."

I laughed and shook my head.

"I'm serious, man." Just then, his phone buzzed, and his jaw dropped open. "I...uh...it's..."

"Natalia?" I supplied.

"Yep. Her," Ethan stammered, sliding a folded twenty onto the bar. "Shit. I'll...uh...I'll see you around." I nodded, more content than I could have predicted to stay at the bar a while longer nursing my own beer. The poor guy clapped me on the shoulder as he made his way out, and I felt comforted that at least I wasn't the only one suffering from woman-related confusion.

I spent a long time at specialty grocery stores that night, killing time. I'd learned how to make sushi during a Japanese culture filler course at Stanford, and even though I hadn't tried my hand at it since I was twenty-one, and had kind of sucked at it back then, I decided to fill my evening trying it again. Maybe Liz loved sushi. Maybe she would love having the supplies lying around. Maybe we'd make it every Friday night and I'd stand behind her with my arms draped over hers to help her roll the bamboo mat even though she didn't really need me to. Maybe we'd use the excuse to stay in Friday nights. Maybe the whole weekend. Maybe we'd feed it to each other naked in bed.

Or maybe I was just going to way too many grocery stores to fix dinner for a girl who might not even be interested in spending a ton of time with me. A girl who was my roommate, and I would have to see every day for the next twelve months regardless of how—or whether—things progressed with us. A girl whose job was to date other guys.

Whatever. Traipsing from one grocery store to another to pick up sushi mats, a rice cooker, seaweed and fresh fish, plus the three-store hunt for perfectly ripe avocados, filled up my evening decently. Yeah, I felt a little weird being the only brown-skinned, curly-haired, over-six-feet-tall guy in most of those stores. Not to mention that most guys my age would have been getting ready for a night on the town instead of solo shopping for domestic goods. But it was all worth it when I realized I wouldn't be home until nearly 8:00. Just that much less time for me to figure out what the hell I was going to do with myself while I waited for Liz to come home.

I winced when I reminded myself that she might not come home at all tonight.

Once I'd stashed the refrigerated stuff away and slid the box holding the rice cooker onto the counter, I collapsed on the couch, only then realizing how tired my feet were from so much walking. Philly was different from Stanford in many ways, but the amount of walking required to get around was one of the most glaring. Not that I minded, exactly, but I'd definitely have to get better shoes.

I toed off my sneakers and let out a deep sigh as I settled into the large armchair. I wasn't even that hungry, having picked up a couple incredibly delicious spring rolls from a Chinatown food truck..

The apartment was too quiet. If there were going to be many nights like this, I'd have to get a fish tank or a white noise machine or something just to fill the space.

Maybe I'd make friends in my program, but the truth was that I'd never been a guy with tons of friends. It was almost like I didn't have enough brain space to maintain that many personal and social connections, and when guys I'd gotten along with moved on to a new program or moved out of my apartment building, we sort of fell out of touch. Maybe once I got my PhD, things would change.

That's what you need to be doing, JJ. Focusing on your damn studies. Classes started in two days and the only prep I'd done was buying a bunch of books and printing the syllabi. I eyed the stack of paper and a few of the books that sat on the coffee table, right next to my reading glasses. I'd meant to scan through them earlier so that I could email my professors with any questions before Monday rolled around, but of course I'd been too damn distracted.

I blew out a long breath as I grabbed the top syllabus on the stack and shoved on my glasses. Maybe returning to the language and form of academic paperwork after so many weeks off was exactly what I needed to get my head on straight.

I'd only read the name of the class and the professor's name when a key ground in the lock of our front door. Before I could even get to my feet, Liz slumped in, dropping her bag and her keys just inside the door like she'd been through the longest night of her life, even though it had only just started to get dark outside.

I had to fight to keep myself from grinning. She was home, and she clearly hadn't had a very good time. At all.

"You're back early," I said, keeping my butt in my seat even though every instinct told me to get up and pull her into my arms. She was headed right for the couch, anyway. She collapsed onto a cushion, stretching her body across the full length of the couch, slung her forearm over her eyes, and groaned.

"It feels late," she muttered. "Do you know where they sent us? She dropped her arm and lifted her head just enough to look at me. I tore my eyes away from the strip of skin that had been exposed where her shirt had ridden up over the waistband of her jeans. Really damn cute jeans that perfectly clung to her hips, like they were inviting me to hook my thumbs into the belt loops. "Uncle Phil's Philly Phun Zone," she said before covering her eyes again.

"I don't know what that is but I'm guessing it's like...a garbage dump? Or maybe a fish cannery?"

She puffed out a laugh, and then brought her hands down to rest on her stomach with a smile still lingering on her lips. Her eyes drifted closed, like she could fall asleep right there. "It might as well have been. It's local, obviously. Arcade games and skee-ball and pizza."

She drew up her legs and pulled off her shoes, dropping them on the floor. When she stretched out again, I saw their half-moon outlines where they had cut into the top of her foot, some looking close to bleeding.

"Jesus, Liz. What the hell kind of shoes were you wearing?"

She laughed, her eyes only half open. "It's one of those mysteries of girls that we never tell you. Flats are actually not all that comfortable. Especially when they're new."

"Okay, that's ridiculous. Hang on. I'll be right back."

I rummaged around in one of the handful of boxes I still hadn't unpacked and came up triumphantly with my first aid kid, which resembled a tool box more than it did most household Band-aid and Neosporin outfits.

"What in the world?" Liz asked with a soft chuckle, now propped up on her elbows. I dropped the kit at the foot of the couch and slid my palm under her ankles, lifting them up and sitting under them so they lay across my lap. "Who are you, Mr. Safety? God, I remember you mixing chemicals and blowing stuff up in the kitchen sink without so much as your glasses on!"

I winced at the memory. "Yeah, and it only took one time in chem lab singeing my own eyebrows off doing exactly that to get me to keep burn cream close at hand."

She craned her neck and peered into my med kit, which I'd now opened and pulled some bandages out of. "That's a lot more than burn cream."

"Yeah, well there was also the time I sliced my thumb open on a vernier, and scorched my arm with sodium hydroxide, and branded myself with a soldering iron. Nobody told me when I went for my engineering degree that I'd be training to be a lab medic at the same time. But there it is."

I slid my hand along the bottom of her foot, and her leg jerked.

"Ticklish?"

"Shut up," she said, smiling at me with sparkling eyes.

I gripped her heel firmly with one hand and spread some antiseptic cooling salve over the largest of the raw spots. She let out a long, gentle sigh, with a soft smile that could only be relief. Once her poor feet were all bandaged up, I slid my palm around to the arch of her foot, digging my thumb in. She groaned when I stroked against a tight muscle, and I suddenly remembered that her feet would be able to feel the effects of that groan was having on my crotch. I adjusted a little bit, then pulled a throw blanket over my lap, just to increase the buffer zone just a little.

She looked so comfortable, I expected her to drift off to sleep, but a minute later, I caught her studying my face, like she was on the edge of asking something.

"What?" I asked.

"Just...have you ever gone on a blind date—on a first date—and been a totally self-absorbed asshole?"

"Not...that I know of," I said carefully. "I guess I've been on a couple dates where I never heard back from the girl. But those dates seemed pretty normal. I guess I always just tried to be myself."

Liz snorted. "I guess that makes sense, then. This guy - *Brad* - was definitely not afraid to be himself."

"But I assume, from your tone of general contempt for him, his true self is a complete douchebag?"

She sighed and let her head tip back again. "I don't know. Maybe we were just *that* incompatible. Just...I thought I looked cute tonight. Not gorgeous, obviously, we were going to a freaking arcade - but he was clearly not admiring my outfit. Like, at all. We're talking actual disdain coming from this guy."

"You're kidding me, right?" Liz looked incredible. As far as I had seen, she always did. Her outfit tonight - a flowy, silky blouse with form-fitting jeans - was perfect. In fact, the only thing a little less than perfect about it was the way the loose and flowy bottom hem of her top was practically begging me to let my fingers slide up under it. It didn't help that I already knew how completely perfect her stomach was, with her skin so smooth and that adorable little mole just an inch above her belly button.

Dammit, JJ. Calm. The fuck. Down.

"It was like...he was weirdly transfixed on my shoes? That they weren't heels? And he said more than once that I just didn't look like my picture. You know, the one on the Philly Illustrated site. Which I guess is true because I don't have on the cutesy dress and dangerous heels and gobs of makeup. And Photoshop."

"Of course you don't look like the picture," I said. "You look like you. Like a real girl. Uh, woman. A real one."

She raised an eyebrow at me.

"You look *better* in real life than in the picture," I clarified. "You look almost like a Barbie doll in that picture. Who wants to date a doll?"

"Him, apparently. He kept talking about all his magazine modeling work. Commenting that I was wearing a different outfit, my hair was different... Maybe all the other girls he's ever met transfer flawlessly from the page to real life."

"Mmm. So his type is *paper* dolls, then."

That earned me a real laugh, from deep in her belly. I swore that genuine smile of hers was one of the most beautiful things I'd ever seen.

Liz's head lolled to the side and her eyes drifted shut. I ran a hand down her shin, squeezing her ankle when I reached the end. "Close your eyes," I said. "I have some reading to do. I was gonna be sitting here anyway." It wasn't a total lie.

"If you're sure..." she said, not even completing her sentence before she fell fast asleep. I reached over her legs to grab my stack of syllabi and a highlighter, and dug in.

The next thing I knew, my eyes fluttered open in our dark living room, the light filtering in from the street lamps the only thing illuminating the dark in front of me. My face was smooshed against something warm and soft, and I nuzzled deeper in with a satisfied hum.

Then my pillow started to breathe.

I blinked, hard, then dragged my heavy head up and saw her. Lizzie Palmer, my own personal gorgeous, sweet-smelling body pillow. And I'd snuggled my head right onto her boob.

CHAPTER 14

LIZ

HIS FACE LOOKED EVEN CUTER when he was asleep. The strong jaw that had become prominent since we were kids was somehow softened when his mouth hung slightly open. It occurred to me that he was probably drooling all over one of my favorite shirts in the same moment that I realized I didn't care.

His sharp intake of breath told me he was waking up, and in response, I snuggled a bit further down, trapping his body even more tightly between mine and the back of the couch. I didn't know what the hell we were doing here, but instinct told me that I just wanted him close.

Jordan tilted his chin up and blinked his eyes sleepily. I couldn't help but smile at him. In that moment, the familiarity and sweetness of our past relationship came flooding back to me. Yeah, we'd hassled each other as kids, and I was sure Jordan resented me sometimes just as much as I resented him for taking away from my time with Kiera. But I knew the crinkle of his forehead when he was perplexed and the tone of his voice when he was frustrated. I recognized the t-shirts he still owned, which now fit him much more snugly. When he smiled, his eyes crinkled up at the corners like they always had.

JJ may have been a new, incredibly sexy force in my life, but Jordan—the guy who fell asleep on me and drooled on my shirt —he was home.

"Mmmph," he said, leaning his forehead against my collarbone for a second before starting to push himself up. My heart sank, and my arms tightened around his waist. Either I was stronger than I thought or he hadn't really wanted to get up in the first place, because he came crashing back down on me, smooshing my boobs into his chest and his lips into mine. Something about it felt desperate, fleeting, like if I didn't hold onto it, it would float away.

So, in that split second, I decided to hold on—tight. I moved my hands to his head, letting one comb through his hair and the other cup his jaw. I barely noticed that he tried to pull away for a breath before pressing just as hard into the kiss as I was. His hands snaked under me, his fingers gently digging paths through my shirt, catching on my bra clasp. Everything was too hot, too encumbered - I wanted both the shirt and the bra gone.

Finally, my 30-minute sculpt class from my UPenn days paid off—I used my stronger-than-average abs to pull myself up, and him along with me. He managed to get his legs under him so he was sitting straight up against the back of the couch. I grinned. Exactly where I wanted him.

I pushed up on my knees and swung one leg over his lap, spurred on by the thick outline of his cock through his jeans. I let out a breathy moan as I settled myself over it, satisfied, if only a little bit, by the pressure of it between my legs. In one smooth motion, I tugged my blouse up over my head, saying a prayer that the way the movement mussed my hair was sexy and not disastrous. I bit my lip and ran my fingers under the hem of his gorgeously-fitted tee. "Now you."

I was more than a little disappointed when he hesitated. For the first time since he'd woken up, I dared to look into his eyes.

One of his brows raised and tilted his head a bit, searching my eyes, too. His lips pressed into a thin line, and my heart twisted. He was going to reject me. That would make two guys in one night. Awesome.

"Lizzie, are you sure?" He traced my jaw with his fingertips and ran his thumb once across my chin, like he was priming my mouth for more contact.

"I don't—It's not really *wrong*, is it?" My lips twisted and I felt my throat tightening. "Tonight...he was so clearly not for me. I didn't even kiss him. I... I didn't even want to." With every word, I willed him to understand what I couldn't bring myself to say—he was the only guy I could imagine myself kissing. At least for the near future. I wiggled my hips, pressing my crotch further down onto his hardness.

He sucked in a breath and his eyes fluttered shut. I smirked. Every time we were together, I loved that look a little bit more. I watched, mesmerized, as my fingers seemed to drag themselves through his hair. He'd learned how to take care of it since he was a kid. His blond dad wouldn't have known how to teach him even if he had still been alive, and his mom had always wanted it buzzed short. I leaned down to kiss him.

He let out a low hum, like he was pausing to savor this. I pulled back just enough to smile at a memory that just poked its way through the lust-induced fog in my mind. "Do you remember when you went to that wannabe barber when you were sixteen?" I asked.

He gave me a quick, soft kiss and then returned my grin. "And I came back with that terrible excuse for a fade? My head looked like a damn layer cake."

I kissed him again, harder. "You didn't want your mom to see it because she'd say 'I told you to just cut it short," I recalled. "So I buzzed it down for you."

"I didn't appreciate you then," he replied. "Did I even say 'thank you?'"

"Can't hold it against you," I said, shrugging. "It was a truly horrible fade."

Jordan narrowed his eyes at that and then dug his thumbs in under my ribs. I squealed with laughter. The jerk *knew* I was ticklish. Even reflexes didn't make me pull away from him – instead, I pressed into him closer so that his arms instinctively circled my waist. I melted into his kisses, mesmerized by the stroke of his tongue against mine. We were hot and heavy again in no time.

"Do you want a condom?" he ground out as his thumbs dug into the skin just over my hips.

I leaned down, pressing a smirking kiss to his lips. "Only if you do."

He growled in response, moving as if to flip me beneath him, but I stopped him. "No, " I said. "I want you just like this." I leaned to the side and his tight grip moved to my thigh, pressing so hard even through my jeans that I half expected a bruise to form there.

That just reminded me that my jeans were in the way, so I peeled myself off his lap and stood, shimmying out of them. They brushed against the bandages he'd so lovingly applied to my feet and his sweetness coursed a rush of warmth through me. Right before climbing back over him, I made the call to pull my panties off as well. The past week with JJ, plus a full future docket of dates, had inspired me to step up my grooming game, and I happened to know exactly how cute this particular view of me had been just this morning.

I had to swallow down the extra drool that watching him tug off his own pants and boxer briefs caused. Most girls I knew thought dicks were ugly, and I tended to agree, but something about his was beautiful. It was certainly big. Maybe it was just that looking at it brought back the memory of how it felt inside me, and I was wearing sex-fogged glasses.

It didn't matter one bit.

I straddled him again, and the slide of his cock through my wetness brought a groan from both of us. He mouthed at my neck, then at the base of my throat, then down to the swell of my breast, sucking a mark there. I wondered if anyone would notice at work, and what they would think it meant about how my date had went. When he slid the strap of my bra down my shoulder, then thumbed at my nipple through the lace, I decided I really, really didn't care what anyone thought. I arched my back, pushing my breasts right in front of his face, leaving no doubt about exactly what I wanted him to do.

"It's not really fair that you took your panties off but left this on," he murmured, tracing the bottom edge of the bra strap around to my back, then flicking the clasp open with his deft engineer's fingers.

"Your shirt is still on," I countered, struggling to get words out as he pulled the bra completely off, shoving it onto the couch cushion. My fingers tugged pathetically at the short sleeves while he latched onto the side of my boob, drawing deeply on the skin, almost certainly leaving a mark that I'd feel for days. Every time I turned, I'd think of this moment.

"Patience," he said, chuckling as his lips moved farther in. He flicked his tongue against my nipple and I whimpered, clawing my fingernails along his scalp to signal my approval. "I want you to know how beautiful you are," he said before taking my breast in his mouth and sucking hard. "How perfect," he said as he moved to the other side, then driving me wild with the same treatment on the other side. "I want you to understand," he said when he finally released me with a loud pop of lost suction, "that anyone who doesn't want you, doesn't want to touch you, or kiss you, or talk to you, or be with you, is one hundred percent idiotic." He alternately licked and kissed his way back up to my neck, then to the space just behind my ear. His breath blew hot there, ruffling the little hairs there and sending electricity skittering down my spine. "Pizza bloating or not."

I threw my head back and laughed, the spell broken, but not at all in a bad way. I grabbed his face with both hands and kissed him, hard and messy. "That's why it's good we had a nap. The pizza bloat is gone."

He wrinkled his nose and groaned.

"Too soon?" I teased. "We could kill time by taking this off..." Finally, I tugged his tee off over his head, smiling fondly at the way his hair stood up every which way when I did.

I tossed it to the side, then resettled myself on his lap, making his cock drag through my folds and nudge against my clit in the most delicious way. I let my nails trail over his pecs and trace the slim muscles on his stomach. I'd painted them a soft pastel pink before my date, and they looked gorgeous pressing against his warm brown skin. I wanted to take a picture of my pale freckled arm draped over his chest, forever remember how it looked like part of him had blended with me, like I'd have a reminder of his skin pressing against mine forever.

I gasped as he gripped my hips, shifting me slightly backward and then tugging me forward again. His cock pressed against the little bundle of nerves, and it was like he'd flipped a switch. Suddenly I was frantic, grinding my hips down and tossing my head back, then forward once again to give him another desperate kiss. I gasped out every word. "Need to feel you—" while he groaned,

"Need to be inside you."

Things seemed to happen in warp speed then. I was so hyper focused on getting him where I wanted him that it was like every one of my senses became eagle-sharp.

When my fingers reached the curls at the base of his cock, reflex pushed me up off my heels. His groan when my fingers wrapped around him filled the room and resonated with something deep inside me. Everything converged into one overwhelming, crystal-clear feeling—this was so undeniably, deliciously *right*.

I guided him to my entrance and slowly, slowly sunk down, allowing him to fill me bit by perfect bit. God, he was perfect. The friction of him inching into me traveled across every nerve ending, leaving me breathless, not knowing whether I wanted more, faster, or whether I needed a moment to catch my breath. He wasn't quite in all the way to the hilt when he bumped against my cervix, sending a jolt of pleasure-pain through me that made me cry out.

He froze, cupping the back of my head with his palm and looking into my eyes. "You okay?" The intensity of the connection between us in that moment made my heart swell, so full it felt like it would burst.

"Perfect. Amazing. Don't stop," I whispered as I leaned down and brushed my lips, feather-light, against his. Just that slight forward lean changed the angle between us, and something about that set him off. His hands slid down to cup my ass, tugging my body up and pulling it down onto him again in a rapidly increasing rhythm.

"Lizzie," he moaned, before peppering my neck and shoulder with hot, messy kisses. "You're sure about the condom. Right?"

"There hasn't been anyone else in months," I groaned as he dragged himself in and out of me.

"For me either," he grunted. His breathlessness made me feel like a goddess.

I hooked my arms under his, to get better leverage, the noises coming from my throat on each thrust growing louder, more desperate. The heat building inside me licked at every inch of my skin, a warning of the coming devastation, but somehow all I wanted was more.

I felt my nails dig into his skin, heard his low growl when they did. "Jordan. I'm..."

"Come on. Let go. I've got you." He slid his hands up and looped his arms around my waist, pulling me tight into him, supporting me as the pleasure crashed through my veins and left me shaking and gasping. A moment later, he thrust so hard into me that I saw stars. His shout when he came sent pride coursing through me. I wanted to grab his ass and beg him to keep going, but I also kind of wanted to cradle his tall, lean body against mine and lick lazy kisses over every inch of his skin.

This combination of arousal and affection was strange. The other times I'd slept with a guy, it had been either because it was expected of me, or because I wanted to make him happy. Because I liked him. Occasionally, I would get drunk or have such an amazing time partying and laughing that I'd get carried away and have trouble keeping my hands off a guy - Josh used to buy me drink after drink for that reason - but I'd never felt anything close to the pleasure I felt with Jordan. JJ.

We sat in the same position until we caught our breath, aiming kisses at each other's mouths and sometimes missing, which made us laugh and try again. The sensation of Jordan's lips vibrating against mine, his breath puffing into my mouth, made me feel warm all over, in a completely different way than his cock had just a couple minutes ago. This felt like something I wanted to wrap around me, to claim as my own and no one else's.

Finally, when I realized how badly my quads burned, I shifted to the side to stand up.

"Noooo," JJ complained, still grasping one of my hands as I got to my feet. It was a good thing, too, because my legs were like jelly. It had been a simultaneously terrible and incredible night for my lower half, that was for sure.

"I'm just cleaning up a little," I said with a chuckle, and made my way into the bathroom.

I flicked on the light and stared into the mirror. I blinked at my reflection and startled. In the harsh light, I could see what a terrific disaster I really was.

My hair was rumpled in a frizzy half-wave mess, with one knot so impressive on the side JJ had pressed himself into that I'd need half a bottle of conditioner and several very patient minutes to remove it. My mascara was smudged and my lips were dry. Red spots where I'd gotten rid of my monthly couple of zits glared out at me in the harsh light.

Forget the photoshopped Barbie doll in the "Liz Dates Philly" article. I didn't even look like the "first date Liz," who Brad thought was so reprehensible. I looked like I'd been dragged through the gutter and then ridden on the back of a motorcycle for a few miles.

I couldn't go back out there like this. Whatever JJ had been able to turn a blind eye to in the midst of what I thought was pretty hot couch sex would not cut it for very long. I scrubbed my face and ran a toothbrush through my mouth.

I checked myself in the mirror again. Not much improvement, and it felt pretty freaking stupid to think of putting on makeup now. Same with detangler and busting out a straightening iron. Didn't change the fact that the thought of JJ seeing me such a mess made butterflies of doubt flutter in my belly.

I shouldn't have come to the bathroom. It ruined the mystique, and our dreamlike, just—roommates, absolutely freaking incredible midnight couch sex was just that—like a dream. At the last moment, I grabbed a towel from the bar behind me and wrapped it tightly around myself. It still smelled like JJ's shampoo. I breathed in deep.

Stepping back into the hallway after turning out the bathroom light made the dark seem pitch-black. I tiptoed over to the wall, hoping JJ had fallen asleep and I could pass safely to my room without him seeing exactly what my date that night had seen—a mess. Maybe he'd gone to his own room, hoping to sleep quietly without me drooling on him.

Why did that idea make my breath hitch in my throat, and my heart twist with dread?

But he wasn't gone, or asleep. Instead, he was in his boxer briefs, picking up every article of clothing we'd tossed on the coffee table, floor, and... doorknob? Wow.

"Hey," he said with a warm smile. "Now that you're back, you can decide which clothing you want. If any. I mean, clothing is optional. Obviously. I just didn't want to leave this..." he motioned down to his crotch "...well, you know. Out."

That made me giggle. "Um... toss me a shirt?"

"Yours or mine?" His eyebrows arched up and a smile flickered at the corners of his mouth. My eyes were adjusting to the dark again, and with the dim blue light coming in from the high windows, his expression looked almost like hope.

"Yours," I practically whispered. He tossed it to me, and I dropped my towel with a squeak when I went to catch it. I fumbled with it for several seconds, gracelessly searching for the opening and then tugging it down over my head. After I tried to smooth my hair down, again, I looked up to JJ still standing there, still looking at me, with a shit-eating grin on his face.

"You tossed it on purpose," I said as my grin slowly grew to match his. "So I'd have to drop the towel."

He shrugged and stepped closer to me until we nearly stood toe to toe. "Can you blame me?"

"I... um ..."

He held his hand out, palm up, and my own hand shook as

it slid into his. He squeezed, then turned it enough to link our fingers together. "Your room is really hot, I noticed."

"Yeah?" Even that one word came out sounding breathless.

"Yeah. I think the AC is messed up. Stay in my room? I won't steal the covers."

I was pretty sure that was bullshit. The AC had been working perfectly that morning. I was also really, really relieved that he was offering me an excuse to do what I desperately wanted to do anyway—tangle my body with his while we slept.

"Okay. I'll call the landlord in the morning," I said softly as he tugged me along behind him.

"Don't worry about it," he said, giving me a wicked smile.

There were a dozen reasons we shouldn't be doing this. But right now, I had no idea how I'd be able to stop.

CHAPTER 15

JORDAN

I WOKE the next morning to hear Liz, in the kitchen, again.

I didn't know what I wanted out of this, or what exactly I expected her to do in this weird morning-after space. Still, the memory of the last time, when she'd been fixing coffee and ready to run out the door and - worst of all - pretending that nothing had ever happened between us, put me on guard.

Sure enough, she looked almost exactly as she had in that memory of mine: wearing a flowy dress and fitted jacket this time, but still obviously headed to work. She was pouring coffee into two mugs, and I slid into one of the chairs at our tiny table and gratefully accepted one.

We sipped in silence for a few moments. She stood the whole time.

"I have to write about my date today. Deadline's at 5."

"On the weekend?"

She shrugged. "I guess they want it ready to run on Monday. Thought I'd head to the office so I could..." her eyes flicked to mine, "focus."

Disappointment washed over me. She felt weird around me. How could she not? She was just trying to do her job and here I was, making out with her, and more, whenever she'd let me. Hell, I'd even tried to rig the damn date. She wasn't my property.

"If this isn't what you—"

"This is weird, isn't it?"

Both of us blurted out those half-thoughts in the same instant. The pink flush on Liz's cheeks bloomed immediately, and I realized that it must happen in any variety of over-whelming circumstances. She blushed when she was flattered or turned on, I knew, and now I could see that her face reddened when she was embarrassed, too.

She took a deep breath and started again. "I know we agreed that this apartment, and everything that happened here, could be like our own little bubble, but...I also know it's weird. I'm dating other guys and writing about it for all of Philly to read. It seems like common sense that I absolutely should not be doing... what we were doing...while I'm going out with other guys. Right?"

Before I could answer, she pressed her lips together and nodded firmly. "It's weird," she repeated, "and I'm sorry."

Deep down, I'd known that the whole 'friends-slash-room-mates with benefits' thing wouldn't work for me for very long. Whatever feelings I thought I could push off were relentlessly bleeding through at the weak edges of this relationship, that much was clear.

It might have been weird for her, but it was dangerous for me.

If this wasn't what she wanted anymore, and it wasn't what I could handle, there was no way I was going to push her. And really, I shouldn't push myself.

By instinct, I stretched my hand out to touch hers, letting my fingers brush the back of her hand before I pulled it back. *Focus, man.*

"You have nothing to be sorry about. Pretty sure I was just as equal a participant as you were, in...you know. Everything." I said, adding a chuckle in hopes of sounding more convincing, even though I couldn't bring myself to look at her when I did. Her eyes flashed to mine in a way that told me that she didn't totally buy my feigned nonchalance but was choosing to accept it anyway.

It wasn't like I could really tell her that I'd been daydreaming about her nonstop since the first time we'd slept together.

I made some excuse to take my coffee back into my room, and plunked myself back down on the bed for a few minutes of staring at the wall. The coffee didn't do anything to erase the scent of her shampoo on my pillowcase.

Thankfully, the next couple weeks had me spending most of my time on UPenn's campus and addressing all the work on my busy Engineering PhD. schedule.

Okay, Maybe I didn't *have* to volunteer for an inner city junior high's LEGO Technic state competition team. Maybe I didn't have to spend quite so much time in the library, or make sure I held long office hours and met each and every one of the students I TA'd for. But there was just something unbearable about being in the apartment with Liz and hearing her talk about work. It was almost impossible to be in the same space as her, watch her walk around and bend over when she picked up her laundry and slowly eat a popsicle, without wanting to grab her and kiss her. And, obviously, more.

There was just one problem—neither one of us had been fully aware of ourselves the last time we'd had sex. I knew she'd wanted it in the moment, just like I had. But if we were in danger of something as innocent as falling asleep on the couch together turning into a full-blown, clothes-on-the-floor, frenzied session of lovemaking, I hated to think what would happen if we ran into each other unloading groceries, or happened to be alone watching TV, or—oh, God—bumped into each other to or from the shower?

I lamented the problem to Ethan at Joey and Hawk's, the same bar where we'd first met, later that week.

"I don't know what to tell you, man. If you can't predict the outcome, you should absolutely not be putting yourself in the circumstance." Ethan was taking a break from a long day of studying insurance policies to hang out with me. Of course he'd be talking about a relationship like this.

"Oh, I can predict it. The likelihood is high that we'll have sex. There are just too many other variables."

"Like..."

"Well, condoms, for one."

"Jordan Jacobs. Bro. Do not tell me that you went bareback with her. The incidence of sexually transmitted diseases in urban populations of under-25 females alone is—"

I shrugged. "I trust her."

"She's dating all of Philly. Publicly. Everyone reads her column."

My eyes narrowed. "Who's everyone? You?" I was happy that Liz was getting readers, but at the same time, hearing about them broke the illusion that I was getting exclusive, intimate details about her life by living with her. Things nobody else could know.

"Well, vicariously. Natalia read her intro, and the first date column."

"Natalia. Isn't that the bullfighter? Who you've known for, like, two weeks?"

Ethan nodded forlornly.

"I thought you weren't going to see her anymore, man. Too risky."

"I wasn't. But she decided she was gonna see me. And then she sort of held me prisoner in her bed for a week and a half." The words were harsh, but he said them with a slight smile.

I raised my eyebrow. "You don't sound too upset about that."

Ethan sighed. "I don't know what I think. I never don't know what to think. That's what this girl does to me."

"Well...tell her thanks for reading. I guess."

Ethan just slumped his shoulders a bit and ordered us both another beer.

It turned out that Natalia wasn't the only one reading. Liz's boss declared the column an instant success and got right to work setting her up with more guys.

The second date she went on, just a week and a half after the first, had been the result of a rather entertaining variety of choices. Maybe readers thought Brad was too blah, because the guys up for vote this time were a yacht-owning young tycoon cruising through life on his daddy's money, an artist whose bio was penned in iambic pentameter, and an environmental activist. It was hard for even me to choose the most awful one between these guys. In the end, though, I chose to try to stack the vote in Mr. Environment's because his leather man-necklace and facial hair annoyed the hell out of me. I idly hoped it would have a similar effect on Liz.

I fell asleep reading some atrociously boring book on structural engineering theory and woke up to the sound of poor Liz retching in the bathroom.

It turned out he'd taken her to a back alley Indian restaurant he swore was authentic, where she'd eaten some chicken tikka that tasted off, while he insisted it was fine.

I held her hair back while she emptied her guts into the toilet, and we ended up spending the night trading college party-puking stories between her bouts of vomiting. After the fifth time she puked, she pressed her head to the cool tile of the floor and let her eyes flutter shut. "Thanks for cleaning the bathroom yesterday. And holding my hair. You're the best," she said in her raspy voice. "You know what Kiera and I always said back in high school?"

"Hmm?" I said, feeling my eyes drift shut, too, as my own sleepiness finally started to claim me.

"A clean toilet to puke in says 'I love you.'"

My eyes flared wide at those words. Did she mean that? Because even though we'd only been back in contact for a month or so, I couldn't help but wonder if my feelings for her were...

But when I turned to respond, my heart softened. She was fast asleep, her face smooshed against the base of the toilet.

"C'mere, sweetheart," I said, standing and then bending over to brace her shoulders with one arm and thread the other under her knees. I hoisted her up with a grunt and managed to get her to bed without jostling her too much.

She'd washed and folded the bathroom towels the other day - not just hers, but mine too. It had struck me as sweet, so I'd left a packed lunch in the fridge for her in return. I grabbed the stack of them and laid them all around her on the bed, tucking the edges in under her sleep-heavy frame. She could probably use some water - I ran to the kitchen to get her a fresh glass, then set it on her nightstand.

I brushed a stray strand of hair off her face and bent down to kiss her forehead. I pulled away quick. God, she smelled absolutely disgusting.

Right before I turned to leave, I decided it was probably best to stretch out next to her for the night. Just in case she needed me.

I fell asleep with the lingering scent of Indian-food vomit filling my nostrils. Right before I drifted off, I decided that however difficult it was to be around Liz while still wanting her so very badly, it would be even more painful to stay away.

Days later, I fidgeted in the kitchen, watching Liz fix herself a cup of coffee with milk. I'd downed my coffee quickly, and now my stomach was queasy. Or maybe it was nerves, instead of coffee. Being a teaching assistant at UPenn was a big deal.

Her eyes drifted down my neck. "So, is this how all engineers dress?" She stretched a hand out and flipped the corner of my collar up with one finger.

"What are you talking about?" Kiera and Mom had looked at the clothes I was taking to Philly and said they looked good.

Liz raised an eyebrow. "The weird prints? The slightly loose tie? The old man cardigan? JJ. Please. You should just wear what you always wear. You know..."

"T-shirts and jeans? To TA a class? Figured I had to grow up sometime..."

She looked at me for a moment, nodding slightly. "I guess it's easy to forget that we're real grownups now. I keep forgetting that about myself, with this ridiculous assignment...barely passing for a journalism job..."

I wiped my mouth, mumbling into my napkin, "I just don't want the kids I'm teaching to think I'm a loser, you know? It's hard enough to get respect in engineering when you're a black guy. If I wore clothes that casual to the office, they'd think I was the janitor or something."

Liz's mouth curved down. "Oh, Jordan. No they wouldn't."

"You'd be surprised," I muttered, gathering up our trash and shoving it into the white paper bag printed with the red-and-turquoise Joey and Hawk's logo. Ethan had introduced me to it the first time I met him, and I was addicted. "Anyway, I just sort of copied the outfits my Stanford TAs wore, I guess. My students seem to like me so far."

"Of course they like you," Liz said as she stood up and slung her work bag over her shoulder. "And you know what?" she said, tilting her head. "You look just like every engineer I've ever seen on TV."

I chuckled. "Not sure that's a compliment."

"I'm not sure either. But you look nice all the same," Liz said, squeezing my shoulder before standing up to grab a stack of napkins. "Cute. Which, you know, is in stark contrast to Milton."

"His name was *Milton*?"

She nodded slowly, handing me the latest issue of Philly Illustrated. "Hand to God."

I read over Liz's account of sitting across from Indian-food-dude, who not only ate exclusively off food trucks and occasionally out of dumpsters, but also smelled really, really bad, I was laughing so hard that tears streamed from my eyes.

"That is good. Really, really good."

"Yeah? Or is it really bad?" Liz tore off a bite of the bagel I'd brought for her from her favorite shop down the street and chewed, waiting for my response with lights dancing in her eyes. I'd be lucky if I could stop watching her lips move long enough to formulate a response.

"Uh...well, obviously, it's so bad it's good. The date was bad. Not the writing."

"You know," she said after she swallowed her mouthful of bagel, "I'm starting to wonder if that isn't what Philly wants. I mean, nobody is trying to help me find true love, are they?

They're not even lying about it like on that stupid dating show, what is it called?"

"Meet Mr. Right?" I supplied.

"Yeah. That. Where he dates twenty-- girls and falls in love with three of them, somehow, but then has to decide to give the tiara to one, and they all cry half the time and snarl at each other for the rest."

"Yeah. Except, so far, you're just going on one awful date after another."

"But what if I *wanted* to find true love?" she asked, taking a sip of coffee and staring at me over the rim of her mug. "Then all of Philadelphia is just playing a really shitty joke on me for their own amusement."

I shrugged, trying to ignore the pit that formed in my stomach at her words. I'd been working on the assumption that she was only doing this dating thing because Philly Illustrated wanted her to. It helped that she was damn good at doing the write-ups. The way she weaved a narrative was so engaging that I'd finished reading the column in minutes, and almost wanted more.

If 'more' "more" didn't involve Liz dating a guy that she might actually fall in love with. I thought about Ethan, afraid of seeing a girl because she was thinking of maybe doing something that might get her killed a year from now. I'd never thought of falling in love as something dangerous before, but between Liz and Ethan, I was starting to think twice.

"Well...do you? Want to...um...fall in love?"

Liz looked down at her hands, suddenly very interested in removing a little patch of old polish on her thumbnail. She shrugged. "Maybe. Doesn't everyone?"

I watched her for several seconds, until she finally raised her head and looked right at me.

"I guess so," I said quietly.

"I know we didn't decide anything definitive about...you know. Us. Last time we talked." . I tried not to wonder if her glistening eyes meant that she was trying to hold back tears, or whether her trembling lip meant she was nervous about what I'd say.

But Liz knew that she was in control. She knew that I was unattached, and that the barriers to us keeping up this arrangement of roommates-plus-sex were largely on her side of the fence.

The only barrier for me was the one that scared me most, though. If I kept having incredibly hot, runaway-train, mind-blowing sex with Liz, I would just keep falling more and more in love with her. Maybe so deep that I wouldn't be able to pull myself out again.

If Liz did end up finding true love during her Liz Dates Philly escapades, she'd still be my roommate. And seeing her with another guy when I was already halfway to head over heels for her? That would destroy me.

"Honestly, if you're looking for Mr. Right on these dates... maybe it's best for us to call it quits."

"Well, it's not like you're volunteering for the position. Right?" She stared at me boldly, and it was clear that she needed an answer from me. Now. She was asking me if she should pull the plug on Liz Dates Philly, for me. My heart pounded.

I stirred the half-inch of coffee left in my cup, just to give my eyes somewhere to focus except on hers. I wouldn't mind at least trying my hand at a real relationship with Liz, but I couldn't promise that I'd fit the bill as her one and only. I knew that she was a nice girl, that she was talented and funny, and that she was amazing in bed. But that wasn't enough for me to ask her to gamble her professional future on. I had to make her think I didn't care about keeping whatever we might have had going.

Cowardice won out. I forced a chuckle. "To be the subject of your dating column? Absolutely not."

The corners of her mouth turned down for a split second before she nodded. "I don't know what I'm looking for. I guess there's always a chance to find the right person for you, no matter how little you expect it. Right?" My heart sank as she stood decisively from the table and deposited her coffee cup in the sink. Seconds later, she was headed out the door, with a soft, "See you later."

My stomach felt like it was dropping to the floor. I'd fucked everything up. It hurt that she'd given up that easily, and I hated knowing I'd never stare into her hungry eyes as I plunged myself into her again. I wished I'd stolen just one more kiss from her before I cut off that possibility completely. But I'd done it because I cared about her. I didn't want to see her ruin the chance she had to win a long-term position with a paper where she could start her career.

That's what I told myself, anyway. I knew it was because I was selfish, scared bastard.

Thinking about Liz's next date, though, made me grimace. Once she'd finished the "Liz Dates Philly" series with wild success, I'd be free to tell her how I really felt – as long as she hadn't met the perfect guy along the way. What would be the harm in trying to vote so that her dates continued to be more hilarious and less swoony?

As soon as she left, I whipped out my phone and laptop started my voting for the day. Alec the filmmaker looked high-maintenance and egomaniacal enough to get rejected by Liz right off the bat and still give her good fodder for the column. Win-win.

Still, I wasn't sure my voting alone would do the trick this time. Liz's column was bound to draw a ton of readers, and they'd all be voting for the next date. I texted Ethan. Being in the actuarial department, he knew algorithms and coding like the back of his hand, and I'd considered asking him for his help on this for a while.

JJ: Hey Ethan - how difficult would it be to rig lots of votes to an online poll?

CHAPTER 16

LIZ

LIKE EVERY OTHER warm-blooded college woman in the United States, I'd watched my fair share of that dating reality show, "Meet Mr. Right." In the end, he always fell in love with one of the girls, and sometimes, their relationship even lasted long enough to make it to the cover of People Magazine. My sorority sisters and I had always joked that the producers of the show must have hand-picked the most ridiculously dramatic girls possible, just for the added publicity.

I was beginning to think the same thing about Philly Illustrated's approach to finding men for me to date.

Yes, Monica always ran a rough sketch of the guys in each poll by me - "Entrepreneur in his 30s," "Hipster Musician," "Eclectic Adventurer" all sounded just fine, even exciting. Then I would go on the date, and it turned out to be a complete disaster.

As early summer turned into fall, I went on date after date with guys who weren't just awful matches for me - they were awful matches for *anyone*. There was Rich, the guy who was cute enough despite his rumpled shirt, who I found out spent approximately 18 hours a day playing video games in his parents' basement. Where he lived.

There was Alan, who was a very successful hedge fund manager, who traveled so much that he really just wanted to keep a girlfriend in every city. I would make a perfect "Philly fuck-buddy," he informed me. I asked him if we could spell it "Phuck-buddy," for the sake of alliteration in the write-up. He failed to understand that I was joking.

There were a couple more self-absorbed douchebags - the original underwear model Brad; Louis, the suffering artist; Neil, the plumber with dreads; Jack, who moonlighted as a stripper, which would be totally fine if he didn't offer sexual services for extra tips on the side. Then there was the mayor's nephew, Trent, who I would have loved to have a conversation on politics with if he would have let me get a word in edgewise. Most recently, there was Harry, the conservationist who said that any girl he dated had to be willing to eventually move into the tiny 250-square foot house he built on the back of a trailer with him. He cheerfully told me I'd be allowed to bring any of my personal possessions, as long as they would fit in a single storage tote.

I never called any of them back.

Instead, I poured my frustrations into my column, which got funnier every week, if I did say so myself. All the guys went by pseudonyms, and Deanna was super skillful at snapping photos that expressed the atmosphere and feel of each date without actually showing the guy's face.

Basically, Liz Dates Philly was about as pain-free as it could get for all parties involved.

That is, unless you counted me, when I had to go home after the date was over and share space with the guy I actually wanted to be with.

"It really is just what you read in the column," I explained to Kiera one day on the way home from the office, my phone wedged between my ear and shoulder, making the ache in my neck even worse. "These guys are entertaining. And that's about the most complimentary thing I can say about them."

"I just find it seriously difficult to believe that you haven't at least gotten into some heated make-out session with at least one of them."

"Yeah, I was just dying to run my fingers through Neil's dreadlocks. Right after he listed the top five most common cloggers of residential toilets."

Kiera let out a short laugh. "Okay, but Trent? He was cute. He liked the same things you do."

"I know, just...it's hard to explain. Just not in the same way?"

"The same way as who? What impossible standard are you comparing these guys to? I know it's not Josh, because you have hardly mentioned his sorry frat boy ass in the past two months. But I am one of your best friends, and I know you are pining for someone. It is clear as the day is long, even in your voice! So maybe you should quit looking around Philly for a guy if you already know the right guy for you, babe. Because whoever it is..."

"It's my *job*, Kiera! And besides, there is no 'whoever,'" I hissed, cutting her off with no room for response.

It wasn't technically a lie. I wasn't dating, or even sleeping with, anyone on the side. Not anymore.

"Well, all I'm saying is that if there *was* a 'whoever,' I'm sure it wouldn't mean losing your job. Liz, I've read your columns since you were writing them. Remember when you started with the mystery of the tack on Mrs. Rigby's chair for the school paper in 5th grade?"

I laughed. I remembered, vividly. That was some freaking good writing for an eleven-year-old. At least high school level.

"Yeah. So, I know you can spin anything. I've seen the readers' comments, too. They think the dates are funny, yeah, but they all say they want you to find true love. That's all they want. A good love story. I really don't think they care how you get there. Follow your heart, you know? It's never wrong."

"Sure, Kiera. I'll follow my heart and then my fairy godmother will drop by with a brand-new car and a designer gown for my date with the prince."

"I'm serious, Liz! I mean, yeah, shit happens, but this Liz Dates Philly thing? This is a story, entertainment, escapism. Give them a good narrative and they'll eat it up, whether they voted for the guy or not."

I sighed. "I know you're usually right about everything, but I hate to break it to you—nobody is asking to be in a relationship with me. Zero guys. From anywhere."

That wasn't technically a lie, either.

JJ was utterly inexplicable to me. He never asked questions about the guys in each week's dating pool but seemed to know all about the one who had been chosen when he read my column on Monday. And he always read my column on Monday, out loud, right after I got home from the office and plopped down on the couch.

JJ managed to strike the perfect balance between teasing me and complimenting my sense of humor or admiring a turn of phrase and nudging me to try to add even more projects to my Philly Illustrated workload. "I'll cook dinner for you. Twice a week, if you need the extra time," he encouraged, squeezing my foot where it lay next to his lap on the couch.

"I don't know," I grumbled, letting my head loll back on the arm of the couch. I didn't miss how he stared at my exposed collarbones when I did, and I couldn't decide whether that was satisfying or frustrating.

Jordan hadn't tried to so much as kiss me since the last time we'd had sex. The memory of that night on the couch, feeling so desperate to have him inside me, wouldn't leave me alone. I was pretty sure you could have put People's Sexiest Man of the Year in front of me, naked and ready, and the sight of him wouldn't make me want the guy on the cover nearly as much as just that one memory of me and JJ together made me want him.

If only JJ felt the same about me. Sometimes he squeezed my foot, or nudged my side with his elbow when he needed to step past me in our tiny kitchen, or gripped my shoulder in encouragement when I hunched over my laptop at our little table, frustrated with a sentence or paragraph. Every single time he touched me, goosebumps broke out up and down my arms, and I had to fight to keep from turning to him, grabbing his shirt, and pulling him down for a kiss. I knew without a doubt that I wanted more of what we'd done so many weeks ago.

Yes, it would be complicated, but these Philly Illustrated dates weren't going anywhere. They were one hundred percent for Phil-Ill and zero percent for me. I needed to talk to Monica about what exactly the plan was for this series - whether there was an end game like a grand date-off or whether she just wanted to draw out this misery - and the increasingly impressive advertising it attracted - indefinitely. After working on the project for four months and eleven dates I had to at least be getting close to building up some journalistic capital with the magazine. Every week more and more people voted in the column. Maybe if I got the click-through data for my column, I could float the idea of ending this project and starting on a new one. Maybe reporting on something that had any actual significance for this city.

I couldn't deny that a side factor in just wanting Liz Dates Philly to be over was being able to kiss Jordan again, and hopefully more. Or at least to try getting back what I thought we'd had, weeks ago. Every day I thought of a new way to broach the subject with him. Every day I chickened out.

It wasn't that I wanted to be able to act on my crush on my roommate, on my childhood bestie's brother, on the one guy in the city that I shouldn't have been fantasizing about day and night. But I did, and the crush was starting to crush me.

CHAPTER 17

JORDAN

SLOWLY, I'd started to admit to myself that my feelings for Liz weren't going away. She really was as irresistible as I'd feared. Not only had we had incredible sex, but she was adorable and funny and smart, too. And she lived in my goddamn apartment, so I was reminded of her awesomeness every single day.

Didn't change the fact that she'd made it abundantly clear that the possibility of us being together had ended the day I'd told her to keep going with Liz Dates Philly. She went on date after date, looked incredible for every single one, no matter how awful the guys were. (I made sure they were awful, with the simple programming hack Ethan helped me with weeks back). I may have been disappointed, but I wasn't a bitter jerk. Rigging her dates to be ridiculous wasn't exactly something a good friend would do, but it wasn't really malicious, either.

At least, that's what I told myself.

So when the next dating poll came up two days later, I tried to skew it again - in a direction I thought Liz might like.

I only knew bits and pieces about her ex-boyfriend, Josh. From the photos on Facebook and what Kiera had told me about him over the years, he was a typical white-bread frat boy who got decent grades and managed a seat at a good law school thanks to his daddy's connections.

She'd been with him for three years. I knew from Keira that she'd been expecting a proposal the night they actually ended up splitting up.

That was the split that opened up a spot for me in this apartment.

The more I learned about Josh, the only guy Liz had ever liked enough to want to settle down with, the more melancholy I felt. Looked like I really wasn't her type at all. I tried to push down the memory of her moaning my name all those weeks ago, of the exquisite pleasure-pain of her teeth scraping my skin. Sex was different from relationships, and she clearly was not interested in one of those with me.

Maybe Liz really *was* looking for love by dating every guy in Philly she got her hands on - no matter how awful each one was turning out to be.

As difficult as it was to be around Liz, as the weeks went on, it seemed like I couldn't stay away. She was addicted to Joey and Hawk's – everything from the craft beers they featured to Joey's small-batch artisan scones in flavors like blueberry mascarpone and Brussels sprout and cheddar. After Liz gave me a taste of one of hers – key lime, that day - I was hooked too. I found myself stopping there and grabbing something new for her a couple times a week. I'd be lying if I said it wasn't partly to see the look of ecstasy on her face when she had the first taste.

Then there were her periodic Netflix binges. She didn't just veg out in front of the TV—she was a participant in the shows she watched. There was The West Wing, The Good Wife, Scandal, Homeland, Designated Survivor, Madam Secretary, and even Jack Ryan—anything and everything to do with politics and Washington fascinated her. For how invested she was, you'd think she was a character on the show that none of the others happened to ever acknowledge. She engaged in (one-sided) dialogue with them, shouted at them about what policy and strategic decisions they should be making, sighed and shed tears over their defeats. It was a stunning thing to watch, mostly because it was a perfect showcase for her passion and knowledge.

She belonged on the political beat, that was for sure. It was evident even in her column. She spun each and every negative quality from every guy into something entertaining, without actually lying about what a tool he was. Watching her watch political shows gave me a glimpse into what her life would be like when she finally got her dream job, and it was beautiful.

We watched other stuff, too. I loved comparing our favorite childhood cartoons and movies. Forcing each other to sit through and watch the whole thing, no matter how ridiculous it seemed, brought a new level of flirty teasing to our relationship. I may have been making fun of how much drama a Saturday morning superhero cartoon involved, and she may have rolled her eyes at the sheer volume of clichés in The Princess Bride, but I never saw her smile as much as when we were immersed in a fictional world together, teasing each other.

Besides that, I cooked for her. Liz took on as many extra little assignments at Philly Illustrated as she could, hoping to make the right connection or impress the right people. I encouraged her to do it every chance I got, and if that meant sussing out her favorite dishes and perfecting them for her, just to watch her wrap her lips around the fork and hum in approval, well, I'd happily suffer through it.

I still tried to fill every moment we weren't together with things to distract me - schoolwork, lesson prep, even more volunteering positions with high school LEGO clubs and the Boys and Girls club after-school program. That, and voting for the worst option in the Liz Dates Philly poll every week, and setting Ethan's rudimentary algorithm-run program to do the same.

I was clicking those poll buttons enough times that I almost stopped feeling guilty about it.

I blew out a long breath. I couldn't think about that now. She was the one whose job was making this whole situation impossible. She would have to be the one to make any more moves. If I let any more amazing- and I mean, *amazing* - sex happen between us, and if I let any deeper feelings grow between us, I would bear responsibility for messing up this job for her. She so clearly wanted to protect it, and I couldn't blame her. Journalism jobs were never easy to come across, and in this economy, you had to hold on tight to any job that came your way.

Even if holding on tight meant dating a bunch of randos and then letting your boss publish pictures of the whole thing.

I was glad for the pictures, though. They let me see what a total loser Indian-food guy, whose name was, hilariously, Milton, actually was. The looks on Liz's face as she watched him talk made it that much funnier. She looked so different from the Liz I knew on that date, with her lips pursed and her brow furrowed, like she was trying so hard to get through every single minute she spent in that place.

I also kind of liked knowing that, at the end of that date, she'd ended up in bed with me. Even if it wasn't exactly the way I would have liked it.

Even if she'd gone on at least six more dates without the same thing happening again. I heaved a frustrated sigh.

It wasn't like I had fought it, beyond rigging the votes. Wasn't like I *could*.

I was staring at this week's Liz Dates Philly choices while waiting for students to trickle into office hours. The Engineering department's main building was in the middle of some very dusty construction, but the promise of nice new offices a year from now didn't do very much to make me feel better about being cubed off inside one huge office with every other Engineering major at Penn.

That day, though, it kind of worked out for the best.

I had been randomly shoved in next to a Sound Engineering Ph.D. student I hadn't even met yet. I rolled back in my chair and peered in quizzically when a tiny slip of a girl with a waist-length waves heaved her bag on the desk and collapsed into his chair with a soft groan. "Damn cobblestone walkways," she grumbled as she slipped one high heel off and rubbed the joints of her toes.

"Can I help you?" I asked, leaning my head into the doorway. "I haven't seen Mr. Eisen at all today. Don't know when his office hours are."

She raised an eyebrow behind her bright red frames. "Mr. Eisen?"

I pointed to the name plaque. "Toby Eisen? Your sound engineering TA, the guy I assume you're waiting for? I don't know when he'll be in. Been here for two months and haven't even met him yet."

She smiled and tilted her head, like she felt sorry for me. Like if she used words instead of her eyes, she'd be saying, *Aw, bless your heart.* Slowly, she stood up, her bare feet showing lines where her shoes had dug into them, just like Liz's had the other night. "Toby. Short for Tovyah. This is my little cube of engineering office heaven. I'm working under Doctor Hollis."

I scrambled out of my chair, my heart pounding in total mortification. "Oh, God. I am so, so sorry. You know, I'm not the kind of guy who—I mean, I have a sister, and a single mom, and they would beat my ass if they found out I did or anything remotely sexist—I should never have assumed."

She watched me, her smile of amusement making her eyes dance with light. "Well, are you gonna shake my hand, or...?"

"Yes. God, yes. I'm sorry." Her grip was vice-like for being so tiny. At least she didn't have sharp nails to dig into my palm.

Then, I gasped. Something about the way her smile crinkled her eyes...

"Toby. You used to go by T."

"Have we...?"

"You had a short red bob, and a lip ring. Right? Stanford?"

"JJ!" she said, her confused expression melting into a smile. "God, it's been forever!"

Yeah, forever since my freshman year roommate had dragged me to one of those weekend-long outdoor concerts, I'd smoked some pretty potent weed, and ended up fucking T – now Toby - in about six different public places, including against a tree and next to someone sleeping in our tent.

No, they hadn't noticed. No, I hadn't called her again after our first non-high date—and fantastic Netflix and chill—the following weekend. She had a fantastic body and the lip ring had done amazing things when it glided over my cock, but when we weren't high, it turned out we couldn't find a single damn thing to talk about. I hadn't even bothered to learn her last name.

She sure looked different now, in professional clothing, with her name on a plate above the "PhD program" designation.

"I...uh...I had no idea you were in engineering. I'm in aerospace, working under Doctor Phillips."

She giggled. *Giggled.* "Well, I wasn't, really, when we...uh... met. I was just a sophomore then. That concert, where we..."

"Yeah," I stammered. "That was..."

"That was where I decided to look into music careers. I have an aptitude for math and science, so...audio engineering was a good fit." She craned her neck into my cube, where the Liz

Dates Philly page was up and open to the poll for her next date. "Whatcha working on?"

"Oh, that? I just...um...well, it's..." Dammit. The first one of my colleagues I'd really met in this office, and I was dicking around reading a tabloid. "She's my roommate, actually."

"Elizabeth Palmer is your roommate?"

"Yeah. You know her?"

"I've been following her column since it started. I read it after her first date with that underwear model. She's funny."

"Yeah, she is," I agreed. I felt a sigh escape me. It was a strange feeling, admiring a girl who I really wanted but couldn't have. If we had a straightforward breakup, or any separation at all, it would be easier to talk about her with someone.

"So, did you vote yet? For her next date?" Toby shouldered her way into my cube and motioned for me to scroll through the date options. "Oooh. Some good choices this week. And by good, I mean hilarious."

"I know. There's some body builder guy, right?"

"Yeah, but after the model, I think she's had enough self-obsession in a guy for a few weeks, don't you? Or, like, a lifetime."

"Good point. What about...?" She reached over me and slid her hand over mine where it cupped the mouse, nudging my finger out of the way. She scrolled down the page and circled the cursor around a picture of a dude wearing a dark suit, half-unbuttoned dress shirt underneath. His skin was pale as a freaking vampire's, his cheekbones were steep enough to base-jump off of and he looked like he'd spent hours strategically mussing each individual chunk of his hair. "Can't go wrong with Mister Emo. He's suffering for his art."

She pointed at his profile, and I leaned in to read the single quote, "There is nothing more truly artistic than to love people."

I pulled back and grimaced. "Didn't Van Gogh go crazy and cut his own ear off?"

"Mmm. And mailed it to some girl, I think. He loved her. This guy seems to sympathize. He's *perfect*." Toby stood up again, making whatever perfume she wore waft out in front of me. I swallowed and tried not to let my gaze travel to her chest, which I'd already noticed straining against her button-down. I loved women's perfume. I didn't know if it made me sexist, but it always made me wonder if their skin smelled the same as their clothes or their hair...

"Well? Aren't you gonna vote?" Toby was tapping away at her phone, apparently doing just that.

"Yeah, I'll vote for the vampire emo artist guy. What's his name?"

Toby peered at her phone and snorted. "Alex. It's so normal. Maybe he's trying to compensate with that severe suit and the vague quotes."

"Or maybe he's just too dense to think of anything original to say. Even so, she should have fun with him."

"Aw," Toby said, cocking her head at me and pulling a softly pitying look at me. "You're so sweet. Let me tell you, these guys are a dime a dozen in this city. This date is going to be miserable."

As she sauntered out of my cube without another word, I tried to sigh as quietly as possible. I could only hope she was right.

I voted for Emo Alex at least five hundred more times that day.

CHAPTER 18

LIZ

I COULDN'T HAVE BEEN MORE underwhelmed about date number twelve. Thousands of Philly Illustrated readers had spoken, though, and here I was, going on my dozenth date with a very pretty, but seemingly very moody, guy.

Alex was objectively handsome, but his pale, perfect skin and flawless suit made me feel like I would need permission just to touch him. The Picasso quote on his profile meant he thought he was really smart, and maybe really emotional, but it was impossible to tell at this point. I glided on some long-wear red-lipstick and tugged down my curve-hugging little black dress. I was meeting him at the Blue Elephant, one of swankier bars Philly nightlife had to offer, and I knew this dress wouldn't ride up or down too much no matter how awkward the seating or how crowded the dance floor. The Elephant had done a small advertising deal with Philly Illustrated and created a limited edition cocktail named after the column in exchange for our attendance on this date, and, of course, my favorable review.

I sighed as I stepped into my heels, then cast a longing glance at the empty couch, with my favorite knitted throw draped over the back. I would so much rather be lounging with

JJ in front of the TV tonight, even if every time we'd done that since the last time we'd slept together it had been nearly impossible to keep my mind off of ripping his clothes off. Still, it was never a bad way to spend an evening. Not in the least.

Maybe the date would end early.

I arrived at 8:45 for a 9:00 date, after picking Deanna up a block from the club. "Is it crazy living down here?" I groused as I trudged down the sidewalk next to her, shivering against the already pitch-black autumn night air.

She shrugged. "There are people who like to party, and people who like to chill. If you're the type that likes to chill," she said, gesturing to herself, "the partiers don't bother you that much. It's a nice kind of symbiosis."

I raised my eyebrows, then nodded. I knew Deanna was a veritable connoisseur of pot, just from random bits of conversation she dropped here and there. She never came to work high, and I told myself that even though I wasn't a fan of lighting up for a good time, I had to admit that her photography had this otherworldly quality to it that the pot-smoking definitely didn't hurt. Maybe snapping photos while high on various strains could be her sell to major galleries when she finally graduated and broke free of this Philly Illustrated internship.

"Just try not to stick out too much," I said, shooting her a kind smile.

"Never a problem," Deanna said proudly. "This'll be a nice challenge, with the smoke and the darkness and the neon. I think this is one of the clubs with glowing drinks."

I wondered what color the Liz Dates Philly cocktail would glow.

"Well, I'm glad at least one of us is happy about this date

location, then" I said before pushing my way to the front of the club's line, as Alex had directed.

Deanna rolled her eyes at the collection of girls waiting to get into the club. "All these girls are, like, college grads. Did you realize that?"

I furrowed my brow. "So? I am, too."

Deanna snorted. "Nah. You're a graduate now. You know why there aren't any eighteen-year olds waiting in this line?"

"Because...?" I didn't have much patience for this conversation. I also felt older than my years, not knowing the answer to this immediately.

"Because they let all the youngest girls in first. This must be one of those 'barely legal' clubs. Ugh."

"Well," I said, pulling out my I.D. and showing it to a burly, tattooed guy in a black button-down, "then it's a good thing you're just here to take pictures. You don't actually have to enjoy the club."

"Not even supposed to," Deanna said as she gave the bouncer a wan smile and held her camera up to him for illustration. He, in turn, whispered something to a woman wearing a sleek black pantsuit standing behind him with a clipboard. She gave him a curt nod and he lowered the rope separating the crowd outside from the interior of the club, dark and pulsing with bright lights.

I hoped Alex the tortured artist was worth it because the inside of this club—smoke, darkness, constantly moving neon lights, music loud enough to reverberate through my bones—was a recipe for an instant migraine.

A hostess led us on a winding path around low-slung couches and groups of girls writhing on the dance floor, wearing glow-stick jewelry. Deanna had been right. They all looked like they'd just left high school. Disturbingly, this dance floor seemed to have a ratio of about five girls to one much older-looking guy. Most of these guys looked like they were nearing thirty.

My spirits lifted a little bit when the hostess stopped in front of a curtained-off section at the back of the club. Inside, everything seemed relatively calm. A few girls who looked closer to twenty-five than eighteen dotted the booth seating at a round table, each nursing a drink and chatting with a guy.

I only had to scan the small group for a few moments before my eyes landed on Alex. It was uncanny - the gaze with which he met mine looked almost exactly like his picture. He wore the exact same outfit as he had in the picture, and I made a mental note to joke with him about whether that was intentional, so I could recognize him, or whether that was his standard uniform.

Alex smiled at me, the corners of his lips curving up in a gentle smirk, and stretched both arms out to me in greeting. "Elizabeth," he said, his voice warm and smooth as honey.

"What is he, the motherfucking Godfather?" Deanna mumbled in my ear. I snorted, luckily not loud enough for Alex to hear over the blaring music.

"So great to see you, my dear." He wrapped his hands around my fingers, holding them like they were fragile little birds.

"How long have you all been here?" I asked as he led me to a seat.

"I've been here since right after opening, and all of these lovely couples are my new friends."

I nodded at Deanna as she took a shot from behind Alex while he spread his arms wide to gesture to the whole table. As if I couldn't see the people there. "So, wait...you guys don't know each other?"

"We do now," Alex smiled. "They've all graciously agreed to become participants in my latest project, and I hope you will too."

Well, this was shaping up to be the most *interesting* date I'd been on, if nothing else. "What kind of art do you...do?"

"I don't really like the word 'art,'" he said, and I tilted my chin down to look at him skeptically.

"You're an artist, right?"

He sighed and looked at me like I was a simpleton. "Yes, but what I do is so much more than art. It can't be experienced in a gallery or through a pair of headphones. Even in a theater would be insufficient."

"So...how are people supposed to...you know...experience it?"

Alex snaked an arm around my shoulder and chuckled. Deanna got a snapshot of that, too. "It's about couples. The human condition when life is lived in tandem. You see, I believe that none of us walks through life alone, that every moment is tempered by the influence of someone else."

"And you plan to share it...how?"

"You mean, with the public? I haven't decided whether or not to take applications for the experience. Regardless, this particular project will be prepared for viewing in a small, enclosed space by couples only."

"Because we're all affected by someone else." My eyebrow raised slowly. I hoped it communicated more interest and less of the disdain that was starting to creep in.

"Exactly! Our orbit through this universe is steady, but it can wobble when someone else gets near to it. That's transcendent."

"Huh." I nodded slowly. I had to admit, most of my dates had started off with small talk and fidgeting and awkward laughs. This one felt decidedly more grown-up, and a bit out of my reach. It was like I'd walked into a spy movie crossed with a philosophy department lecture hall.

"This is Romy and Tom, Tara and Helen, Leo and Laura, and then, of course, you and me."

"We're not a couple, though."

Literally every person in the room besides Deanna and I burst out laughing.

Alex smiled at us gently, then announced to the three other 'couples,' "She missed the prologue."

They nodded understandingly. One of them—Helen, I thought, a woman with long blond dreads and a sequined t-shirt dress—slid me a drink, glowing blue. "This is the one named after you, darling," she said in a deep, cloying voice. I took a sip and the stinging heat of it going down my throat nearly made me splutter.

Luckily, that meant I didn't drink anything else that night.

Alex explained how he'd submitted his profile to Liz Dates Philly weeks ago, narrated to the group how he'd been taken by my photograph at first, then my 'sweet' sense of humor, then my extensive vocabulary. It was sort of an odd list, but I'd rarely had a guy get so specific about why he was attracted to me. Except—I gulped at the thought—JJ. That first night, when he'd treated every inch of my skin like it was precious...

A sharp fingernail poked into my upper arm. "Liz? Still with us?"

I shook my head, bringing myself back to the moment, and Deanna tilted her head toward Romy and Tom, who had just started enthusiastically making out.

"Wow, they're..."

"They're the newest couple here. Well, besides you and me." Alex smiled like he'd just said something brilliant enough to add to the Bible. "The project explores the way time affects our connection with one another. Time is a real thing, but it's an illusion, you know?"

I didn't know, but my brain suddenly started to feel very,

very tired. My mouth dropped open the slightest bit as I searched for a response, but he jumped in again before I could give one.

"It's just that it's fucking *right there*, you know, this ephemeral time-relationship-*being*, and I'm trying to fucking capture it, you know? But it's like a puzzle. This'll be the sixth installment I've done."

"Soooo cool," Tara, Helen's other half, drawled, and then put her head down on the table, heavy-lidded eyes drifting shut.

"She's baked," Deanna said, stating the painfully obvious.

"So what do you say? Are you game?" Alex trailed his fingertips over the back of my hand, and looked at me with such openness that it felt weird saying anything but yes. Plus, with all these people here, what could go wrong? It might be really cool to be part of his art, or experience, or whatever it was. At the very least, it could make this my most hilarious column yet.

"So, to my studio, then." The other couples started collecting their stuff, and stood to walk out. "It's too far to walk, but that's better. It's down on Washington and 6th. I chose it for the way the street lights filter in right around this time of night. We have perfect timing." Leo and Laura nodded solemnly. "They've been there before," Alex said, like it explained their apparent reverence for his apartment.

"The bill?" I asked, slightly dumbfounded by this whole date. If you could call it a date. It had barely lasted fifteen minutes.

"My grandfather owns the club," Alex said, waving a hand airily over the whole dim, writhing place.

"Now it all makes sense," Deanna grumbled as she got down on the ground to take a picture of the other couples' shoes. At least that's what I thought she was doing. She heaved herself back up again just as Alex was fitting my coat around my shoulders.

JUST DOWN THE HALL   173

At least I didn't have to dance. That, at least, was one positive outcome of this whole weird night. Alex's hand grazed the small of my back while we walked out. My skin crawled.

All nine of us stood on the sidewalk, waiting for Alex's car to pull around. Deanna tugged her phone out of her coat pocket and tapped something out on the screen. After a few seconds of wiggling in place to try to keep warm, Deanna looked up at me with a decidedly guilty expression.

"What?" I asked her. I was becoming more aware every second of how intensely uncomfortable this whole thing felt. But I wasn't drunk, or drugged. Neither Alex nor any of our companions seemed dangerous.

"My roommate is texting me. She's always losing her key, but now she's lost the backup key.

"And you're the only backup now?" I guessed.

"Yeah, and she just got off a long shift, and it's cold..." she trailed off.

"Go let her in."

"Will you be okay, though?"

"Totally," I said. "You know where I'm going, in case anyone asks, and honestly, I think these guys are harmless."

"I'll bring her home when we're finished, of course," Alex said. It was only then that I noticed that his eyes were slowly raking over my body, down and then back up again. He met my eyes and smiled the same smile he had when I'd first arrived. "Beautiful," he said with a decisive nod.

"Um...thank you?"

"You're welcome," he said with a soft, smug smile, letting me know that I'd made the appropriate response. Okay then.

"What about the pictures?" Deanna groaned. "I have to have photos of the whole date."

"I'll snap something on my phone. Alphonso won't even notice."

"If he does, he probably won't even care," Deanna offered.

"We're good," I said with a reassuring smile. It was the right thing to do. I'd want Jordan to bail me out if I was locked out of the apartment. I squeezed my eyes shut, trying to push the image of Jordan opening the door to our place for me, welcoming me in with a smile. The more I thought about it, the more I'd crave him. This was not the time or the place to be lost in thoughts of what I wished he was doing to me with his mouth and hands.

Whatever. He'd closed the door on any possibility of us being together weeks ago. I was on a date with another guy, and I was going to try my best to enjoy it.

Deanna was happy to wait outside the club within eyesight of the bouncer for her ride, so I climbed into the back of Alex's suburban, squeezing in between Alex and Helen. Leo and Laura had taken their own car. Alex murmured something to his driver - yes, *driver* - and we were on our way.

Now that we'd left the bustle of the bar, an eerie quiet hung in the air around us. I'd come to depend on Deanna's company for a certain security more than I'd realized. My gut twisted, telling me that going to Alex's with a bunch of strangers may not have been the greatest idea, after all.

It only took about ten minutes to arrive at Alex's place. I couldn't have been happier about that fact, since Alex had spent the whole time speaking low in my ear about the rhythm of the breaths of all humanity ebbing and flowing in tandem. Or something. He also informed me that he mixed a totally ethereal cocktail whose name had something to do with clouds, because it would make me feel like I was floating.

I was definitely not going to be drinking one of those.

The apartments were newly built, the biggest thing standing on this particular corner. The contractors had lined the sidewalk around the apartment building with trees, which stopped abruptly at a decrepit parking lot that led to a small grocery store. Across the street was a row of businesses - a medical supply shop, a nail salon, and some kind of cafe, their backlit signs looking dusty and exhausted. Alex led us through a heavy wooden front door with brushed silver handles, motioning for Leo and Laura, who had just pulled up down the street, to join us.

"So when we get to the studio space I'm going to explain the whole process, okay?" Alex said as we walked into the brand-new building. "Keep your shoes and coats on, please." I looked around. His place was minimalist, clean, with polished concrete floors and pale wood accents.

"So, this is your place?" I asked, trying to steer the conversation a little bit.

"Yeah, well...mine and my parents'. It...uh...well, it had the optimal studio space on my budget, and I like to be near my work at all times. In case inspiration hits. They mostly leave me to my work, though." He pulled open a door and clicked on a light that illuminated a set of steep stairs.

Oh my God. Alex the artist lived in his parents' basement. How did I get stuck with not one, but two of these guys? Couldn't Philly Illustrated at least vet them for shit like this? I needed to have a talk with Monica, first thing in the morning.

The entire basement was painted white - ceiling, walls, floor. There was zero furniture, no TV, nothing except a tripod set up with a small video camera. "The space actually has surround-sound mics that feed into my system." Alex gestured toward the corner of the expansive, chilly space, where he had a huge computer screen set up next to a simple bed with white sheets.

"So, we're gonna start with Romy and Tom, if that's okay? Since they just met, like, when? A couple days ago?" The two of them interlaced their fingers and giggled, pressing their fore-heads together.

"Last night," Romy murmured as she stood on tiptoes to give Tom a long, languid kiss. He cupped her jaw and bent her back-wards, responding in kind, for the longest twenty seconds of my life. Finally he pulled away with a section of her auburn hair wrapped around his hand.

"Okay, so if you can just stand about four feet in front of the camera, we can begin," Alex said. "Just face each other and follow my instructions. Okay."

Romy and Tom barely broke eye contact with each other. They just stared into each other's eyes with goofy grins. Not that I envied these two, exactly—they were clearly on a completely different plane of awareness from most of the world —but I had literally never been into someone enough to want to look at them and smile forever.

Well. Except for one guy. The morning after with JJ was the smiliest I'd ever felt in my life.

The other couples watched Romy and Tom with fascina-tion, like their makeout session was the only event occurring in the world. I mostly felt like I was intruding on something.

"I just want you to take turns. Go at your own pace, okay? I want each of you to undress the other, one item of clothing at a time."

Wait, *what?*

"There's just one catch. You have to try your hardest not to touch each other while you do. I'm trying to capture the tension of desire and longing or perhaps unexpected distance, to put it in tangible form, all right?"

"So I can't touch her?" For the first time since I met him, approximately forty-five minutes ago, Tom didn't look like he was totally on board with what Alex was asking.

"When you absolutely have to, you can touch her."

Tom grinned. "Solid."

I had to admit, it was kind of fascinating watching Tom gently unclasp Romy's necklace and let it drop to the floor beside them. She did the same with his button-down shirt, giggling as he shivered at her almost-touch. When Tom pulled Romy's sweater up over her head, making her hair stick up in a staticky halo, I thought for sure that Alex would tell them to stop. But he didn't. Romy had her hands pulling at Tom's belt, and then his fingers brushed gently against the back of her bra strap.

This was like watching porn. Really slow, sensual porn on a white backdrop. I couldn't decide if I wanted to look away or just let the train-wreck nature of it all wash over me.

Once Romy's bra dropped, though, Tom couldn't keep his hands off her long enough to leave her exposed for much time anyway. His hands flew to her waist, and she sighed in relief, and then his mouth was on her neck, then he hoisted her up and sucked one of her nipples into his mouth.

Okay. This was when they deserved their privacy. If not from everyone else, at least from me. I turned, and Alex stayed stock still, peering into the camera and nodding slightly as Romy and Tom started to let some distinctly sexual noises loose.

"Is it okay if I have us go next?" he asked me in a casual whisper.

"I guess. What are we going to do?" I knew what he was going to say. I'd only asked because of how desperately I was hoping to be proven wrong.

He turned his head slightly and flicked his gaze to mine. "The same thing. Everyone's doing the same thing."

Of course. My gut feeling had been right. My head started to shake of its own accord. "Uh...no. You never said anything about undressing."

"I didn't say anything to anyone. That's the fucking *point*, Elizabeth."

"Well it's not like anyone would have figured that out from your freaking circular philosophical bullshit "project" or "experience" or what the fuck ever this is!"

The truth was, it had sounded interesting, when he waxed eloquent about it at the bar. I might have even agreed to participate, if I hadn't been basically tricked into doing it.

By this point, Romy was completely naked, and Tom was tripping over his jeans, which had slid down to a pool of denim around his ankles.

"Look," I said, bending down to grab my bag, "I'll just... show myself out. Thanks for...well, just...thanks. I guess." Damn the little Miss Proper manners my mom had driven into my psyche since I was little.

I scrambled up the stairs in my spiky heels to the sound of his shouting that I'd ruined everything and this night would be impossible to replicate and I was murdering his art. Or something.

I didn't really care when I made it back to the sidewalk. I'd never been happier to escape a place in my life.

I'd also never felt farther from anything I knew, or anyone I loved, or any sense of myself. Apparently dating a bunch of random guys for the sake of Philadelphia's sadistic voyeuristic entertainment could do that to a girl.

Without warning, all the feelings crashed over me in an overwhelming wave and I gasped against lungs that suddenly felt crushed. I had to get home.

I clicked on my phone and checked the time. How had it gotten so late? Was Alex's weird basement studio some kind of time warp machine? Were Romy and Tom's sexual performance skills really that hypnotic? Had I completely lost all grip on reality?

No matter the explanation, it was dark outside, getting colder by the second. Wearing these stilettos, I could probably make my way to 34th street station in fifteen or twenty minutes, but I knew damn well at 10:15 PM that I'd be waiting on the next train for far too long. This wasn't known for being a bad part of town, but I still didn't want to hang out here for very long.

I pulled my phone out to open a ride sharing app, but the damn thing refused to load. I helplessly watched the icon in its "please hold" phase for several long seconds before heading to the app store to download one for a different service, but the damn store wouldn't load, either. One glance to the top menu of my phone confirmed my worst fear – there was no reception here. On top of that, my battery was hovering at a terrifying seven percent. Even if I wanted to wait for one of the apps to become functional, it would probably waste too much precious power.

My only chance for a ride was to call the operator and get a taxi. Within a few minutes, I had a cabbie promising to pick me up within ten minutes, and my phone still wasn't dead.

Not a total win, but better than nothing.

I killed the time by pacing rhythmically back and forth down a small stretch of sidewalk, muttering "heel-toe, heel-toe" with each calculated step in these freaking impractical shoes.

Soon, the cabbie pulled up and I gratefully tugged open the door and collapsed onto the warm seat.

"Where to?"

I gave him our address in University City and grunted out a sigh of relief, letting my head fall back on headrest.

"That'll be twenty," he said, turning around and staring at me.

"Oh. Right." I fished through my purse and pulled out my

credit card. Monica would probably gladly reimburse me in exchange for tonight's doozy of a story.

"Cash," the cabbie said, with a look that told me he had very little patience left for anyone's bullshit. Maybe less patience than I had, which was saying a lot.

"Oh, sorry. I don't have any." I gave him a weak smile, hoping to communicate just how grateful I was that he understood.

"Cash only, honey." He pointed a stubby finger at a sign right on the dash controls that confirmed what he was saying. "It's on the site, too."

"I...I didn't have the site, there's no reception here, and –"

"Not my problem," he cut me off with a shrug.

"But I...how the hell am I gonna get home?" I couldn't help it. My voice broke on the last word.

"Not my *problem*, sweetheart."

I sat bolt upright and glared at him. "I'm not your honey. Or your sweetheart."

He shrugged and just looked back, nonplussed. "Cash only," he repeated.

"Asshole," I muttered as I yanked the door open yet again.

He let out a few choice words of his own when I got out and slammed the door behind me. The cab sped off and I was alone again.

I didn't realize I was crying until a tear rolled down my cheek, then dripped off my chin onto my dress.

I really, really didn't want to call Jordan. I'd been hanging out with him enough to trust myself not to throw myself at him under normal circumstances, but this was different. He would see me vulnerable. Needing him. If he came to my rescue, I might not be able to help myself.

But at least I could trust *him*. That was one thing I knew for sure. So, without a second thought, I dialed his number and lifted the phone to my ear.

"Liz?" His voice was scratchy and distracted when he picked up. Shit, had I interrupted him? Or...was he *with* someone?

"Hey, um...are you busy?" Dammit, there went my voice, modulating and cracking again.

"What's wrong?" I heard the rustle of sheets, or maybe the couch fabric, on the other end of the line. *Please don't let him be in bed with someone else.* The thought pierced my mind, blocking out all others in a jarring flash. Luckily, I gathered my wits quickly.

"I'm...uh...I'm on the other side of town, and I don't have a ride back. I called a taxi, but it's cash only, and..."

I heard more fumbling on the other end. Then, "Okay, just send me your location through the maps app. It'll take me straight to you."

"My phone's almost dead, and the reception sucks. I'm on the other side of Center City," I rushed out, hoping to give him a location before my phone crapped out. "At, uh...7th and Chestnut," I said, catching sight of the street signs at an intersection a short block away.

"Looks like I'll see you in about...ten minutes," he said.

"Thank you," I said as my throat tightened even more. No questions, no fuss, no argument. He was coming to get me. Right now. "See you soon."

"Soon," He promised, then hung up.

Checking my surroundings one last time to make sure I was relatively safe, I backed up against one of the skinny trees stuck in the middle of the sidewalk and then slid down to sitting.

And then, without really knowing why, I started to cry again.

I knew my dress was showing most of my thighs and my hair

was limp and my mascara was running. I knew I was in a state of serious emotional distress that I could only sort of start to explain. I didn't really care about either of those things, though, because one thought kept running through my mind over and over - I couldn't do this anymore.

Tomorrow, I'd ask Monica for another assignment, or I'd walk away from the position entirely. Nothing was worth exposing myself to the weird quasi-sexual intentions of the rando freaks who applied to date me. Now that I thought of it, it was a miracle I hadn't been murdered or tied up by now. This was insane.

CHAPTER 19

JORDAN

I WAS REALLY DAMN glad I'd splurged for a parking spot when I first moved here. My car was only a couple blocks away, and I made it there as fast as my legs would carry me.

The bright lights of the city blurred together as a misty rain started to fall, and I found myself gunning on the gas as I drove over the river and speeding through yellow lights.

Liz hadn't said she was in danger, but she hadn't sounded okay on the other end of the phone. And she called me to pick her up. Me. Whatever weird tension there was between us didn't matter. In this moment, I wanted to be whatever she needed, and I wanted to be amazing at it.

Finally, I pulled up to the location she sent me. I watched her scramble up from sitting on the ground against one of those pathetic sidewalk trees Philly had apparently planted to show they gave a shit about the environment. I would have jumped out to help her to the car if Liz hadn't been so quick to grab the handle.

She tumbled inside, sighing against the cushiony seat. "You okay?" I reached out my hand to touch her, but when I saw her hands twisted up in her purse straps and how short her skirt was, leaving me no choice but to feel up her knee, I pulled my hand back to the wheel.

She turned to me and all I could see was her red-rimmed eyes, trembling lip, framed by the rain-frizzed dirty blond halo of her hair.

"Yeah...No..." She sighed. "I don't know."

I waited for long moments to see if she'd say anything else. When she didn't, I put the car in drive. This time, I went slower than I needed to, and took a route that curved back and forth through the Philly streets and added a mile to our trip. I remembered my mom telling me that, when I was a kid, she loved driving me to weekend science competitions because, after enough time sitting in silence in the car, I would start to tell her things.

It was kind of astounding how badly I wanted Liz to tell me things. Real things. Things that would make me more a part of her life than I was now. Cups of coffee and Netflix and leisurely homemade dinners were good. The sex had been *really* good. But I couldn't shake the feeling that there was something more, a deeper level I could get to with her, and I wanted to. Desperately. I couldn't explain it.

Liz didn't speak the whole way home. I didn't hear a thing from her except for the occasional sniffle or small sigh. When we got inside and she dropped her bag at the little table beside the door, she didn't move toward her room or the couch like I would have thought. She just stood there, looking at me, grasping her upper arm with the opposite hand and watching me as I locked up the door.

"You okay?" I asked again, battling how badly I wanted to step up to her, hold her in my arms, and kiss the top of her head. Maybe tell her that, if she wasn't okay, I wanted to be the one to help make it better.

I wanted that more than anything, I realized. My stomach flipped.

"I can't do this anymore." Her voice was raspy, weak. God, it just hurt to see her like this. "I just...I'm just *done*, you know? How hard can it be to find one freaking person I can get along with? One person I want to actually *date*? Am I that big of a freak, that not even the entire city can find someone I'm compatible with?" Her voice was heavy, wet. Exhausted.

Maybe Philly would have been able to find someone for her, if I hadn't weighted the votes so heavily in favor of the most obvious losers.

Holy shit. I was the biggest asshole on the planet.

Her fists clenched and unclenched at her sides in a steady rhythm, and the furious white spots bleeding in and out over her knuckles were like flashing warning lights. She needed something, and she was confiding in me because she thought I could give it to her. I wanted to know so many things about her, wanted to spend hours and days and weeks getting to know her deepest thoughts. I wanted the obstacle of my guilt over trying to throw her dates to the guys she'd hate to melt away, somehow. I had no idea what she would do if she knew that.

But from the way she was approaching me, little by little narrowing the space between us, I knew that now wasn't the time for guessing games.

"What...um..." I sighed, gathering my courage. "What can I do?"

"You've done plenty. Thank you for coming to get me, Jor - JJ. I should just..." she leaned her head toward her bedroom door and took a dragging step in that direction. She looked up at me, her eyes watery and tired. "Thanks. Really."

She crouched down and fumbled with the small buckles on her heels, stepping out of them and leaving them in the middle of the floor. Once again, the straps had left crisscrossing red marks over the tops of her feet. Once again, I was hit with the overwhelming need to tend to her, to take care of her. Not because I thought she needed me to, no. Because I knew she deserved it.

Tonight, she might even be craving it.

But my feet remained rooted in place as I watched her duck into her room and heard the rustle of her body settling onto the comforter. I inflated my lungs, slowly, then blew out all the air over the same number of seconds. I'd never felt so torn.

One more time. I'd just check with her one more time, and then I'd leave her alone.

Before I could change my mind, I kicked off my shoes, tossed them to the mat beside the front door, and did the same with hers.

I stepped quietly to her door, which she'd left open. Not just a crack, either. Wide open. Like she really had wanted me to stop there. Her breathing was quiet, but not the heavy, steady rhythm it took on when she was sleeping. I knew that one by heart already.

"Liz, sweetheart? You need anything?" My heart lurched in my chest as I heard myself use the term of endearment for her, the one I'd stumbled into using months ago. *Sweetheart.* It felt so right.

She turned her head on the pillow so she faced me. Her words, muffled against the pillow, were quiet but decisive. "Help me with my hose?"

I stepped closer to her, until I was an arm's length from the bed. "You want me to...?"

"Take them off, yes. Please." The last word was twisted, choked.

Another step, and I was an arm's length away. I reached down to brush my fingers along her shoulder blade, then touched them to the small of her back. She seemed so small right now, a quiet, defeated girl wrapped in a dress designed for a life she didn't want.

I knew that I had to reach up her dress to roll the thin stockings down. I'd watched one of my ex-girlfriends do it, but never done it myself. A slow breath in through my nose, then a quiet exhale through my mouth, and I let my hands travel under the hem of her dress.

She made the most delicious sound then - a cross between a sigh and a moan. My dick strained against the fly of my jeans and I ran through every stern lecture I could think of to get it to calm down. This was not the time. She was tired, and sad, and I was partly at fault.

Did she know what she was doing to me, asking me to help her get out of her pantyhose? Did she care?

I thought about baseball, math competitions, and my high school track coach in her underwear on a steady loop as I gently peeled the thin nylon down over her thighs, past her knees, and finally, off her feet.

She really did have beautiful feet. I'd never been that taken by any girl's feet, ever, but it was like every part of Liz's body had its own siren song. I could get lost in her, if I let myself. Too bad she didn't really want to let me. She'd said as much. Hadn't she?

I cleared my throat. "Feel better?"

Liz grunted, and wiggled in place. Jesus Christ and all the angels, her ass was perfect. I wanted to give an award to whatever genius had invented skintight satin dresses. The sheen of the fabric accentuated the flawless slope of each cheek into the valley of her thighs, and to make matters worse, I knew exactly how butter-soft it would feel beneath my fingers.

"This dress is so freaking tight," she murmured. "Can you help me with the zipper?"

My fingers shook. Just listening to her say the word 'tight' while she laid on the bed like that... *No.* It didn't matter. I'd never been anything less than a gentleman with any woman I'd been with, always double checking exactly what it was she wanted, whether every move was okay.

Liz couldn't be any clearer with her request, and yet this still, somehow, felt wrong. I brushed her hair away from the neckline of her dress and gingerly gripped the slim metal zipper pull. "Just pull it down?"

"Mmmhm." Her voice rasped into the pillow. I could practically feel the cloud of heat her breath created there just by listening to it.

Her skin was flawless. Even the scattering of moles across her creamy, smooth, lightly tanned back seemed to be placed there, just so, in some perfect design. I wanted to glide my finger from one to the next, drawing a picture, mapping her so that I could commit her to memory.

My throat suddenly felt like sandpaper. I stood up, pressing my hand firmly to my side, mentally reciting statistics from the 2011 World Series games.

Liz shifted, turning her head to the other side, making some long strands of hair hug her throat, with a few strays teasing along her shoulder. My breath caught. I would have sold my soul in that moment to be one of those strands.

She rolled one of her shoulders back, whimpering against the stretch. My thoughts immediately shot to what it would feel like if she let out that sweet, sexy little noise with her lips wrapped around my cock. I clenched my fists, then stepped backward. I had to get out of here.

Before I could take another step, though, she spoke again. "Could you just...get my bra, too? Freaking itchy clasp."

I walked right back into the danger zone, a moth toward a flame that would most likely kill me. I couldn't help it. Her pull was just too strong.

As my hands hovered an inch above the tempting red satin strap, I decided I wasn't too proud, and it wasn't too late, to beg. I let out a shuddering breath. "Liz, I'm trying to respect you, here. Respect what you want."

"Obviously you're not," she shot back, all softness gone from her voice.

My heart stopped and threatened to jump into my throat. I counted five seconds, one deep breath in and out again. "Then I don't know what you want, Liz." It took everything in me to keep my voice from breaking. "You have to tell me."

Her breathing had gone shallow, too, and the tension hanging between us seemed to stretch out the seconds into endless moments.

"You make me feel like a person. Not like an object or a goal or a toy. Or a freaking conquest."

"Yeah, Liz. Because I respect you. I'm trying really hard to be a gentleman right now. Please, help me."

"I would, Jordan. So I really want to know...do you want me? Even when I'm this much of a mess?"

"You know that I do. Jesus, Lizzie, you must be able to tell how badly I do."

"Even though it's been so long since...?"

"God, yes," I answered, before she'd even finished the question, in a needy exhalation.

"Then, you know what I want you to do? What I need from you right now?"

"Tell me," I practically begged.

"I want you to show me. I need you to. Touch me, Jordan. Please."

That was all I needed to hear. In a split second, my knees were planted on either side of her body. There was only one word to describe how I felt in that moment - *hungry*. My hands plunged into her dress, palming at her hips and framing her navel with fingers digging deep into skin.

CHAPTER 20

LIZ

JORDAN'S HANDS on my body were heaven. The way they dragged against my skin felt like magical life-giving warmth pushed through every pore, invigorating me. I couldn't help the way I moaned as his powerful hands tilted my hips back so that my ass pushed up toward his cock, which strained against his jeans. It was one of the things I found most attractive about him - that big, beautiful dick of his couldn't even be really hidden by boxers and a solid layer of denim.

If he was mine, every girl would be able to guess exactly what I had, exactly what they were missing out on.

If he was mine.

He couldn't be mine. I knew that. He didn't *want* that - he'd told me as much months ago and hadn't tried to make a move since. It wouldn't be wrong, exactly, but there were too many things making it weird.

I knew what this was about, my impulse to make him hot and bothered to touch me. I'd been on enough dates in the past four months to know that a guy being good looking, or having a good job, or being really nice or really interesting, wasn't enough to create what I really wanted—a chemical reaction bordering on explosion that I just couldn't stop myself from getting myself mixed up with.

It was wrong to get so close to JJ when I knew I was just chasing that feeling, circling a grenade that could explode at any second. But that was the problem with explosions - once they started, it was impossible to stop them. Seeing JJ rush to my rescue tonight, cataloging the concern and care etched into his expression, had lit a spark inside me.

It didn't matter how hard I tried to avoid it. This spark between us was going to turn into a full-blown fire no matter what I did.

Within seconds, his mouth was on my neck, licking and sucking in exactly the right way to make me absolutely desperate for more. Well, I'd already gone this far. I'd already lured him here and made it impossible for him to keep from touching me. I might as well go balls-out.

"Goddammit, Jordan," I gasped as he stretched one hand out over my belly, fingers splayed far enough to brush my ribs, and dragged the other hand up to my chest, twisting a nipple and squeezing hard.

"Tell me what you want," he rasped in my ear. "I'll do anything. You know that, Lizzie. Anything for you."

His words were sexy and tender all at once, and my mind exploded with dozens of visions of what he might have meant by his willingness to do anything—anything at all—for *me*.

Only one of those visions was going to win out now, though. I took a deep breath and thrust my ass up, loving the almost-painful press of his hard shaft between my cheeks. "Fuck me, Jordan," I murmured, just loud enough so that I knew he heard me. *Make me believe that at least one person can sweep me off my feet, forget every other shitty situation in this world.*

"That's not what you want, Liz," he groaned against my neck.

"It is," I insisted, bending my neck back to press my cheek to his, relishing the pressure it added to his delicious weight on top of me. "Those times we...did this? That's the only time I've felt what I was supposed to feel. The first time. And the last." I squeezed my eyes against the tears burning at the corners.

Jordan planted his hands on either side of my shoulders, and suddenly, I felt his weight shifting off of me, punctuated by a cool breeze swirling through the space he left behind. I pressed my forehead into the pillow and squeezed my eyes tighter, waiting for the sound of the door falling shut to gasp into the sob I already felt coming.

Instead, I felt the blessed sensation of Jordan's knee making the mattress dip on one side of me. Then his breath ghosting hot at the back of my ear.

"If we do this now, it's not gonna be me fucking you."

I drew a shuddering breath. "What...what are we doing, then?"

"I will give you whatever you want. Fast and rough or slow and deep. I'll suck your tits or lick your pussy until you scream my name, or I'll swallow every one of your moans with a kiss. Anything you want, Liz." I could have sworn I heard his voice break there, just a bit. He swallowed, hard, and brushed his nose up and down my neck. "But I won't fuck you. Because that's what you do when it's desperate and thoughtless. When there's nothing behind it except wanting to get off. I can't just fuck you, Liz. You're...you're more than that. To me."

I held my breath, waiting for him to say more, trying to put my thoughts in any sort of order. My chest constricted with the sudden realization that I felt exactly the same way.

Somewhere in between multiple-orgasm tutorials and frantic couch sex and going on dates with a dozen other guys, I'd fallen in love with my roommate—so deep in love there was no hope of digging myself out. I gasped at the realization, but

Jordan seemed to take it as encouragement. He settled himself back over me, his chest pressed to my back, his cock parting my legs. "Is that okay with you? Can I make love to you now, Lizzie?"

"God, yes," I moaned, "Please."

"What do you want first?"

I wanted out of this dress. I wanted to be truly bare before him. But more than anything, I wanted my panties, which were now sticking to the slickness between my thighs, off. And I wanted his hand in their place. "Touch me," I managed, my voice breathy, like the next time I tried to get words out, I wouldn't be able to remember a single one.

When he knelt over me and his hands brushed over my shoulders, I thought he may have misunderstood. I wanted his fingers inside me, slicking through the wetness at my core. I knew, somehow, that he would feel parts of me that other guys hadn't even bothered to consider, and use them to make my whole body sing. It was all I could think about, and I opened my mouth to demand it.

But then I realized he had read my mind.

His fingers hooked into the straps of my dress and slid it down, his palms smoothing over my hips as he revealed my skin, inch by excruciating inch. By the time he tugged the satin down my calves, the coolness of the fabric making me shiver, I was desperate for him on top of me again. I craved his weight, wanted to be held down, to be claimed, needed to be tethered to one certain place in this crazy life.

"Jordan, *please*," I moaned. Another night, I would have been loath to beg him. I would have wanted to be an equal player in every move we made. Something about tonight, though, had me desperate for him to prove himself to me. In what way, I couldn't articulate. I just knew that after what happened between us tonight, I would have to make a decision about what we were. If we were anything.

Obediently, he straddled my back again, and I thrilled at the solid weight of his body sandwiching my thighs against the sheets. Instead of putting his hands where I so desperately wanted them, though, he slid his chest over my back, and stretched his legs out against mine, blanketing me completely. Between checking on me and being propositioned by me, he had taken off all of his clothes, too, aside from his boxer briefs. His hands snuck under my arms and cupped my shoulders from the front. I shivered at the proximity of his arms to my nipples - just a few inches and my scrap of a bra stood between them. Even though we were both almost completely nude, this was an embrace of reassurance, of comfort.

The dissonance between the two was driving me crazy.

He shifted to the side, lying on one arm and lifting the other to brush my hair from my face, sending his legs slotting between mine. I left my eyes closed. I was afraid of what I'd see if I looked in to his. Sadness? Pity? Or, my greatest hope—something more?

I felt the unmistakable brush of his lips over my eyelids, then their press against my forehead. The perfect mix of warmth and wetness, solid pressure and inviting openness. He moved down, ghosting half-open kisses over my cheekbone, my chin, and the opposite cheek. Another light kiss against my nose made me gasp, so desperate was I to have his lips devouring mine.

He must have read my mind again, because in the next breath, he was drinking me in, running his tongue over my bottom lip, then along the roof of my mouth, making me feel like he was everywhere all at once. I nipped at his top lip, and in that instance, all of his maddening, gentle control fell away. His free hand gripped at my ribs, then palmed my hip, fingers digging in so hard they could have left marks there. I hoped they would. Tomorrow morning, I didn't want there to be any doubt that this had happened, that it had been as real and solid as any other part of my life.

That it would still be there in the morning.

I squeezed my eyes shut, tight. *Don't think about that now, Liz. Be here. Feel him. Figure this out.*

Jordan notched his thumb into the space right over my hip bone and gripped me there, hard. In a flash, his muscled arm had flipped me to my back, and his mouth was dancing over my abdomen like it had been drawn there by a magnet. His tongue dipped into my navel and he groaned. The vibrations from his chest buzzed against my thigh, and I felt myself growing even wetter. "I want to taste you," he growled as his fingers dragged up to my chest, practically tearing my bra off. "It's been too long."

I wouldn't argue with that. I wiggled my arms like a damn octopus, all in an effort to finally get my bra off and be bare before him that much sooner. His palm cupped my breast as his fingers dug into the top of it, and I arched my back, purring at the contact.

This. This was exactly what I wanted, what I needed - for Jordan to show me that he could make me his, and that I was allowed to crave him this desperately. There was a certain comfort to this frantic push and pull between us, and I wanted to wrap myself in it.

He shifted over me again, letting his chest fall between my legs with a soft grunt. He licked at the seam where my thigh met my center, rasping his teeth against the tendons there, and I cried out. "I need you, Jordan," I said, breathless and hungry for his mouth to taste the spot where every nerve in my body seemed to lead. He moved his lips in a circle, its diameter drawn an inch from where I really wanted him on all sides. His teeth sunk gently into the flesh of my mons, and I felt a tremor from deep inside me. Hell, he could probably make me come just like this - with his noises and vibrations and all-encompassing closeness.

It was that thought that had me nearly coming undone at the first pass of his fingers down my slit. Every cell of my core was a live wire, and he was turning each one on like a string of so many lights on a freaking Christmas tree.

"Fuck," I hissed. He seemed to take that as a cue to spring into action—in that instant, two of his long, beautiful, expert fingers pushed into me and his mouth fell on my clit. He lapped at it insistently, his breaths coming faster in time with his hand pumping in and out, the edge of his palm smacking my ass with every pass.

My walls squeezed in syncopation, making my channel tighter as I anticipated each of his thrusts. I was slowly combusting, every process in my body an inevitable series of reactions that would completely unravel me, and I was feeling it all happen, second by second.

Then, something I didn't expect—he flipped his hand, palm up, and curled his finger against my upper wall, pressing into the spot just inside my pubic bone. It was like a match dropped in a puddle of gasoline. A scream tore out of my throat and filled the room, the energy pouring itself out of my body and continuing in a long, satisfied moan of shocked, all-encompassing pleasure.

I whimpered as he slowly drew his fingers out of me, even as he left his mouth open and licking gently over my lips. When my breaths slowed, he slid his body up to align with mine again, then drew his hand up to his mouth, slowly pushing the two fingers he'd just had inside me between his lips. A fresh wave of desire flooded me, so intense that I couldn't even make myself move. My answering whimper seemed to satisfy, him, though, and he moved his hand to cup my jaw and slotted his mouth over mine in a long, soft, slow kiss, filled with emotion.

I squeezed my eyes shut, knowing that if I looked into his right now I might cry, or look away, or be too scared to figure out what the hell I was supposed to do next, and ruin everything. Whatever this was, besides me being in love with my roommate, I certainly didn't want it to stop right now because of my own senseless tears.

"Please, Jordan," I whispered, begging him for what I'd so desperately wanted since I'd laid eyes on him tonight. I couldn't do it anymore. My breath stilled in my throat for agonizing seconds of nothing—no answer, no contact—from Jordan. And then his hips notched over mine, and relief sank into my stomach, bleeding over my entire body.

"Liz," he said, his voice rough but somehow quiet. "Lizzie." His knees pressed deep on either side of my thighs, trapping me there. I had no desire to escape. "Liz, look at me."

I snapped my eyes open, powerless under his command, those words spoken in that voice. Really, I *wanted* to look at him. I wanted this to be honest in whatever way it could be, even if that was only through a teary gaze. He had just given me the signal I needed to be brave enough to do it.

"Oh, Liz," he groaned. All at once, he kissed me, his tongue plunging into my mouth, my fingers fisted at his hair, and he surged straight into my dripping wet center.

We moved together in what was the most desperate, yet intensely focused, experience of my life. He plunged in and I clenched around him, welcoming his invasion, desperate for him never to leave. He pulled out and I spread wide, hungry for him to fill me again. Every moment with him was lived in pursuit of the next, because I knew it would be even better than the last.

We were chasing orgasms together, both for ourselves and

each other. It seemed that any movement that sent me hurtling even further down that path elicited a proportional groan from him. It was just motivation to get him to make a louder, more interesting sound with the next rock of my hips into his.

For the first time in my life, the challenge of dancing right on the edge of orgasm was fun. Like even if it took a while or something weird happened or even if the whole chase failed miserably, I would still have thoroughly enjoyed myself, tangled up in a pile of sweaty, naked limbs with Jordan. Just being with him, so close, so intimate, struck me as a worthy activity all on its own.

Though, that didn't matter right now, because the rock-hard, insistent stroke of him in and out of me, the way he filled me perfectly and kept my body dancing along that fine edge of just-enough and too-much, was not even close to failing. The only thing I was failing at right now was lasting longer than a few minutes of this.

That brought a little smirk to my face. Usually, it was the guy who had trouble lasting, and here I was with a boyfriend who had me completely satisfied and spent, twice, within a handful of minutes.

Except he wasn't my boyfriend. And he couldn't be.

Dammit.

Any emotions I might have had the chance to feel over that, though, were interrupted by Jordan sucking love bites up my neck, then worrying at my earlobe with his teeth. He hit a nerve that ended way south, and I arched up and moaned.

"Tell me what you *want*, Liz."

"You. Just you." The words fell out of my mouth before I could even think of saying it, like it was waiting on my tongue for my guard to be let down for just one second.

He stopped moving and propped up on his elbows, staring down at me. I was terrified to look back. I didn't want to see disappointment, or stress, or, honestly, negativity of any kind. When I finally brought myself to raise my eyes to his, though, the only thing written in his expression was patience. Openness. A quiet stare that brought my heart to a stuttering stop.

Bending back down to me slowly, he pressed a firm, quiet kiss on my mouth, then dragged his lips just enough to the side to let him get the words out. "Me too. You."

"I'm yours," I replied, my voice trembling. "Take me."

Jordan's demeanor shifted then. Instead of focused and relentless, driving into me like it was the last thing he'd ever do, he settled against me, bracketing his chest to mine with arms hooked behind me, fingertips pressing firm into my shoulders. He propped his forehead against mine, gave me another slow kiss, and started to move again.

This time, he rocked steadily into me, slow and strong, like we had all the time in the world, like this was the first of thousands of times we'd have the luxury of figuring out all the different ways we could make each other come.

And oh hell, was this ever a different way. Instead of his hips snapping a maddening rhythm against my clit, they were now engaged in a slow, soft grind. The sensation of it was dragging me back to the top of a climax so steadily, yet deliciously, that I wasn't sure whether I wanted to get there or just stay in this warm, tingling, teasing suspension of almost-bliss.

His forehead remained pressed to mine, occasionally moving down to my temple when he would groan or shift, and I took advantage of that perfect full mouth hovering over mine to aim kisses at. Some instinct I'd never felt before overtook me, and I took my time licking my way past his lips, cataloguing the frequency of the hums and moans moving from his throat, swallowing them eagerly.

If we hadn't been going so slow, or pressed so close, I never would have felt him becoming even harder inside me. But he was, and I did, and now, in addition to the pressure on my clit, there was a new something his cock was doing inside me. The hot friction against one spot on my inside upper wall scratched a barely-there point of need that I didn't even know existed, and with every point of contact, I lost more ability to breathe, to see, to think, to remember my own name.

I'd had orgasms before, of course. I'd even had some incredible ones with Jordan. But none of them had ever felt like the one that overtook me then—like my entire body had been replaced with some ethereal substance and I had completely ceased to exist.

I didn't even recognize the noises coming out of my own mouth.

None of my senses returned back to normal until Jordan lay on top of me, panting, his erection softening slightly between my legs. The sounds of his breathlessness mingling with mine only turned me on for another round I knew I was too exhausted to take part in. I couldn't bring myself to care, really.

After what had been a crazy few months, I was overwhelmed with the feeling flooding me now—that I was really, truly comfortable. Finally home.

I didn't want to let him go, but the boneless, satisfied feeling he'd given me wouldn't let me keep my eyes open much longer, either. I pressed my face into his neck, giggling at his quick breaths slowly spacing out, and kissed him there. I didn't know how to define what had just happened between us, but I knew for sure that I wouldn't be able to talk about it until I'd gotten a good night's sleep.

A few hours later, a chill skittered across my skin, and I shivered, pulling his silky sheets up over my waist. I felt his name dropping off my lips, and then heard the distant echo of his voice ricocheting in a coarse, short whisper off our walls. "I don't fucking care, you don't leave a girl on her own on the streets of Philly."

He sounded so pissed and so anguished at the same time. I didn't know exactly what it was, but I felt all warm and fuzzy all over again, and drifted back off to sleep.

CHAPTER 21

JORDAN

I WOKE UP, once again, to bright sunlight warming my body, casting mesmerizing patterns over my crumpled sheets and, best of all, over Liz's soft waves of golden hair currently blanketing my chest.

Fuck friends-with-benefits arrangements and internships and relationship rules. Fuck it all. Fuck everything except how perfect it felt to be snuggled up with this perfect creature.

Liz stirred then, and with her eyes still closed, pressed a kiss against my chest. That was all it took for my dick, which was already in alert mode just by virtue of it being morning, to twitch happily.

I tilted her chin up with two fingers, bringing her lips to mine for a long kiss, savoring the soft "mmm" she hummed against my mouth. I didn't care about morning breath, not today. The knowledge that I was kissing Liz was so delicious that I barely noticed the soft ping of my phone at my bedside.

Liz tensed, under my hands, not much, but enough for me to feel it. "Need to get that?" she asked with a tentative smile. I shrugged, hoping to stretch out this moment even longer, but Liz had already done a fast ninja roll over top of me and down my other side, snatching my phone. She nuzzled her face back into my chest and pressed the phone into my hand. "Who could be calling you on a Saturday morning?" she asked.

I blinked, hard, fumbled for my glasses where I swore I'd felt them next to my pillow, and shoved them on my face. I moved the phone in and out in front of my face a couple times before I could focus on the words in the text, and grunted out a laugh.

"What?" Liz asked, craning her neck up to look.

Kiera: How was Lizzie P's date last night?

"She probably wants the scoop before Philly Illustrated gets it. Here, give it to me."

Before I could protest, Liz yanked the phone out of my hands and hit a bunch of thumbs-up emojis, then pressed send.

Seconds later, the phone dinged again.

Kiera: ???
Kiera: Call me.

I chuckled, hoping it sounded casual enough that Liz would interpret Kiera's message that way too. But I knew that when Kiera demanded a call from me, she meant business. Somehow, some way, I was in trouble.

I pressed a kiss to the top of Liz's head and then slid out of bed, snagging a pair of pajama pants from the floor and stepping into them as I stood. "I'm gonna go grab some breakfast. From Joey and Hawk's, of course."

"And I'm gonna go back to sleep," she murmured with a sleepy smile.

My shirt from last night was crumpled on the floor, and I snagged it in one finger before putting my hand on the doorknob. Liz was already drifting back off to sleep, her makeup-free face sweet and without worry against her pillow. The sight of her, the memory of what we'd done last night, and the lingering scent of her perfume on my skin all mingled together, hitting me hard in the chest. I staggered backward, bumping painfully into the corner of my dresser beside the door.

I really, truly loved this girl. It was more than an infatuation, more than an afterglow-clouded fascination—I *loved* her. I actually wanted to bring her baked goods, and sit in bed with her while she ate hers and talk with her while our coffee got cold and lay her back down on top of the crumbs I knew she would leave in the sheets and spend hours kissing her from head to toe.

I wanted the rest of the day, the rest of the year, the rest of my foreseeable future with her.

And her job was dating someone else—lots of someone elses. A job which, by the way, I had been making harder and harder on her for months, just so I could keep her for myself.

Sighing, I grabbed my keys and toed into my shoes. I stabbed at the screen of my phone with the dexterity of a caffeine-deprived lovesick idiot. Which I guess I was.

Kiera was screeching in my ear before I even had the door shut behind me. "JORDAN ALBERT JACOBS WHY WAS ELIZABETH PALMER TEXTING ME FROM YOUR BED???"

I scrubbed my hand over my face as I strode to my car. I slumped in and let the door fall shut behind me. I didn't know what the hell I was going to do about this whole situation myself yet, and I sure as hell didn't want Liz to think I was going to consult my baby sister, one of her best friends, about it before I got up the courage to talk to Liz about it.

Even though that was exactly what I was doing.

"I don't know what you're talking about," I said, trying to make my voice sound groggier than panicked. Of course she knew there was something going on between Liz and I—my sister was some kind of a relationship psychic, and her powers only got stronger the closer she was to the people in question. There was probably some alarm bell or something in her head that woke her up as soon as I'd decided that I had fucking fallen hopelessly in love with Lizzie Palmer.

"You slept with Lizzie. And then she texted me from your bed this morning."

"How in the world could you possibly know that? If it was even true?" I mumbled as I turned the key in the ignition and started to drive in no particular direction. This conversation might take a while and I wanted to come back to Liz calm, happy, and fueled by enough coffee to be coherent.

"First, it's 8:45 on a Saturday morning. You never wake up until eleven on a Saturday, not ever, not even for the SATs. Remember how you lied and said you were Jewish and had to take them on Sunday because the idea of waking up that early on a Saturday had you so emotionally compromised you said you'd mess up the test?"

"Yes," I grumbled.

"So I know you were in bed. And I also know that you would have never sent me a text message like that."

"Like what? Some stupid emojis? KiKi, I send you those things all the time!"

"Excuse me, asshole, I am a mathematician. A statistician, actually. Which means that I can tell you that exactly forty-one point six percent of the messages Lizzie has sent me in the last three months consist of four thumbs-up emojis in a row. Do you know how many of your texts have given me the quadruple thumbs-up, Jordan?"

"Um. One. Because I just sent it to you."

"Jordan..." Kiera's voice was full of warning. She was giving me one last chance to come clean. I didn't want to, but even I had to admit it—I needed her help.

"I hope you feel bad about what you've been doing," Kiera said, her voice suddenly somber. "I know I've been teasing you about all this, but honestly you've been dragging her along in more ways than one for a while."

My heart twisted. "Have you been talking to her?"

"Not about you. Exactly."

"About who? Is she telling you about her dates? Like, more than she writes in the column?" Suddenly I felt like I was going to throw up.

"Jordan. Please. Don't do that. Jealousy does not sound good on you."

I growled. "You know what I mean, Kiki. You said I was dragging her along and I didn't know if she thought..."

"No, Jordan, I don't know any details about the crazy sex you've probably been having all over your new apartment with one of my best friends that I haven't even been invited to visit yet, thank you very much. She wouldn't even admit to playing tonsil hockey with you, though I have no idea why."

"No, Kiera, I can't imagine why Liz wouldn't want you to be deeply, painfully involved in whatever relationship she's having."

"Fuck you, Jordan. I'm just trying to help. What I *do* know is that Liz has been dating all these gross, weird, or generally awful guys and it's your fault. So, do you want to be with her, or not? Because I know Lizzie and she hasn't fallen for any of those guys she's been on dates with, but she's got a thing for *someone* and I would bet my bank account it's because she's falling for you."

Thank God I'd come up to Joey and Hawk's parking lot by the time she said that, because I had to stop and clap a hand to my chest. I knew what it had felt like when I was inside her, knew that the way she stroked my face and moaned my name meant more than just good sex. I'd just always assumed I was the only one feeling it.

"JJ? You okay, there, buddy?"

I wanted to tell Kiera this wasn't a damn joke, but somehow I thought that would make it even worse. "I'm fine, KiKi. I just don't know what to do."

"About what?"

"About any of it."

"Can I give you some advice? Even though you're the big brother and I'm your baby sister?"

"We're both kind of grownups now, aren't we? And you're only younger by fourteen months so I guess it's practically nothing." I scrubbed my hand over my face again. I just wasn't used to feeling like this - like any decision I made could have far-reaching consequences that I might come to seriously regret.

"Figure out what you want, and then tell her." I could hear Kiera slumping back against something, her chair or a couch, and I could just see her being all smug and confident that this advice would actually work.

I, on the other hand, could only think of all the different ways I could screw it up. My answering sigh blew static into the phone. "Thanks, sis."

"Keep me posted? Please? I am stuck here in the 'Burgh with no dates and even fewer prospects. And that's not even mathematically possible."

"Yeah, I will." I sighed long and loud into the phone, still a little annoyed but mostly loving my baby sister for her kind heart and persistence. Even when they made me do really uncomfortable, ridiculously tough things. "And Kiki?"

"Yeah?"

"I wasn't lying. She was texting you from *her* bed."

"You are the literal worst, Jordan. And I love you anyway."

I laughed as I parked and headed into the bakery. Coffee helped. I sucked the ultra-sweet hot liquid with its bitter after-taste through my teeth. Sip by sip, my thoughts were becoming clearer, my determination stronger.

I knew how I felt about Liz. I knew what I wanted. All I had to do was figure out what I wanted to do about it - and I was almost certain that was to stop this stupid dating thing and be with her, we'll figure out everything else after.

Yeah, we shared an apartment, and a little bit of a past, and she had a conflicting job right now, but there was something between us, something I'd never felt with any other girl. She made me feel happy and self-assured in a way I never had. More than that, if someone had told me she was the only girl I'd ever be with for the rest of my life...

Let's just say I wouldn't have objected to a life with Liz at all. I probably wouldn't even freak out if someone had dropped in from the future and showed me our wedding pictures.

Well, now I was getting ahead of myself.

All I knew, with coffee and Liz's favorite blueberry mascarpone scone in hand, was that this girl had given me a home where I had none, and just maybe a new outlook on life to go with it. I could do this—I could be honest with her, lay my feelings out at her feet. What could possibly go wrong?

CHAPTER 22

LIZ

ONCE UPON A TIME, I thought this would be complicated.

Having a massive lust-crush on my new roommate who I also happened to have grown up with while it was my job to date other people should be complicated. And maybe it was. Maybe it was weird that I went on dates with other guys and came home to Jordan.

But just that thought, *coming home to Jordan*, filled me with such warmth that I couldn't help but grin. I buried my forehead in my pillow and let out a half-scream, half-squeal, kicking my legs against the sheets. Right now, in the afterglow, basking in the streaming sunlight and tangled in his bedding, it didn't seem complicated at all.

What had Kiera said just the other day? *The voters probably just wanted me to follow my heart. All anyone wants is a good love story.*

The only problem was that Liz Dates Philly was working, at least on one level. Sponsors were rolling in. Monica had been beside herself when Cosmo called to say they were looking into featuring the column, and then there was the interview with the National Inquirer...maybe all this wouldn't get me a spot at the political desk, but it might be good enough to at least write the relationship column I wanted. Maybe I could spin it. An epic love story, G-rated of course, and then let the readers vote again on dates for Jordan and me to go on. I could work with the food critics. Day trips around Philly would be good topics for columns too, and maybe, just maybe, when the time was right, I could review some caterers, bridal salons, jewelers...

My head shook back and forth rapidly at that thought as I blew another long breath into the pillow. That was so far off I had no business even thinking about it. If it was going to happen at all. If I wasn't imagining that Jordan felt the same way about me as I did about him.

It wasn't the craziest thing to imagine. We got along so well. He knew how I liked my coffee and always remembered where I'd left my hairbrush. He understood my jokes and appreciated my political geekiness. Hell, he participated in it with me, at least in the fictional worlds on Netflix. He knew embarrassing things about me as a kid and he still wanted to hang out with me.

In the other room, my phone pinged with a text. I growled into the sheets. Probably Kiera. The last time Jordan and I had discussed our between-the-sheets relationship, it was casual, just for fun and blowing off steam. By the time I talked about my Liz Dates Philly conundrum with Kiera, she could tell something was up. Sure, that girl had a radar for relationships - she could sniff out a couple from farther distances than merely across the state. My feelings were leaking out, staining every word I said.

When the phone pinged again, I thought about getting up. When it sounded the tone for three more text messages, right in a row, I started to tug the sheets around me and drag my torso off the bed. I shivered against the chill in the air - November in Philly this year was colder than usual, and with our wonky radiators, it was almost impossible to keep the place at a steady temperature. I was just thinking about collapsing back onto the sheets when my phone started to actually ring with an incoming call.

"Geez," I muttered as I wobbled up onto my feet and stumbled over the bunched-up sheets and articles of clothing strewn everywhere to the door. The ringer stopped before I found my phone buried inside my handbag. Just as I was about to try to find some real clothes, it started ringing again.

"What the hell?" I hissed. Why was Monica calling me on a Saturday morning?

I pasted a smile on my face - everyone said that it affected your tone so that the person on the other end could "hear" your smile. If I had any question about how important this job was to me, this gave me an answer. I was standing in my living room, wrapped in a sheet, fake-smiling into my cell phone on a damn Saturday morning.

"Hey, Monica. What's up?" Don't sound annoyed. Do not sound annoyed.

"Elizabeth Palmer. Get in here. Now." I couldn't quite place Monica's tone, but I could tell there was a tight jaw and slight growl involved.

In other words, this could not possibly be good.

"What's going on?"

"I just need you here. *Now*. You have a ride?"

"Jordan...I mean, my roommate...should be back in like 20 minutes. He can drive me."

"Nope. Need you sooner. Take the train."

"On Saturday?" This was truly getting ridiculous. "You can't just tell me what's going on?"

"I'll send Alphonso for you." Then the phone clicked off.

I groaned and ran my hands down over my face. Alphonso lived just a few blocks north of me - something I was distinctly aware of whenever I took the train, because I did not want to end up sitting next to him. Our relationship had gone from antagonistic to awkward to tolerable, but I still didn't want to chat him up on our commute.

He was honking his horn outside the apartment ten minutes later. I slumped into his passenger seat. He was dressed casually, in a form-fitting hoodie, jeans, and bright white sneakers, but somehow still looked just as polished as he would any other day in the office. He smelled good, too. Damn him.

"I didn't think you had a car," I said awkwardly, at a loss for any polite words before coffee.

"It's my boyfriend's. Who's still snoring away in bed all by his lonesome," Alphonso replied with just an edge of bitterness to his voice. I was guessing he enjoyed the drama by association of this situation too much to be truly angry.

"Well, thanks for doing this. I guess."

Alphonso scoffed. "What the hell did you *do?*"

"If I knew, do you think I'd tell you?"

He whistled, low, and pulled back out on the road. "You don't even know, and Monica sounds like that? Can't be good."

"She sounded like that on the phone with you too, huh?" I bit my lower lip and worried it with my teeth.

"The last time she used that tone of voice was when our last intern forgot to renew one of our domain names and an anti-Planned Parenthood propaganda group bought it and plastered gross pictures all over it."

My eyes went wide. "That's horrible."

Alphonso nodded, slowly, as the building came into sight and he pulled into the parking garage. "My point exactly."

I'd planned on going up to face Monica alone, but as we parked, I found myself wanting to grab Alphonso's arm and drag him in with me. Luckily I didn't have to - he was such a busybody he'd already gotten out of the car and was waiting for me to join him.

I sighed heavily as we stood in the elevator.

His eyes flicked over me. "You look like hell." He was right, I knew - no makeup, hair a mess, and jeans I'd worn for too many days in a row already. He turned and brushed the collar of the shirt I'd grabbed - one of the plaid ones JJ wore to TA his classes - and raised an eyebrow. "At least last night's date was a good one, huh? Did you have to leave the poor guy all alone at your apartment?" The corner of his mouth quirked up in the beginnings of a laugh.

"Oh, shut up," I grumbled, stepping off the elevator with Alphonso at my heels.

As soon as we walked into our little area of cubicles, I knew Monica was the one sitting in my desk, in front of my computer. Shit. Shit shit shit.

I scanned my memory for possible infractions. I hadn't looked on any porn on there, that was for sure. Maybe the occasional picture of a hot shirtless actor, but...

Monica held up a stack of paper, her lips pursed, and stared at me for a beat. Then she held it out to me and said, "Wanna explain this to me?"

"Monica, I...I honestly have no idea what that is. You've got to believe me."

"I'll summarize for you, then. This is the printout that shows every single vote in every single Liz Dates Philly poll that has been cast on our site. Our auditor noticed an anomaly on the visitor logs when she was updating our SEOs last night."

I blinked. With no caffeine coursing through my veins, I barely understood the individual words in Monica's sentence. "Okay. Are all our voters from the closest prison, or something?" I still didn't see why that would have her dragging me out of my house and away from a great morning of napping in some amazing afterglow. And maybe pulling JJ back in bed when he got back with that blueberry scone.

Monica barked out a laugh. "I wish. I *wish* that prisoners had rigged the vote, because at least that would be a fun story, wouldn't it? Something we could all laugh about?"

I snuck a glance at Alphonso, who was craning his neck toward the stack of papers, and elbowed him hard in the side.

"No, no. Please, Alphonso. Take a look." Monica picked up the papers and shoved them at me.

It was row after row of numbers, and I didn't understand a bit of it. "Are these...phone numbers?"

Now Alphonso was literally breathing down my neck, so I turned and shoved the papers at him. "You read it. Because seriously I have no idea why Monica is so pissed and I just want to know what I have to apologize for."

He ran a hand down his cheek, shaking his head. "Oh, man. Oh, *geez*, Liz. You were the one doing all the voting?"

My stomach swooped down as I tried to process the words he was saying. "Me? No! What the hell? Where are you getting that?"

"There are like a hundred random IP addresses here, and then like three hundred some that are all identical. And they belong to a router at your address."

I stared at her blankly for a single, shuddering breath. "So you're saying..."

"YOU HAVE BEEN RIGGING THE VOTE, ELIZA-BETH PALMER!"

My heart stuttered, then kicked into high gear, like a butterfly flapping around my chest. "Okay, I don't know what's happening, but I promise you I have not been sitting on a laptop in my house voting for myself to go on dates with these ridiculous guys. I *promise*."

Monica stared at me. "What the hell am I supposed to believe, Liz? How am I supposed to explain something like this to the sponsors, who poured money into this column? It was all a lie? Nobody actually cared as much as they thought they did? The magazine isn't exactly rolling in cash, it's not like we can pay them back!"

I started pacing back and forth, my hands over my face. I mumbled through my fingers. "I have no idea what's going on, I promise you. Maybe it's some software on my work computer glitching? Or...I don't know!"

"I asked Mandy - the auditor - about that. She says that she'd see something like a computer glitch, that it'd be obvious."

Alphonso nodded. "Yeah, it'd be happening every fraction of a second, or something. Even if it was a virus, it'd happen at regular intervals. This looks like someone sitting at the computer with a mouse, refreshing, and then clicking over and over."

"I still swear on everything holy - on every episode of the West Wing, Monica - I really don't know. But...maybe we can just...not tell anyone? I mean, how would the Liz Dates Philly sponsors even find out?"

"Alphonso? Care to explain Amanda the auditor's personality to Liz?"

"Amanda is a bitch," Alphonso deadpanned. "We hired her because she's the owner's niece and some idiot never made her sign any non-disclosure agreements with her contract. It wouldn't be the first time she's leaked information to other publications before we could print it. But this makes US look bad. It would ruin our columnists' credibility across the board. She'd have a field day."

"Amanda would collect the cash from the tip, and still get to keep working here, even after making us look like a much of manipulative shit heads. Dammit, Liz." Monica slammed her hand on the desk and I jumped.

"Wait a minute, though." Alphonso finally plunked his skinny-jeans covered ass on a desk chair and flipped to the back of the document. "There's another IP that voted like a kajillion times, too."

"As soon as Amanda called me with this, I grabbed the papers from her. So we just saw the one. Where's the other address, Liz? Your favorite coffee shop maybe, hm?" Monica asked, glaring at me.

I sighed. "I only work at home and in the office. I swear." The tension had dissipated just enough for me to find a place to sit, too.

"Yeah, this address...it's actually on UPenn's campus. South. That's the science campus." He smirked over at me. "I used to date a guy in the Biochem program there. Well, 'date' isn't exactly the right word. We mostly met in the stacks of the chem library."

"Ugh, TMI Alphonso, that's..." and that's when it hit me. Nobody I knew on Penn's campus was in a science major. There were no apartments or sorority houses near there. The only person I could think of who spent any time on campus at all anymore was...

"Jordan," I breathed. "Jordan." The second time I said his name came out as a growl. Spit gathered at the corners of my lips, like I was frothing at the mouth. And it tasted like blood.

Monica dropped the papers onto the desk and slid them over to me. "I'm giving you three days to figure this out, figure out how to fix it. You told me you loved politics, right?"

I nodded numbly.

"Well, politics is about spin. So is column-writing. So is saving your ass when you or your—*whoever*—is dumb enough to get it in deep shit. Figure this the fuck out."

My whole body shook as Alphonso drove me back to our place. My fists clenched, making white spots bloom over my knuckles, and my nails dug into my palms. I was so rigid from head to toe that I almost felt like I wasn't making contact with the seat. I was ready to unleash an avalanche of shit on Jordan Jacobs, dickhead extraordinaire, and none of it was good.

Alphonso went to turn the ignition off, and my hand shot out, slapping his forearm. He hissed and rubbed at it.

"You are not coming in with me. This is personal."

"That's exactly why I want to come in!" he whined in protest. "Can I at least come stand outside the door and eavesdrop? It's for journalism, Liz! And I drove you!"

"In your dreams," I grumbled, launching myself out of my seat and onto the sidewalk. After a step toward our building, I stopped and turned, went back, and wrenched open the door. Alphonso was smirking at me, holding my bag up on one finger. I'd left my damn keys inside it. In the car.

"Thank you," I said under my breath. "And thanks for the ride. You saved my ass this morning. I think."

My quads burned as I stomped up the stairs - there was no way I was going to wait for the creaky, slow elevator today. I pictured myself pacing in front of it like a caged animal just waiting to be let out for the kill.

I would not be that girl today. I would be a grownup. Most importantly, I would not let Jordan know he had hurt my feelings. This was about work, and only work. This was about my one good shot at a journalism job that he had taken away from me, why? Because he wanted to keep fucking me.

I scoffed as I started on the last flight of stairs. After all his sweet talk last night, about how you only "fucked" someone you didn't care about. How he couldn't possibly fuck me, because I was more than that. Well, maybe what we did in bed wasn't fucking me, but he'd certainly fucked my career over.

And then confusion swarmed my brain. Which one was it? Did he care about me, or not? Because sending me on awful date after awful date was not something someone who cared about you would do, unless they wanted you all to themselves.

All these weeks, I'd been operating under the assumption that Jordan didn't want a relationship with me – that's what he'd told me. So why would he go to so much trouble to rig Liz Dates Philly so that I only dated cringeworthy guys?

Maybe he just got off on controlling me. I didn't know whether that made me want to cry or rage.

Armed with that thought, I jammed my key into the lock and gave it a good twist. I hoped he heard me. I hoped he understood just exactly how pissed off I was when I finally let loose on him.

I never expected what I saw when the door swung open. Jordan, sitting on the couch, across from a girl with a shocking bright red bob. With her feet in his lap, and her hand on his shoulder, and a dopey smile on her face. Jordan most certainly wasn't trying to get her to move.

All rational thought blew out of my mind then, the new sense of betrayal and heartache mixing with my previous anger. At that moment, the only thing I could manage to say flew out of my mouth with a cracking, high-pitched gasp. "What the *fuck*?"

CHAPTER 23

JORDAN

I CAME HOME to an empty apartment, which worried me for a second, until I realized that there were no signs of forced entry, Liz's keys and bag were gone, and she'd left her typical hurricane-strength path of detritus in her wake. A Chapstick cap here, a stray receipt, a dime and penny flung from her purse or pocket in her rush to get out. I smiled softly and set her scone out on a little plate on the table. I could wait for her to get back. Maybe she was buying more condoms. The thought put a smug smile on my face, and I got busy settling in for the rest of what would hopefully be a lazy Sunday with Liz. Hopefully one where I'd tell her how I felt.

I'd managed to brew myself a second cup of coffee, set Liz's down and get settled with a stack of grading I had to do for the class I TA'd with Toby.

It was difficult to focus with thoughts of last night with Liz running on a loop through my head. The way her little pink tongue licked her lips when she was getting excited about something I was about to do to her, her little whimpering moans in time with my thrusts, her breathlessness when she was close to coming...it all added up to something I had never known was my ultimate fantasy.

I blew out a long breath. If I focused on grading now, maybe I could spend the rest of my weekend getting tangled in the sheets with Liz. I flipped open the manila folder of lab reports, and as soon as I scanned the first one, let out a long groan. Instead of my name at the top of every piece of paper was Tovyah Eisen's.

I was just about to shoot Toby an email, hoping she answered sooner rather than later, when there was a light, rhythmic knock on the door. That had to be Liz, coming back with condoms and maybe snacks in tow. (Hey, a guy could dream. If anything could make her more perfect, it would be running out for Saturday sex supplies.)But instead of Liz's bouncy golden waves on the other side of the door, all I saw was Toby's chestnut locks.

"Oh. Hey." I scoured my memory. Had I even given her my address?

"Don't sound so excited to see me, Mister." Toby shouldered her way into the apartment, drawing the tip of her index finger along my jawline as she did. After scanning the floor to see the trail of Liz-stuff, she called, "Morning, Liz!"

"Oh. She's not home."

"That's what I was hoping you'd say."

I scrunched up my eyebrows and gave her a side-eye.

Toby giggled and rolled her eyes, as if her entire manner wasn't dripping with innuendo. "I just meant that we'll work better if the apartment's quiet." She plopped down on the couch and pulled out a manila folder of lab sheets identical to mine out of her bag, flipping it open.

My eyes narrowed with the memory of her assortment of crazily-patterned folders strewn all over her cubicle in the engineering department. "Didn't you just tell me that you have the folders with the designs on them so that they don't get mixed up with anyone else's?

She shrugged and grinned. "The one time I run out, and look what happens. Lucky mine got mixed up with yours. You're my favorite fellow TA. Favorite guy in Philly, too." She paused, then sniffed the air like a bloodhound. "Would you be a sweetheart and grab me a cup of coffee?"

I shook my head in disbelief, but wandered to the kitchen anyway, pouring her a cup of black and bringing it back to her where she'd already snuggled into the couch cushions. "Thanks, hon," she murmured, leaning forward to rest the cup on the coffee table with one hand and pat the couch cushion opposite her with the other. "Come on, sit by me. It'll be fun. Like old times."

The only time I'd ever been on a couch with Toby, we most certainly had not been grading papers. Old times? More like orgasm times.

More innuendo.

For some reason, though, I obeyed. It only took a second for her to stretch her long, pale legs out across the couch and rest her ankles on my thigh.

It only took a second longer for the doorknob to turn and for Liz to burst in, her gorgeous hair wild and her eyes wide with fury. Clutched in her hand were a dozen or so pieces of paper, which looked like they'd once been stacked neatly. Liz's eyes darted to Toby, then back to me, then down at Toby's feet in my lap, then back to Toby.

The sound that came out of her mouth then was something I would have imagined coming from a hellbeast or a harpy in one of those campy fantasy movies from the 90s.

"What the *fuck*?" Liz screeched as her tight grip on the papers loosened and they went fluttering down to the battered hardwood floor.

Terror ripped through me. I shoved Toby's feet off my lap, barely registering the squeak that came from her side of the couch. I stood and carefully approached Liz, but her eyes went even wider and she backed into the door. I was thankful it had shut behind her. At least she couldn't escape that easily.

"I can explain, Lizzie, okay?"

"Explain what? How you've been fucking rigging the voting every single goddamn date I've been on? Or why you're snuggling with some other girl on the same damn couch where you fucked me senseless?"

Liz's eyes flicked to Toby. "Sorry. I'm sure you're very nice," she seethed.

"She's just a friend," I said quickly, waving Toby off and half-wishing she'd just disappear with a flick of my wrist.

"I'm sorry, *what?*" I heard the thunk of Toby's folder on the floor, and turned to see her standing up and taking on an offensive stance, too.

Nothing like being trapped in the middle of your living room by two girls you'd slept with, claws out and snarling. This was terrifying, but if there was ever a time I needed to be brave, it was now.

"You're just a friend," I repeated, turning to Toby, registering the remarkable way her expression mirrored Liz's. Either they were about to tackle each other or bond over how much they hated me and become best friends. I wouldn't have been surprised by the latter, at this point.

At least I knew why Toby was pissed at me, so I took a deep breath and continued, "We slept together four years ago -"

"Three and a half, and it was awesome," she growled, her eyes narrowed and fixed on my face like she wanted to shoot lasers at it.

She was right. It had been awesome. The flash of memory made me pause for a second, which brought a smirk to her face.

Liz threw her hands up in the air, letting out an indignant squawk.

"That is not the point, Toby. The point is," I said, turning to Liz, "that Toby and I TA the same class, she just dropped by to give me some papers, and we are not even remotely close to sleeping together. It's only you." On the last sentence, I softened my voice and pushed my eyebrows up while letting my mouth turn down. *Please let the puppy dog eyes work.*

Liz's eyebrows went up then too, and together with her little surprised gasp, it meant that I'd hit some emotional chord. Which meant that she felt something for me, too. I moved toward her, starting to lift my arms to embrace her, but she only stepped away again.

"Yeah. It's only me. And you made damn sure of that, didn't you?"

My eyes flicked down the papers scattered all over our floor then. They were filled with lines and lines of IP address read-outs. "Where were you just now, Liz? Philly Illustrated? A sour sinking feeling sloshed in my gut. I knew that's where she'd been as soon as I asked it. And I knew what those sheets represented. Every single damn vote in Liz Dates Philly. Even without a good look at the papers, I knew that a good half of the IP addresses listed there were mine.

My mouth dropped open, then shut again. Finally, I managed to say something. "Liz, I can explain." Dammit, I'd already said that about Toby, and she hadn't bought it then. Clearly stacking the votes in Liz Dates Philly was a far worse transgression than having my ex fuck-buddy's feet in my lap, and I'd been an idiot and used the same intro line.

"I seriously doubt it," she growled. Behind her glare, which she was still terrifyingly maintaining, her eyes glistened. I wanted to go to her, to hold her, to give her tears permission to fall, to kiss and apologize each one away. But Liz was a viper right now, coiled and ready to strike, and behind my very real love for her and panic to make everything between us better, there was intense and total fear.

"I just thought..." I thought a lot of things, or, rather, gave myself over to my emotions on a lot of things. "I don't know. At first, all the guys seemed so awful, so...I didn't think it would make a difference. Maybe give you some funnier material for the column. And then...then I just...I wanted..." I couldn't summon the words for what happened next, even though I knew damn well what had happened. I had been slowly falling for her and I wanted her to myself. I knew it wasn't okay, and even if I hadn't, my own sister had told me to cut it out. I didn't really have any excuses.

Except now I'd gone and let myself fall in love with her. It didn't matter that she clearly wanted to claw out my throat at this moment. I still wanted to hold her, needed her to understand, was desperate for her to forgive me.

I just couldn't figure out what to say to make that happen.

"What the *fuck,* Jordan?" she repeated, and something small inside me was satisfied that she didn't really have anything coherent to say about this whole situation, either.

"Toby, could you...?" I turned back to see Toby stuffing folders into her bag and her feet into shoes. "Just make sure you get the right papers this time," I said, keeping my voice low and timid. She glared, pulled the folder out of her bag, double checked in, slammed it down on the couch, and grabbed the one that I'd left shoved between the cushions on my side of the couch.

She stalked past Liz and I, her steps so forceful that her hair made a small breeze as she walked by. When she was almost to the door, she turned on her heel and looked Liz square in the eye. "He didn't say a word about you, by the way. So I kind of seriously doubt that 'only you, Lynn,' or whatever the fuck your name is, he's feeding you."

Liz looked down at the ground, swallowing audibly in the suddenly, horribly quiet living room. "It's Liz," she said in a near whisper. "My name's Liz." Then she looked up into my eyes, and they were all pain. Betrayal.

That was when my heart broke.

"Toby, could you just—I'll see you in the office." I didn't even try to keep the bitter edge off my request. Toby huffed, but finally left.

Liz was right. She was right, and I was so, so wrong. Of course, my stacking the votes was wrong, but it was so much more than that. I'd kept Liz all to myself, kept our relationship and my feelings for her limited to these four walls, like she was Rapunzel in a damn tower.

Liz stared at me, her eyes red and watery her lip visibly trembling. I couldn't stand to watch her like this, had no idea what to do to fix it. Worst, I didn't even know if I could fix it.

I finally met a girl I really liked—probably, no, *definitely* loved - and I'd done pretty much everything in my power to communicate that all she was to me was a game. A diversion. Something fun to pass the time, since we lived in the same place anyway.

"I don't know what to say." My voice cracked at the end of the sentence. It hadn't done that since I was seventeen.

"Is there anything *to* say?" Liz's words were a half-broken whisper dancing on a knife's edge, holding on to the thinnest string of hope.

I sighed heavily, feeling the weight of my shoulders as they pulled down, a burden I couldn't shake. "I'll move my stuff out tomorrow. While you're at work, so you don't have to see me."

She nodded, swallowed hard. "And you'll pay your share of the rent while I look for someone else."

"Do you think I'll be easy to replace?" I asked, the words falling out more easily than anything I'd said to her, ever. I stared at her, desperate for her to respond.

She swiped at her cheek with her fingertips, trying to keep the movement subtle. It didn't work. I'd made this strong, sassy girl cry. A small part of me hoped, pathetically, that at least some of the tears were due to a broken heart.

I took one more tentative step her way. She didn't move back this time, but she didn't acknowledge me, either. I watched a tear roll down her cheek, heard the whisper-quiet sound of it plopping on her shirt. "I really am sorry, Liz. I'd give anything to—"

"You've done enough," she ground out through her teeth.

I nodded, then took a step back. I should have said something else—*anything* else—but she was so closed off that I didn't think she would have really heard me anyway. Every second standing in front of her while feeling like she hated me was one second too many.

So I quietly walked back to my room. Just as I was about to open the door, she said, "You know, you really did have me fooled. The whole time I was dating these other guys, I kept thinking that it proved something, about how perfect you were for me compared to anyone else, and about fate and inevitability or some shit. Like it was serendipity that I happened to move in with a guy that was perfect for me. I thought that since Philadelphia could only find me guys to date that I hated, and then I came home and had such a good time with you, it meant that I could never get along with anyone as well as I got along with you."

"And?" I asked, my eyebrows up, my heart begging for this to be my second chance.

"And what you proved instead was that you're a creep who was just trying his hardest to keep me to yourself! Or maybe it was all some sort of sick, weird game to you. Either way, I've been jerked around and you are trash." Then, she broke. Her chest heaved in a sob and the tears started in earnest. She looked like she could collapse to the floor at any moment, and I would be the one responsible.

Dammit, she was right. I was scum.

"Liz, I—"

"Just...make sure you're out. Soon."

CHAPTER 24

LIZ

I COULDN'T THINK STRAIGHT ENOUGH to try to make sense of the complete and total mess that was Jordan's excuse for weighting the vote for every single one of my Liz Dates Philly matches in favor of the worst choice. I'd spent the last four months quietly stewing in a detached sort of hatred for the readers of Philly Illustrated for picking these horrible dates for, when in reality the villain of this whole haphazard debacle slept the next room over. And sometimes in my bed. And sometimes naked next to me.

The problem was, that just thinking about Jordan that way made me ache. Thinking about being alone in in our – *my* – apartment was crushing. I had to push through, though. I only had one goal, now - figure out how to make this Liz Dates Philly voting fraud disaster better. But first I had to get myself cleaned up.

Okay, then. Two goals.

As much as I hated the idea of putting my body any closer to Jordan's, whose bedroom door was mere footsteps away, instinct told me that a long, hot shower always made me feel more human and helped me think. I desperately needed both things right now.

Letting the steam fill my nostrils and wrap around my body was comforting, as always, and when I stepped out of the shower I felt less like a snotting, rabid anger beast and more like my determined, rational self. Well, as rational as anyone could have been in my situation. I wrapped myself tightly in my longest, plushest robe - there was no way Jordan was ever going to see those parts of me again after what he'd done, no matter how hot I still thought he was. I tentatively stuck my head out of the bathroom, then darted out to the living room to gather the papers Monica had shoved into my hands just a couple hours ago. I didn't really know what I was looking for, but I knew I had no clue how to fix any of this.

I also knew Monica had put the full responsibility on me.

I pulled up the "Liz Dates Philly" homepage and rolled my eyes at the ridiculous display of guys who had been 'in the running', each picture of a rejected guy crossed off with an 'X' that looked like it had been drawn with red lipstick.

I remembered all of them, some of them more vaguely than others. My eyes landed on Sam, who I thought wouldn't have been a bad choice at all. I scanned the tally of votes he'd received and compared it to the others - they were within dozens of votes of each other. The date could have gone to any of the guys in a matter of minutes.

Which, of course, made sense. Jordan would have started slow, realized he could actually sway the votes in a meaningful way, and then become more methodical about it. Jesus, was he planning to greet me at home after the most awful of dates? Playing the long game of being the understanding, supportive friend for months until my frustration with the awful bachelors boiled over? Waiting to swoop in to my rescue, look like the hero, and then, of course, get laid? Thinking through, step-by-step, the best way to make my eyes rove over his muscles, the quickest way to get me to scream his name?

A whimper broke out of my throat. He was awfully good at all those things. And as good as he was at the actual seduction-and-sex side of stuff, he was even better at what came after. Jordan's fingers smoothing through my hair or his lips pressing lazy kisses to my neck after he came were some of the most calming, warm, loving memories I had. Everything between us had felt so genuine.

How had I been so *stupid*?

I blew out a long breath and forced my thoughts back to where they needed to be. On bringing Monica a solution to all this that would not only let her save face, but be a damn good twist on the unexpected capstone of this whole thing.

I buried my face in my hands and groaned. Being a grownup sucked. I would have given anything to be back in Political stats class, analyzing polls and calculating errors of margin.

Then, something clicked. Of course. This wasn't a dating game. This was a voting game. A shallow one in the form of a voyeuristic popularity contest, sure, but votes were votes. Jordan's vote-stealing was an error, but that didn't mean the whole election was lost. I could still figure out who would have won each date even if the guy I was sleeping with on the side hadn't decided to piss all over my choices.

I sat up and started attacking my keyboard, loving the heady rush that I always got when my thoughts were flying around too fast for me to type. I had to get these thesis notes down if I was going to crunch these numbers with any kind of integrity.

If I took Jordan's votes out of the equation, tallied up the vote totals for each of the guys I didn't end up going on a date with, then removed any outliers within a standard deviation, then quietly deleted any of the guys who just weren't viable candidates because of obvious factors like lack of hygiene or obsession with their mothers, I would have a list of the winners, top-to-bottom, in no time.

Excel spreadsheets would be my best friends today. I opened one, grabbed a highlighter in one hand and the stack of papers bearing IP addresses in the other, and got to work literally erasing Jordan Jacobs from the last four months of my life.

Several hours later, the early November sun had already started its early descent. The darkness edged the sunlight into deepening vibrant stripes of orange and yellow, and exhaustion crept over me, making my head and limbs feel heavier by the minute. I hadn't finished tallying everything yet, but I was getting close. There was a light at the end of this tunnel.

I snuck into the kitchen to heat up some pizza rolls and cobble together a salad. After eating just enough to stop my stomach growling, I slunk into the bathroom, quiet as a ghost, to pee and brush my teeth before collapsing into bed.

Jordan wasn't as quiet - not nearly. He clunked around the bathroom, letting the cabinet slam shut and struggling with the shower curtain. Even the squeak when he turned the handle for the shower seemed louder, even from inside my room.

I smirked at the idea of him standing there under the shower head, shocked by how cold the water was after I'd stood under it for far longer than was responsible given our shitty water heater.

My traitorous imagination, though, worked too fast for my logic to keep up. Because as soon as I opened up to the thought of Jordan in the shower, my brain went straight to Jordan naked in the shower. I'd memorized the planes of his chest, his strong arms, the way those muscles cutting over his hip bones were carved into the most deliciously suggestive lines.

"Dammit!" I hissed into the darkness. The fact that Jordan was a lying, possessive asshole didn't negate the fact that he was the hottest guy I'd ever seen naked. And now I was all hot and bothered.

I groaned and got out of bed, heading straight to the still-unpacked moving box that I knew was labeled "bedside table." It took a few minutes of loud rumbling and cursing as various items crushed or pinched my fingers, but eventually I found the zippered case that held the latex-covered battery-powered column that had, on occasion, been my little workhorse disembodied buzzing boyfriend.

It only seemed right to wait until Jordan was out of the shower to put my memories of his naked chest, his tongue lapping at my clit, his heavy, hard cock rocking inside me to good use. I made damn sure that he heard my vibrator working in and out of me that night, and I didn't even try to hold back on the moans.

Luckily, I came to my senses just before his name came screaming from my lips.

<hr />

It took every ounce of confidence I had to walk into the Philly Illustrated office Monday morning.

I hadn't been able to sleep very well, tossing and turning and reliving my fight with Jordan, and his betrayal, in a dozen different ways - in a fantasy kingdom, where he was supposed to rescue me from a tower and ended up freeing the dragon instead of killing it; in a business office where he took credit for a report I had been the main worker on; in a restaurant where I was the manager and he sabotaged the staff to work too slowly to bring in any real cash.

The betrayal was a shock every time, and that was what upset me most when I woke up, thrashing and fuming mad, from each dream.

Eventually, I forced myself to sit up, rubbed the sleep out of my eyes, and snuck into the kitchen for a cup of coffee. It was still pitch-black outside, and the cold hardwood floor sent a chill up through my legs. I blinked and stared at the clock until the red glowing numbers were no longer a blur. Four fifteen. Great.

French press and mug in hand, I traipsed back to my room, settled myself on the bed, and cracked open my laptop. "Might as well start trying to figure this whole clusterfuck of a situation out," I muttered to myself.

I pulled up the tally of numbers I'd finished before going to sleep last night. The guy with the most votes was one of the main crop of super-generic-looking guys that I'd begun this whole thing with. As the weeks had worn on, Monica had found increasingly...*interesting* men for me to date. This one wore a suit in his picture, but it wasn't a law-office headshot or a drunken wedding outtake. He was at a bar or club of some sort, evidenced by the soft orbs of light in the background and the tumbler of amber liquid in his hand. He had on a white button-down shirt and a skinny black tie, with scattering of reddish-brown stubble, just a shade darker than his hair, over his jaw and chin. He was laughing at someone or something off-camera, and he looked genuinely happy. The light in his eyes was the kind that didn't come from faking it.

He looked real. Nice. Successful, and confident, but good.

Just a basic, good guy.

I could use a basic good guy, I decided.

"Nathaniel Perfect," I murmured as I clicked open the more detailed file buried in the "Liz Dates Philly" folder on Philly Mag's common drive. "His name is literally Mr. Perfect?" I let out a soft, incredulous laugh, and scrolled further down his profile. He was a research geneticist at children's hospital. *Not a doctor, exactly*, his profile said, *but you could tell your mom I help sick kids. That's gotta be worth something.* I laughed. Very cute. Lives near CHOP, so not too close by if things went really bad. I could avoid him in the future. If he was as health-conscious as he seemed, I probably would never see him at Joey and Hawk's.

And he had all those votes. He was cute, and successful, and he took a chance on submitting his name for this dumbassed project with Philly Illustrated that just so happened to be kick-starting my career. Maybe he thought I was cute, too. Maybe he liked my writing or maybe he read my list of interests and thought he'd like dating me.

With that thought, all my dates from the past couple months ran through my mind. How many of those guys had signed up for the project because they were interested in having a conversation with me? Exactly zero.

Which was how you rationalized sleeping with JJ in the first place.

I shook my head back and forth, hard, trying to jar myself from this train of thought. I was a very cute girl with mad writing skills and a varied set of interests in one of the most populous cities in the United States of America. I refused to believe that the only guy in this city that I was compatible with was Jordan fucking Jacobs, especially since he turned out to be possessive and borderline-stalkery. Stacking those votes took hard work and dedication. He had to really want to screw me over.

Or maybe he just wanted to be the only one screwing me.

Either way, I wasn't happy about the deception. Not one bit.

"Okay, Mr. Perfect," I muttered as my fingers began to fly across the keyboard. "I hope you're still up for this."

━━━

Four hours later, I emerged from my room, dressed and as well-made up as possible while avoiding the bathroom. My whole frosty bitch strategy toward Jordan would be messed up if I bumped into him coming out of the bathroom in any state of undress and stammered all over him, so I'd snagged my makeup bag and perched myself on the edge of my mattress with a compact in one hand while shakily applying eyeliner and lipstick.

Damn Jordan Jacobs. He could even force me to mess up my makeup.

Whatever. It didn't matter, not one bit. I was ready for this.

Until, that is, I reached for my keys and my fingers brushed against a white wax-paper bag. Inside was a blueberry scone wrapped in white paper, with two words scrawled on it in red sharpie.

With a pang of sadness, I realized how rarely I'd seen JJ's handwriting. We'd lived together for five months, known each other in so many different ways, and I didn't even know if I'd be able to pick his messy engineer's scrawl out of a lineup.

Just two little words were scrawled on the bag.

"I'm sorry."

I pressed my lips together and squeezed my eyes shut, taking a deep breath. I would not cry. I would not, and I could not. Especially since I was trying to avoid the bathroom.

The first time I'd ordered this and told Jordan it was my favorite, he'd made annoying jokes about Italian blueberries the whole walk home.

A lump rose in my throat, but I pushed it back down with all the fierceness I could muster. I couldn't allow myself to care. I couldn't let him pull me down again and out of a job.

I unwrapped the scone, gently broke its perfectly-glazed, blueberry-drizzled surface in halves, and sighed in sadness over what I was about to do to it. Then, I broke the scone into a pile of teeny tiny crumbs. I moved quickly but precisely for a minute or so, then stepped back to admire my handiwork.

There, in the middle of the little table that had definitely seen the full range of the drama of me and JJ's relationship, was spelled out with purple crumbs,

JJ - Fuck off. <3 Liz.

I nodded, then brushed the stray crumbs off my palms. That should get the message across nicely.

My stomach growled, the sound ripping through our—*my*—quiet apartment.

God, even my appetite was attached to fucking Jordan Jacobs.

I ducked into my cube and opened my laptop, breathing out a long, slow breath before doing a final review of the presentation.

"So you're telling me that your plan for apologizing for all these rigged dates and making it right is to go on another rigged date?" Monica asked wearily, peering at me through the pink-and-purple spectacles slid down on her nose.

"Sort of. It'd be an apology to the voters, because we'd be honoring their actual votes. Nathaniel Perfect would have beaten all the other guys in a landslide if Jordan hadn't been fucking with the poll, see?" I leaned forward and tapped the pad of my index finger to the paper. "They actually really liked him. They wanted me to have a nice time. It's kind of sweet."

"Yeah, adorable," Monica grumbled. "What about the sponsors?"

"That's easy. I go on a date with him every day for a week, where we visit every establishment that paid. We'll start with dinner on Friday and end with dinner on Sunday. Brunch, city walks, and other stuff in between. If Mr. Perfect turns out to be awful, it'll still be enough entertainment to make up for all the dates that both the voters and sponsors might feel shorted out of. If it's great...and I kind of think this guy has the actual potential to be really nice, and a good date—then it'll be romantic and intriguing and all the sponsors will get really, really good reviews."

Monica shook her head, like she was stumped. "There's gotta be something more. Something unique to the marathon nature of the thing, which I'll admit, is kind of genius. If readers don't have to sit down and read one huge-ass piece about it to get a sense of what happened."

"Easy," Alphonso said. "Just live-tweet it. Link to Facebook and Tumblr and whatever and Instagram pictures of you guys at each location. We'll get a hashtag. We'll hype it up hard over the next two days. As the week goes on, we'll get more followers. Maybe even local news coverage if we get on it."

"Alphonso, that's really smart," I said, admittedly a little surprised that he'd pulled something so well-thought out from his brain at just the right moment.

"I can't believe this guy's name," Alphonso said, falling against his chair back in a slouchy mope. "Only you would actually go on a weekend-long date with a literal Mr. Perfect, funded by the good business owners of Philadelphia."

"Oh, relax, Alphonso. I guarantee you, this isn't as fun as it looks."

"It's just that...all this, after Mr. Engineer Hottie was the one spending all this time, rigging all these votes for you." He sighs. "It's kind of romantic."

"Yeah, yeah, super romantic that Mr. Hottie, who's also my roommate, was creeping around online trying to keep me from going out with any guys I might actually like, so he could keep me for himself."

"How do you know he did it because he wants to be with you?" Monica asked. "Maybe this was all a big prank."

"Oh...um..." I stammered, realizing that maybe she really

didn't know the true nature of what was going on between us. "Well..."

Alphonso buried his face in his hands, then dragged them down slowly, pulling his bottom eyelids away from his eyeballs like we used to do when we made silly faces as kids. "Oh my God, Monica," he moaned. "Because they've been fucking. This whole time, she's been sleeping with her roommate and dating the guys the readers picked for her."

I turned to him slowly, my eyes wide with horror. "How did you...?"

"I'm not stupid, Liz," Alphonso said. "Or blind. Honestly, just from the way you talk about him—"

"You know what?" Monica said, waving her hands to cut off whatever he was about to say. "I don't want to know. It's not important. You broke it off with engineer guy, right?"

I swallowed, trying to keep the rising tears from pricking at my eyes just with her words. "Actually, he wants to be an astronaut."

Monica's eyes shot daggers at me.

"Yeah," I babbled. "Broken it off and kicked him out. One hundred percent."

"Okay, then we take the prank angle. You say that he wasn't your boyfriend—he technically wasn't. Right?"

"Right," I nodded, taking another hard swallow, blinking back more tears. "He's actually a friend from childhood."

Monica clapped her hands together, twice. "Perfect. He was just a guy playing a prank on someone he saw as a sister. And, um..." Monica picked up her pen and started scrawling on last page of the paper in front of her, "You should probably say something about how if any of the girls reading this have a boyfriend trying to control them in any way, it's not healthy, not romantic, borderline abusive. Okay?"

God, that made me sad. *Abusive.* After so many good things

had passed between Jordan and I, that was a tough pill to swallow.

I nodded. "Absolutely right. You got it. Should I start in on these calls? I'd like to start planning the dates as soon as possible."

"The sooner the better."

———

I took a deep breath, trying to calm my nerves, as I pulled up Nathaniel Perfect's file one more time. Of course, I was worried he wouldn't agree to go out with me – a guy like Mr. Perfect could very well have found a girlfriend since his application came in. The next guy down on the list would do almost as well, but I had sold Monica on *this* guy. I hoped like hell he'd say yes.

He'd listed a work number and a personal number. It was ten thirty, so I'd almost definitely be calling him at his desk. I could have waited until lunch, in the normal world. But this was journalism, however pithy and trivial, and every second counted.

Maybe speaking from one desk to another would make things more professional.

"Visicom Incorporated, this is Nate." His voice was youthful but confident, just a little raspy with a clear smile behind it. The realization made me smile, too.

"Hi, um, Nate. This is Liz Palmer from Philly Illustrated. I'm calling about a feature you applied to be part of several months ago...."

———

Forty-eight hours later, on a chilly Wednesday morning, I was laughing so hard I was nearly crying into my scone at Joey and

Hawk's. "So you're telling me that you'd never heard of Liz Dates Philly and you had no idea what Philly Illustrated was, and you only found out when the literal guy next door told you, but you still agreed to go out on a date with me if you were voted in?"

He flashed me a wide smile. "I figured the worst that could happen was you were totally crazy and I could just make a quick exit. But hearing your voice on the phone...I don't know. It made me feel like I should take a chance. You sounded smart. And...this is gonna sound weird but... something about your laugh. You sounded beautiful."

I observed the bright pink tinging his ears and smiled a little. Sometimes it felt nice for a guy to be bashful in my presence, even if just for a second.

"Then I realized that my dad was the one who had signed me up, thanks to my kid sister, and I figured, why the heck not? Dad can be annoying but he has my best interests at heart. And, you know, we are the Perfect family, so..."

I balled up a napkin and tossed it at Nate's head. He laughed and caught it in his palm.

"You know, most people would be more modest in the face of such a laudatory appellation," I said.

"Wait, wait," Nate said, pressing his palms to the table and looking around. "They told me this was a modern-day date but now you sound like you're from a Jane Austen novel."

"Shut up," I said, smiling wide at him.

I decided to finish my scone before we talked any more. After all, we had to be at the Franklin Park in forty-five minutes.

Before we left Joey and Hawk's, I pulled out my phone for the first of many selfies Monica and I had agreed I'd be taking today. I stood up and slid in the booth next to Nate, where he put his arm around my shoulders, like it was easy as breathing. I held up the phone and aimed the mirrored camera at us. Right before I took the shot, Nate turned to me and gently brushed a finger at the corner of my mouth. "You had a little crumb there," he said. The camera caught his eyes flitting over my lips.

I smirked at how suggestive it was, how cute he looked with that little smile aimed at me. I marked the location and ended the "Best Scones in Philly!" caption with the hashtag Alphonso had chosen and Monica had grinned into approval - #LizDates-MrPerfect.

When I pressed "share," I secretly hoped Jordan was following along.

CHAPTER 25

JORDAN

I'D CONTEMPLATED about a hundred different ways to apologize to Liz in the last six days. None of them had worked. None of them were good enough, anyway.

I wasn't really stupid enough to think my first actual attempt, the scone, would work out. The girl loved her carbs, obviously, but not enough to quell the lava-hot wrath that she'd shown me the day she'd found out what I'd done to Liz Dates Philly. Then found Toby playing footsie up to me.

Toby was a problem, seriously. I was a smart guy, but I hadn't seen Toby coming. I figured whatever there had been between us was over, but apparently she'd been counting on a repeat performance. . I'd have to figure out whether she'd been coming on to me every time we ran into each other at the office, or whether she was just trying to scratch a suddenly-occurring itch by coming to my apartment unannounced. I even suspected she'd been the one to switch our grading folders, though I didn't have a shred of proof.

Whatever. Toby was an issue for another day. I couldn't decide whether to try to get Liz to understand that Toby didn't mean anything to me, certainly not the same way she did, or whether to never, ever speak her name again in Liz's presence.

If Liz would even give me an audience again.

I hadn't spoken with her since our confrontation six days earlier, which, honestly, could hardly be termed "speaking." It didn't matter - I deserved it. In the three days between our fight and when I'd moved three huge boxes of my shit into Ethan's spare bedroom, she'd certainly wasted no time expressing her displeasure with me. She'd used my towels as bath mats, left my industrial-sized box of Fudgsicles to melt on the countertop, and taped the "for rent" section of the newspaper - which we didn't even subscribe to—to the front of my bedroom door. Oh, and I'd found my toothbrush floating in the toilet one morning.

Ethan's place may have been cramped and run-down and occupied by him and occasionally his maybe-friend-maybe-more, Natalia, who he had already had very loud sex with once since I'd been here, but it was free, and welcoming. Those few times I'd given him a ride home from a late class must have been all he needed to consider me a good friend.

Liz was right. I needed to find a new apartment, not just somewhere to stay while she cooled down. This was not going to blow over. I'd fucked up, and I knew it. I'd decided to make a temporary move out before she started doing...whatever it was she felt brave enough to do. Maybe something with my shaving cream.

I shuddered and settled into one of Ethan's rickety dining chairs with the paper and a red marker.

Just as I'd lowered my expectations from small-and-decent apartment to smaller-and-gross basement hovel, my phone started rattling against the table. Kiera.

I hadn't told her a thing about the fight between Liz and me, and I could only imagine that Liz hadn't either - or else KiKi would have been on the phone with me and screaming in my ear much sooner than now. I had to admit, I'd kind of hoped Liz would call Kiera, just so I'd know she was upset.

Girls trashed your stuff when they were pissed. They only cried to their friends on the phone when their hearts were broken.

The message was loud and clear - no crying on the phone, no broken heart. I really had been just a fuck buddy to Liz, and forty-eight hours was far more time than I really needed to prove it.

"Just move the fuck on, buddy," I grumbled to myself as I picked up the phone. "Liz is not the only woman on earth."

I must have hit the pickup button before the second sentence, because I heard Kiera's biting voice in my ear - "No, but she's the only woman that you've actually liked. Maybe, like, ever. What the fuck were you thinking, JJ? How did she find out? How did you explain it?"

"Too fast, Kiera," I said, running my palm over my face.

"Well, how about one simple question? What the fuck are you going to do about it?"

"Nothing. Not a damn thing. She doesn't want me. She doesn't want me so much, in fact, that she asked me to get a different place, and keep paying for my rent while she found someone new."

"She used those words. Find someone new." Kiera's skepticism bled from her voice through the cell connection.

I sighed. "Yeah."

"Well, okay. She wants you out. You should get out. But what do you want to *do?*"

"I want to respect her wishes. Jesus, I'm not a complete asshole."

"You know that's not what I meant," Kiera said gently. "What do you *want?*"

"I want *her!*" I cried, throwing my hand up in the air. "I'm in love with her."

"You're *what?*"

"You heard me."

"You have never told me that before, about *anyone!*" she cooed. Kiera was incredible in her ability to go from raging mad to emotionally moved in the space of a few seconds. If I didn't love her so damn much, I wouldn't be able to stand a five minute phone call with her.

"I've never told anyone else that, either," I said, the whispered realization stirring something inside me. I'd known it, of course, known that out of all the girls I'd dated in undergrad, I'd never been able to say those three little words to a single one. Now I was saying that, out loud, but not to the girl who actually captured the feeling.

"Maybe it's a good time. You already fucked everything up with her. Might as well toss out this one last life preserver. See if she'll let you float it back to shore."

My head hurt. "Kiera, this is not the time for you to start breaking into poetic metaphors. I can barely keep my thoughts straight as it is."

"What can I say? I've been reading Liz's column."

"She's good with metaphors," I said.

"Yeah, she's been firing them off all morning on this week-long date live-feed."

"What?" My head swam with confusion. "She's doing another date?"

"No, brother. She's doing *the* date. Well, several dates with *the* guy. A week-long affair. I'm guessing she had to do something to make your cheating the polls all better for the advertisers. They called the guy with the most votes that didn't come from you."

"You were stacking the votes too," I grumbled.

Kiera let out a short cackle. "Nowhere near as much as you were. Hey, get this. The guy she's going out with? His name is literally Mr. Perfect."

"Mr..." My voice trailed off as I scrambled to log on to Twitter. I'd opened an account there one drunk night in college, used it to communicate with the girl I'd met at the bar who had nudged me into the mess of social media clusterfuck, and never touched it again. I sighed as I stared at the confusing mess of 280-word messages. "So. You said there was a hashtag?"

It only took me a few minutes to find the beginning of the #LizDatesMrPerfect twitter thread, where the paper had linked to an article explaining what in the hell was going on.

"Dear Philly Illustrated readers,

So many of you have been following "Liz Dates Philly" in the five months since it all began, and voting your little hearts out to help her find Mr. Right! It's been quite a journey, and we've loved watching her adventures getting to know all these great guys as well as our favorite Philly date spots. Fun!

I shook my head. This was the opposite of fun, if you asked me. It was clear as day from the overuse of exclamation points that this was not written by Liz. My guess was on that power hungry pompously-dressed co-worker of hers.

Well, this week there was a big twist in this already-crazy love story. We found out that one of Liz's childhood friends, in town for grad school, decided to prank all of us by stacking the votes this whole time, voting for the winning guy by hundreds of extra each week! Insane!

We enjoyed reading about Liz's dates as much as the rest of you - while Liz's friend made this little adventure entertaining, for sure, one thing it has not been is representative of what Philly Illustrated readers wanted it to look like. Although we didn't know this was going on, it was still misleading, and we're very sorry.

To make it up to you, and to all the businesses that so generously sponsored each and every one of Liz's dates, we've decided to go back over all our records of each and every vote. The lucky guy who got the majority of votes from readers who were NOT Liz's friend from days gone by will be going on a marathon weekend--long date with Liz, stopping at each location that sponsored us from the beginning - on our dime, this time. We hope you'll consider stopping by for your next date or fun evening out, everywhere from 30th Street Station to Uncle Phil's Philly Phun Zone!

For good measure, we'll be asking for your votes for one last thing—the best charity for Philly Illustrated to donate to, on behalf of all these incredible organizations. In the end, Liz Dates Philly may not have been exactly representative of your votes, but we hope you enjoyed the column anyway. Most importantly, we hope that our oversight will end up contributing lots of good to this crazy world.

The lucky guy, by the way, looks pretty incredible. He's a research geneticist, loves his mother, and is darn handsome to boot. The only thing better than all that—for our column-writing purposes, at least—Is that his name is Nathaniel Perfect.

Yeah, Nate's name tells us he's Mr. Perfect in one aspect - but will he turn out to be THE Mr. Perfect for our sweet, good-sport reporter Liz Palmer?

We'll find out today. Follow #LizDatesMrPerfect on Twitter,

Tumblr, Facebook, and Snapchat to watch every step of what we
hope will be her dream date, and weigh in on what you think!

I sighed and ran a hand back through my hair. I had to hand it to
Monica - she'd done a damn good job of handling this whole
mess, even if she did use the word 'crazy" too much for just one
little column.

I scrolled back up through the hashtag. Damn. It was barely
11:00 and they'd already been on three dates? And they were
illustrated with Deanna's photos, too! I knew Deanna was really
good at communicating all the little moments of each date, but
she'd never tweeted them live before now. There was one other
humungous difference - they'd never looked this lovey-dovey-
datey, either. Normally, she would catch an expression of
disgust on Liz's face, the perfect polish of some jerk's shoes, or
the awkward bend of his arm as he tried to play skee-ball or
almost-put his arm around Liz.

But starting from the very first leg of the date, at Joey and
Hawk's, of all places - Liz looked like she was having a good
time. If Mr. Perfect was talking, she was listening intently, her
chin resting on her palm with fingers curled around that
gorgeous jaw. Deanna got a picture of them leaving, too, and
when Mr. Perfect's hand hovered at Liz's lower back, I could
swear she was leaning into it. And then – oh God, the one that
hurt my heart the most – a selfie, taken by Liz, flashing her
cheesy grin to the camera. Mr. Perfect looked smug as hell.

Everything about this damn hashtag was pissing me off, but
I kept reading anyway.

About twenty minutes into my increasingly miserable
surveillance, when I watched Mr. Perfect and Liz stroll down
one of Philly's busiest shopping streets, laughing and smiling, I
realized that I was only following Philly Illustrated's feed.

Through the magic of social media, Liz's readers had started a whole side discussion dissecting every moment of the date.

I should never have looked through there. It only made me more miserable. It seemed the core group of people - a couple dozen - who had been following Liz Dates Philly were more than vaguely interested with the process - they looked forward to each week's update like people obsessed over their favorite TV shows, and some of them even had the crazy speculations and theories to match. There was the group who thought the paper had all the guys hand-picked in advance, and those who tried to dig into each guy's background and life, then wrote their own Tumblr and Facebook posts laying bets on Liz's success with each guy.

There was even a #FrankenPhillyDate sub-hashtag, where each guy was rated by a polling group and then the guys who had the best score in each area—looks, career, family ties, interests, charisma—were re-mixed every week to make the perfect Franken-date.

When I clicked on the responses to the Liz Dates Mr. Perfect hashtag, though, I realized I was reading about myself.

Not in the sense that I looked like Mr. Franken-date—not even close. That guy was blond and muscular and working some job that made him six figures even though he was only twenty-five years old. He also was skilled in bed, but not so skilled that it made him cocky.

Yeah. Right.

As a bonus, the "Liz Dates Mr. Perfect" discussion had a whole, decently robust thread dedicated to the "Jackhole who fucked up our votes." AKA, me. There was a little bit of talk about whether I had managed to mess with the votes *that* much —after all, lots of people had still voted for the guys Liz eventually went out with, they imagined, and the dates hadn't been boring by any stretch. Just a nightmare for Liz. Those people thought that the "childhood friend" was probably one of the kids she'd spent her braces-wearing junior high years with, playing pranks involving each other's bras at sleepovers and giggling over celebrity spreads in teen magazines. Someone like Kiera, I realized, who was friends with her, who knew her well, and was close enough for Liz not to want to kill her at the end of it all, but not close enough that she'd feel any qualms about pulling such an elaborate prank.

That was how I'd started this whole thing, wasn't it? As Liz's roommate, her friend, someone who thought they'd have a good laugh at her expense?

Someone who also happened to be sleeping with her on the side, and falling more in love with her each time we did. God, I was an asshole.

That assessment was confirmed by most people responding to the Jackhole theory—a larger sub-group of hopeless romantics really and truly believed that Liz could have found love through the Liz Dates Philly column, if only she'd been allowed to. And that was where my gut started to twist and I hung my head with guilt. The voters who logged on to Philly Illustrated and voted in Liz Dates Philly every week knew something about the kind of guy she'd want to date. At least it seemed that way, from how cozy Liz and Mr. Perfect looked now that they'd landed at 30th Street Station for a Saxby's latte and people-watching.

When Liz had originally gone to 30th Street Station for the first latte-and-people-watching date of the feature, it had been with some guy named Preston, whose head was shaped like a cabbage, wore a too-tight plaid button-down tucked into khakis, and could barely stop sneezing. *Allergy season,* Liz had explained through her laughter when she re-hashed the date with me.

That night, she'd smiled at me in exactly the same way she was smiling at Nate now—like he'd hung the moon. Deanna was posting pictures at a breakneck pace—one every few minutes—and they all showed things that made me feel escalating degrees of revulsion—Liz beaming while looking into his eyes, Liz laughing so hard she had to wipe under her eyes with a single manicured finger, Liz brushing Nate's knee with her hand to get his attention. (They were looking at a set of toddler triplets dressed identically for a family photo shoot, Deanna's photography breathlessly revealed.) That whole thing set off a frenzy of internet fans mashing together Liz and Nate's pictures and declaring they would make the most adorable babies, like, EVER.

The knot in my stomach twisted tighter. At the thought of Liz having another guy's babies, however fleeting it was. I was so far gone for her it wasn't even funny.

When Liz and Mr. Perfect—every time I even thought his name, I felt sick—parted ways, she breathlessly tweeted that the tag would pick up again when they met tomorrow for lunch.

It was the most miserable night I'd ever experienced. Possible coping mechanisms flashed through my mind in quick succession. I would go work out, but nobody liked to watch a dude lifting weights with tears welling out of his eyes. I could cook dinner in Ethan's kitchen, but not having Liz fawning over how delicious it was would be too damn sad. Hell, I could drink, but that would be sadder than anything, especially with the likelihood that I'd end up passing out on Ethan's floor.

To top it all off, I barely slept, opting instead to stare at the #LizDatesPhilly feeds on Twitter and Tumblr.

Was this rock bottom? I couldn't imagine it getting any worse. That should have been my signal that it most certainly could—and would.

CHAPTER 26

LIZ

"LIZ! WATCH IT!" Nate - as he'd urged me to call him - wrapped my fingers with his. They were solid and strong when they tugged me away from some innocuous obstacle in the middle of the Philly sidewalk. I couldn't help but notice they were slightly sweaty, too.

A small smile ghosted over my lips. Was he nervous? That was so sweet.

"What? Was there an ROUS there or something?"

"A what?" He gave me a bemused smile.

"Uh...never mind." Jordan had assured me that everyone grew up watching The Princess Bride, that I wasn't a freak for loving it so much.

Stop thinking about him.

"No," Nate said, nudging me with his elbow, "there was just a fast food bag there. Didn't want you to trip."

I gave him a quizzical look before I realized—he was just looking for an excuse to hold my hand. Something I hadn't even thought of. I snuck a glance back at Deanna, who was following half a block behind us and across the street with her iPhone aimed at us like a creeper. I'd gotten so used to her paparazzi-like detachable-lens camera that it felt weird for her to be aiming her cell camera at me. But she'd attached some chunk of glass and plastic to the top of her phone and assured me it would help her get the shots she needed.

It had been part of my plan to have Deanna live-tweet, Tumble and Snapchat the whole day—to really spend the day maximizing my time with Mr. Perfect, for the paper's appearances, anyway. Of course, that meant that I was taking extra care with my hair and makeup, not to mention my outfit, since I needed something that would take me the distance of the whole day while still looking cute. It was a tall order, but I thought I'd managed it with some very stretchy skinny jeans, cute flats, and a lace-necked tank with a drapey cardigan over top of it.

From the way Nate's gaze occasionally flitted over my collarbone, and even once or twice below, I figured I did a good job.

Nate, who looked sheepish, squeezed my hand, which he still held in the most awkward of positions. Just like that, I snapped back into First Date Mode, the headspace that I'd learned to put on autopilot over the last few months. I was supposed to be interested, to be flirting, even a little encouraging.

I was expected, both by my boss and by my readers, to *try* with this one.

So I twisted my wrist, which pressed my palm into his, and intertwined our fingers, squeezing a little as I did.

Nate beamed, like I'd just handed him a million dollars or the Nobel peace prize.

"Thanks," I said. "That was sweet."

One thing I'd learned from the last two and a half hours with Mr. Perfect was that redheads—auburns, really—blushed easily. He was the attractive kind of redhead too, his hair ruddy and his skin just the right shade of tan so that it didn't look weird. I was sure he had freckles, somewhere, and the idea that maybe I'd want to go looking for them under his clothing at the end of the night didn't send me recoiling in horror.

Aside from his slightly sweaty hands and awkward first date step-stop behavior of pulling my chair out for me and guarding me from the horrors of stepping in errant trash, Mr. Nathaniel perfect was, well... perfect.

He'd graduated *summa cum laude* from Columbia University, where he'd had a full ride scholarship and earned a biology degree. Instead of using all his free time to study or make extra cash, he'd volunteered with organizations like CityYear and Doctors Without Borders. When Josh and his frat buddies had done community service, it had been in the name of adding something to their resume to aid their acceptance to the best law school or MBA program.

"I could have gone to med school," Nate explained as we sipped our coffee and watched travelers stroll by at the train station, "but this one summer I volunteered in Malawi, I met a family whose baby could barely move. Not because she was starving or had some kind of malaria or something—she had a disorder. She never was able to really hold up her head or even grab things. Two of her siblings had died of the same thing. When I finally spoke with a visiting doctor, he guessed it was SMA-1—Spino-muscular atrophy."

"Genetic, I assume," I said sadly.

"Yep. It's a genetic mutation that keeps their body from producing a protein that lets their nerves control muscles. Kids who have it are weak, so weak they can't breathe. They just... die. Before they turn one, usually. Anyway, I couldn't stop thinking about this kid, and the next semester in my bioethics class we learned about upcoming gene therapy studies. There was this one that was starting at CHOP in two years' time—"

"And it was for this disease?" I guessed, giving him a soft smile. Anyone who hung out with this guy could tell what a good heart he had. No wonder the Philly Illustrated voters had been so overwhelmingly for him. And all this time I'd been thinking they just wanted to screw me over.

All this time, it had been my own roommate screwing me. In more ways than one.

A guy I couldn't stop thinking about for more than five minutes at a time, dammit.

"—and then once we attach the protein to the virus, it just sort of goes through the kid's body and arrests muscular deterioration at that point in their development. We've seen kids who should have been dead at one start to walk by that time."

"That's... wow. That's incredible." I was sure there were girls who would be absolutely salivating to get into Nate's pants after this declaration of medical valor. I thought it was interesting, but not sexy.

"Yeah, maybe once we publish the results of this trial, the rest of the world will agree, and renew our funding. And then maybe I could keep doing this the rest of my life, instead of selling out for med school."

"The rest of our lives isn't that far away, I guess," I mused, letting my eyes fall on a woman pushing a stroller with a baby in front and a preschooler standing on a platform behind his sibling.

"No, but it's not like right now, either," Nate chuckled. "Still, I guess my dad was getting worried enough about my future happiness to sign me up for a very public dating experiment. "

"Well, you don't seem to mind very much. You've been a very good sport about all this, is what I mean," I rushed to explain when his expression softened.

"No, I don't," he said, staring at nothing in the distance with a soft smile. "Can I be honest with you, Liz?"

"Sure," I managed, suddenly stressed about what would come out of his mouth next.

"I was kind of pissed when I found out that I got signed up for this. You know, my dad has no business meddling like that, even if he means well. "Now... I don't know." He shrugged. "I'm glad You're cute. You're fun to be around." His smile was shaky, his eyes sparkling.

But instead of the butterflies I would have expected to feel at hearing those words, the one fairy tales and rom-com movies prescribed for this moment, all I felt was a twisting pit forming in my stomach.

"Aw," I managed. "Likewise."

And he was. Cute. Cute, and smart, and selfless, and open. Emotionally honest. Certainly not the kind of guy who would manipulate a city-wide poll in order to obfuscate any happiness I might have gotten from going on normal dates, screw me once in a while in the meantime, and then bring another girl home, snuggle with her on the couch where I'd had some of the most amazing sex of my life with him just weeks earlier, and pretend that he'd done nothing wrong.

No, Nate Perfect wasn't a manipulative, selfish asshole like Jordan was.

So why couldn't I stop thinking about him and start focusing on Mr. Perfect, who had been served up to me on a silver platter by the blessed readers of Philly Illustrated for the perfect week-end-long date?

Because I was stupid, that's why. Maybe it was our similar taste in movies, or the way he made my coffee, or the way he knew exactly how to tease my body into oblivion with his hands and tongue and cock. Maybe it was the fact that I'd known him forever, that I felt safe with him, that he made me laugh.

For all I knew, Mr. Perfect had those same qualities. Maybe even more so. And I'd never be able to see them if I didn't open up my damn eyes.

So that was why I twisted my hand toward his and let our

fingers twine together. Because I wanted to see. I wanted Nate to actually be Mr. Perfect. I wanted him to prove to me that Jordan was really Mr. Mediocre and Slightly-disturbingly-possessive.

Never mind that I loved "possessive" in the bedroom—something Jordan had taught me.

Dammit. There my mind went again. I sighed heavily, making Nate's fingers twitch in mine. "You okay?"

I forced a wide grin on my face, making sure it reached my eyes, too, and turned my gaze straight to his. *Try, Elizabeth. Don't fuck this up. For yourself or for Philly Illustrated.*

CHAPTER 27

JORDAN

THE NEXT DAY I was so exhausted I could barely move. I stood in front of my Engineering Mathematics students, watching their faces blur together. I mumbled my way through their assignment and asked if they had any questions. Thank God they didn't, because I honestly don't know how I would have answered them. As soon as the first student filtered out the door after I'd dismissed them twenty minutes early, I was back to scrolling through my phone.

I was a crazy obsessed person, and I knew it. I just couldn't get a grip on a good enough reason to stop. I was in love with the girl, and watching her slip through my fingers into Mr. Perfect arm's was going to kill me whether I kept up with every detail or not.

I couldn't stand it when Liz and Mr. Perfect held hands. Their intertwined fingers swung between their bodies as they walked, according to the gleeful caption on Deanna's tweeted photo.

By lunchtime at Nam Phuong Vietnamese I couldn't handle it any more. My brain screamed a hundred responses to each increasingly ridiculous online speculation thread, and I'd started to become more familiar with every person tweeting and Tumbling and whatever the fuck else about Liz Dates Mr. Fucking Perfect than I was with the college students I TA'd. I had to do something.

No, asshole. Back down. "I have to do something" is exactly the attitude that got you here, remember? She likes him. She's having a good time. Maybe he really is Mr. Perfect-for-her.

A much smaller voice told me that that couldn't be true, because of what I knew deep down - *I* was Mr. Perfect. Or, at least, Liz was Miss Perfect-for-me. I wanted to be with her more than anything, all the time, and it wasn't just because she was on a date with someone else. Over the last few weeks, there'd hardly been a moment when I hadn't thought to myself that it would be more fun or at least more bearable if Liz was there next to me.

I absolutely had to do something. Even though I had no idea what.

CHAPTER 28

LIZ

AFTER AN INCREDIBLE LUNCH of spring rolls and crispy tofu, I was grateful for the short walk to digest a bit. The next stop, it turned out, was Joseph Fox Bookshop, a sweet little indie store. Monica text-reminded me that it would be highly encouraged for us to make a book stack of our top ten favorites of all time and take a cute pic for Deanna with them, and for the book shop. The book store had been one of the more forgiving sponsors, and we were trying to strike a better distribution deal for our print magazine, so extra cutesy antics were in order, apparently.

I loved the book store. Any book store, really, because the smell of the pages and the quiet looks of contemplation on the shoppers' faces always made me feel peaceful, happy. A sense that I was among intellectual equals.

But there was nothing like a good rare book store, or even just one of those eccentric ones with a million rooms you could literally get lost in. Which was a good description of Joseph Fox I'd been so happy the first time I'd been on a date here for Philly Illustrated, and then disappointed when the guy, Hank, just sort of hung back while I looked around. The next week, when

Jordan had mentioned stumbling into it and spending way too much time and money there, I'd felt a whole new rush of butter-flies in my stomach, and had a particularly hot dream about him that night.

There my thoughts went again, right after fucking Jordan. I wondered if he was trying to find a new apartment. Maybe he already had. My heart twinged at the thought.

Even though it shouldn't have.

Nate squeezed my hand. "Penny for your thoughts."

"Oh, nothing. Just how excited I am to come here. You ever been?"

He shrugged. "I haven't. I love book stores, though."

That made me smile. I added it to the small mental list of reasons to *try* with Nate. Books. "I don't read, like, ever. But I like being surrounded by books."

Damn. He had to go and keep talking. "You don't read? So what do you do on a quiet weekend morning? Like, after pancakes and before naptime?"

He shrugged. "Watch the news? Clean the house? I guess reading is one of your things, huh?"

It's a human thing. I pressed my lips together. *Try, Liz.* "Definitely."

"Well, you know," he said, leaning in close. "I wouldn't mind watching you read." His breath was hot on my ear, curling around it and making it buzz with his soft, low words.

It made me shiver, but not in a good way. More like there were ants crawling up my neck.

I stood my ground, though, and didn't flinch away from him. He seemed to take it as a positive sign, and let his arm drift around my back, his fingers lightly brushing at my waist just above the hip.

"Lead the way. Show me what you like." His voice was still

low, but he'd given my poor neck some space. He was, however, shooting me some very obvious bedroom eyes.

"Um...lately I've been reading young adult," I chattered. "See, in middle school, we always had summer reading assignments. I read the books without really questioning, but once I got to college I realized they were giving us adult literature to read."

Nate's eyebrows shot up.

"Well, not *adult* adult, but like....written for grownups?"

"And you understood them?"

"Yes," I laughed. "Vocabulary-wise. They were just...maybe...boring? And sometimes gruesome. So I realized a couple years ago that there was this whole age group of literature that I'd completely skipped. I picked up a young adult romance that had been mis-shelved in this very bookstore, took it home, and the rest is history."

"So you like reading about teenagers? Like...kissing?" Nate wrinkled his nose, and though he still smiled, I saw the ghost of a look I'd seen plenty of times over. Judging me. Thinking he was better, or smarter, or more grown-up.

"Well, yeah," I said, finding my ground in a way I hadn't before. "It's sweet." Jordan and I had talked about high school for a couple of hours one night after we'd...well, enjoyed each other...reliving our crushes and all the drama that had seemed so serious then. I remembered thinking that he made me feel that way - not overly dramatic, but like a kid again. Just endlessly happy, like we were the only two people that existed and nothing could ever go wrong.

Nate was still staring at me, puzzled.

"The emotions there are just so pure, you know? When you're a teen, you haven't been through so much pointless adult shit, so everything is just sort of raw and unfiltered. They just

feel everything in a way that grownups have been taught not to.
I think."

I cleared my throat, waiting for his response. He smiled and
dipped his head in a polite nod. "Okay, then. Show me."

That was unexpected. I gave him a small secret smile and
squeezed his hand. We walked quietly up the stairs to the young
adult room. I found a copy of *The Knife of Never Letting Go* by
Patrick Ness, and started reading.

He was actually listening, his fingers trailing a gentle, inches
long path back and forth against my sweater. A smile formed on
my face, unbidden, and I kept going.

Nathaniel Perfect might be worth an honest-to-goodness
chance.

That afternoon, back at the Philly Illustrated offices, I struggled
to do my 500-word write-up for the day. Alphonso glided his
chair back and forth behind mine, humming stupid show tunes
about love too loudly for me to ignore.

"God, Alphonso, could you stop for five seconds so I can
write?" I finally blew up at him after half an hour of self-control.

"If it was a good date, you would have been done with the
column by now," he sang as he rolled back to his desk.

I bit down on my lip and kept my eyes fixed to the screen so
he couldn't see the tear rolling down my cheek.

I missed Jordan. I hated him, but I missed him all the same.

I went home that night and settled onto the couch with a
bottle of wine and the TV remote. I itched to pull my phone out
and call Kiera, but the guy I was trying to avoid was her brother.
Even if she was on my side, talking to her would only remind me
of Jordan. As I sat there mindlessly bingeing shows I'd already
seen, my phone rang from inside my purse, over and over again,

and I forced myself to stay away. I didn't want to know if Jordan was calling – I didn't want to know if he wasn't.

⊏⊐

I woke up hours later in the pitch-black living room with the TV glowing blue, my cheek smashed into the arm of the couch, shivering. I hauled myself in the bathroom to wash my face and brush my teeth, and stared into the mirror, instantly remembering that night with Jordan on the couch.

Freaking hell. I missed him.

The next day, Mr. Perfect and I had a pre-dinner date, taking me back at Uncle Phil's Philly Phun Zone, where Nate played an impressive game of skee-ball and even pulled the age-old flirty move of standing behind me and guiding my arm with his to perfect my skee-ball form. He used the hundred and eighty tickets we won to "buy" me a cheap plastic rhinestone necklace and earring set, which he fastened for me while I held my hair up. "Beautiful," he whispered against my ear, and this time, I didn't shrug away.

Try, Liz.

I'd had to remind myself less and less as the marathon date went on. We had three more stops, over two more days, technically - a record store, a stroll through the Morris Arboretum, and then attending a Philly Flyers game. There was optional dancing at the end, at some new club, which I could choose to take advantage of, or not. Nate didn't know about it.

This time, it was my hand that reached down to twine with his. "Ready to find some tunes?"

"Oh my God," he laughed. "Has anyone actually used that terminology since, like, the 60s?"

I shrugged. "Maybe not. Do you mind?"

"Not one bit," he said, giving me a gentle smile. I noticed his hand getting a little sweaty again, and I squeezed it in response.

"You okay?" I asked gently.

"Yeah, just a little nervous."

"After we've been hanging out for like...what? Day number three and six hours now?"

"Because I've been thinking about doing this," he said, before quickly leaning in and brushing a soft kiss against my cheekbone. His eyes floated up to mine, and he stayed bent toward me, his lips still hovering inches from my face. All I would have to do to turn the cheek kiss into a real kiss was turn my head up to his, stand on my tiptoes a bit, maybe touch his face.

For some reason, though, I just...didn't. Instead, I smiled and squeezed his hand, then stepped toward the waiting cab, called for us by Alphonso, who was stationed back at the office.

We slid into the seats, and I found myself scooting as far toward my door as possible. My eyes found his, which were watching me intently. "No need to be nervous," I said, squeezing his hand again.

He smiled, still looking a little shaky. Poor guy.

"Hey. I was bossy at the book store. Maybe you have a thing or two to teach me about music?"

"Oh," he said, his shoulders relaxing back into the seat. "Absolutely."

CHAPTER 29

JORDAN

I THOUGHT Friday was the worst day of Mr. Perfect Date Week imaginable. I was so wrong. My Saturday schedule was completely empty, which meant I had nothing but time to wallow.

I hadn't been able to tear my eyes away from the #LizDates-MrPerfect tag all day. It was like a train wreck for the very reason that it...well...wasn't a train wreck. I had never seen more pictures of Liz looking gorgeous and smiley and flirty in my entire life. If I hadn't known her in real life, hadn't had the opportunity to touch her and kiss her and laugh with her and really get to know her, I would think she was a character in a movie.

I saw every single detail like it was magnified a thousand times - the way her hair curled and rested just so exactly where her bra strap would be, the glint of her earrings - I almost never saw her wear dangling earrings, but there they were - the perfectly drawn line of her lipstick.

It drove me crazy when she wore lipstick, mostly because it made me think of all the places on my body I'd found hers smeared since we'd become - whatever we were.

Whatever we had been.

Just as I was wincing at the horrible selection of music Mr. Nate Perfect queued up at Long in the Tooth, an incredible record store on Sansom, my phone buzzed again.

Kiera.

I wondered as I picked up if any other guy in Philly had a sister this involved in his love life. Or lack thereof.

"Hey, Kiki," I sighed in to the phone.

"Day three," she jumped in, big guns blazing. "You're not holding up well, are you? It's no wonder. This guy really is Mr. Perfect."

"Wow, thanks. Really encouraging."

"Listen, brother, I love you, and I want you to be happy. But I love Lizzie, too, and you have to admit that you did a monumentally stupid thing."

"Again, sis, it's not like you were innocent."

"Oh, will you stop it? I was messing around. Twenty-five votes is nothing compared to the haul you pulled in. And you had an ulterior motive."

"I would honestly give anything to admit that, if she would listen to me. But she told me herself not to contact her, and now this Mr. Perfect guy turns out to be actually perfect. I mean, what are the chances that she comes back to her apartment in abject misery after this whole thing?" After a second of silence, I whined, "None. The chances are none."

"You mean, like you made sure she did on all those other nights?" Kiera paused, and I heard the sound of mad clicking on her end. I bit my tongue. "I don't know, JJ. She doesn't exactly look thrilled to be with him.'

"Are you kidding me? Did you see her at that cheesy arcade place, with the jewelry? She looked like he'd just given her the biggest fucking diamond in existence."

"Yeah, okay...except don't you think she's smiling too much?

And look how her shoulders are all tense when he does it. Hold on."

More clicking, and about twenty seconds later my phone buzzed with a photo text. It was a zoomed in picture of the delicate line of Liz's neck, framed in wispy blond strands that fell from her hands when she held the rest of her hair back. "See?" Kiera piped in again. "The tendons in her neck. They're sticking out. She's trying not to step away from him, or something. She's not into it. Not really."

I peered at my phone and sighed again. "I don't know, Kiera. That's a pretty big stretch."

She sighed. "Whatever, brother. Just...don't give up yet. Okay? Maybe...I don't know. Maybe email her boss. See if you can explain yourself."

"And meddle even more in her life? Become more of a stalker?"

"I don't know, Jordan. It'd be for love." She drew out the last word and I could just picture her moony eyes as she did. "What if there's still a chance?"

"You're such a sap," I teased, even though I couldn't bring myself to laugh, or even smile.

"Ingrate," she said. "Keep me posted, okay? I worry about you."

"Thanks," I said, my voice breaking. "Hey, Kiera?" I asked in a tone that I was fully aware was pathetic and whiny.

"Yeah?"

"Are you gonna keep following the date?"

"Is the sky blue?"

I grinned, feeling tears of unexplained gratitude forming in my eyes. "Thanks, Kiki."

"Love you, JJ."

CHAPTER 30

LIZ

Twenty-Nine – Liz

Mr. Perfect Date Weekend was going exactly as Monica had hoped. We'd picked up coverage on the Philly morning news show, and for the first time ever, I felt like this job at Philly Illustrated was getting me somewhere.

"I have a confession to make," Nate said as we left the Arboretum early Saturday evening. I'd loved the lush green indoor space even more the second time around, knowing all the cool things I should look for, and the relief of having something solid to write about in my update washed over me.

"You're not actually from Philly, you have a girlfriend already, and this is another elaborate prank?" I tried to keep my tone light. I'd been through so much bullshit during the Liz Dates Philly experience that not much would have surprised me anymore.

Nate winced with a smile. "Yeah, I read about that whole thing. Your friend rigging the votes? You must have been pretty pissed at her."

I reeled back to take him in, the realization that some people thought it was one of my childhood slumber-party variety friends who'd been messing with me instead of someone like JJ. My mouth dropped open to answer that it was a guy who'd messed this whole thing up, but something stopped the words from coming out.

"No," he chuckled, saving me from another moment of awkwardness. "No, just that...well, I was so shocked when I realized I'd get another chance at this whole dating the famous Liz Dates Philly girl thing. And then I spent some time looking for pictures of you, whatever information was out there."

"So you're saying you didn't rig anything, but you are guilty of stalking?" I made sure he saw the gentle smile on my face.

"Geez," he said, running a hand down over his chest in what I'd learned was his chief nervous gesture. "No. No more than anyone else. I mean, no more than anyone does with anyone they're dating on Facebook or whatever."

I raised my eyebrows, maintaining the smile.

"Okay, okay. I'm talking myself into a hole. All I meant to say was... I realized after a couple days that I might actually turn out to like you. I mean, on paper, you're... well, you're pretty fantastic. I guess that's how all online dating works, of course, but I thought, what the heck. Maybe once I met you in person, I'd realize you're even better than everything I'd already learned would tell me."

I bit my lip, letting the ghost of butterflies in my belly turn itself into a small smile. Flattery was nice. Nate was nice. No, Nate was perfect. Butterflies in my stomach were entirely fitting and appropriate in this situation.

Never mind the fact that I'd spent every night this week thinking of Jordan while I lay in bed, wide awake. Missing him.

"So," he continued, "I planned an alternate last date of the week. Just in case a Flyers game didn't fit the mood."

"And?" I asked, still teasing my bottom lip with my teeth.

"I think—and this is only if you agree, of course - that I'd like the chance to take you somewhere else. Someplace nice. Not that the Wells Fargo Center isn't nice, that's not what I'm trying to say... just that..."

I laughed. "I get it. What about Philly Illustrated's agreement with the Flyers?"

He placed his free hand over his heart. "I solemnly swear to whatever Philly Illustrated powers that be that I will personally attend a game at the Wells Fargo Center with at least two friends, sample every snack they have to offer, and write a glowing but accurate review on every news outlet available to me. At my personal expense, of course."

"Of course," I nodded, my lips twitching with a smile.

"But for now," Nate said, letting go of my hand and winding his arm around my waist, "I'd like to go somewhere quiet. With wine, and candles. With good food and fancy desserts. Does that sound like something you'd be up for?"

It was strange, looking at this objectively handsome guy— this good, polite, *perfect* guy—and feeling nothing in my gut, no appropriate reaction to his question. Most girls would have been falling all over themselves for Nate, sweaty palms or not. I recognized the pleasing angle of his jaw, his great taste in clothes, his impeccable manners, his respectful flirting, were all something that would make any other girl in my situation trip all over herself not only to go to a romantic fancy restaurant with him, but to make sure that he didn't leave her sight for the rest of the night and probably many, many days thereafter.

I just...didn't *care*. One way or the other. If Deanna had popped up between us right this moment and said that we had to cut the date short, I'd shake Nate's hand, kiss him on the cheek, and respond noncommittally to his request to call me.

But nobody popped up to end our date, and really, there wasn't any reason not to go to a nicer place than a Flyers game with him. So I dipped my head, made a point of looking up at him through my eyelashes like a girl who was enjoying this kind of attention, and said in a lighter voice than I normally would, "I'd like that."

It wasn't a lie. It just wasn't true, either.

After a day of small talk and gentle teasing, with a little compliment-heavy flirting here and there, sitting across from Nate in an environment that pretty much blocked out all other noise was kind of nice.

"So, what gives with this whole assignment? I've spent—" he checked his watch, a nice grownup one "—nine hours with you now, and I have no idea what to think about the entire premise for this weekend-long date. Don't get me wrong, it could be a very fun story to tell our grandchildren."

I let out a short, surprised laugh, my eyes flying to his.

"Too soon?" he teased. "Anyway, now that I've gotten to know you a little better, you don't seem like the kind of person who went to college in order to professionally date and write about it in possible perpetuity."

"Funny you'd ask," I said, taking a final bite of my salmon and dabbing at my mouth with the fine-woven white napkin. "I am supposed to be writing for the Washington Post, or at least the Inquirer. Covering elections and local issues. I'm a poli-sci major. Big political geek."

"Is that right?" His eyebrows curved up in pleasant surprise.

I nodded. "I could give you a run-down of the most likely candidates for the upcoming presidential election, from their voting records to where they're most likely to land on their party's platform. The ultimate goal is to be a communications director for one of those elections, help win it, and then become the Press Secretary."

"Like C.J. Cregg," he said.

"Yes!" I screeched. "You watch the West Wing?"

"I watched it, yeah," he laughed. "Loved the characters, got lost in the plot, but I'm never opposed to re-watching it. CJ was hot. In a way."

This was the moment. He liked something I loved. A connection, something that we could talk about for hours before slipping into more personal conversations, then something more. Just like Jordan and I had. Well, sort of like we had. Here he was, Mr. Perfect, proof that Jordan wasn't the only guy I could make a connection with.

Except... I still didn't feel a damn thing, outside of polite detachment. Nate might as well have been a statue or a painting I was eyeing at a distance. He was beautiful, even a little interesting, certainly valuable. But I had zero interest in actually taking him home.

"So... I'm confused," he said, interrupting my thoughts. "CJ Cregg never wrote for Cosmo, right? Because it seems like this whole dating experiment thing would be right at home there."

"Cosmo would be a serious upgrade right about now," I said. "Anyhow, in the show, she did publicity for a variety of smarmy actors before getting her gig with the President. You've gotta pay your dues, and I guess these are mine. Turns out I just had lofty expectations. I'm only twenty-three, with almost no journalism experience. My dad is an editor in the Pittsburgh Post-Gazette, and the only gig I could get was editing other peoples' work and writing my own quirky yet insignificant column in the lifestyle section. Now, don't get me wrong. I was smart enough to spin it into something bigger and better. But at this point in my career, this is as good as it gets."

"Seriously, though, Liz," Nate said, all of a sudden getting this solemnly sincere glint in his eye, "I've read your stuff. You're very good at what you do." He leaned forward and held out his hands, inviting me to rest mine against them. Almost reflexively, I did, and the little squeeze he gave my fingers was comforting, solid. Reassuring, and real.

There wasn't a zing of electricity through my skin like I got with JJ, but at least this hand-holding wasn't backed up by lies.

"I truly enjoyed your columns. I even finished reading most of them without wanting to quit halfway through."

"Gee, thanks," I said, cracking a half-smile. "That's a ringing endorsement."

"For a guy who likes reading medical journals more than anything else? It really is," he confirmed.

"Well, maybe we should put that on the intro to this last one."

"Liz Dates Mr. Perfect, who only struggled to make it through reading her column a couple times." I raised my eyebrows, trying to tease him. I wasn't offended—I knew that dating columns weren't everyone's cup of tea, not by a long shot. But the whisper of the memory of Jordan reading my column and cracking up laughing wouldn't leave me alone.

It was because the guys themselves were laughable, stupid. Because he rigged the vote so they'd be that way.

God, he was probably laughing at his own cleverness the whole damn time. Laughing at his ability to pull the wool over my eyes. Not just the wool—the whole damn alpaca.

Nate chuckled, and when I looked at him, he was looking back at me like I was the sweetest, most perfect thing he'd ever seen.

Understand how very lucky you are right now, Lizzie Palmer. Your readers love you, and they managed to find you a guy who's handsome, smart, selfless, polite, and single. He really is Mr. Perfect—maybe he'd be perfect in private, too. And there's only one way to find out. So what are you waiting for?

"You seemed interested in dessert," Nate said, squeezing my hands gently before pulling one of his away, probably to call for the waiter to bring a menu.

That was when I made my decision.

I reached forward, grabbing his hand back with mine, twisting my wrists to intertwine our fingers like we had when we walked together. Just like that, the mood at our table went from sweet and romantic to an intimate bubble, a question I was writing in the air for him to answer.

I caught his gaze and made sure that he heard my next words loud and clear. "I do want dessert," I said, fully aware that I'd pushed my voice lower and softer than it had been just seconds ago, a classic signal of education. "But how would you feel about taking it to go?"

Nate's eyebrows pushed up and I could swear his body jerked in surprise before he tilted his head with a small smile. "Just to be clear, would you like to take it..."

"To your place, yeah. I mean... if that's something you'd be interested in—"

"Yes. Yes, very interested." He looked up at me and beamed, happy disbelief laced through his features. "Yes. Jesus. Unexpected, but yeah. Definitely. Okay."

I giggled at the flush in his neck that rose to his ears, and this time I let him pull his hand away to signal the waiter. "Check, please?"

He stretched his neck out and swallowed hard. Mr. Perfect actually had kind of a cute Adam's apple, one I wouldn't be opposed to running my lips over. Maybe even more so if it was scattered with the next day's stubble. I smiled at him gently as the waiter brought the faux-leather folder to our table and Nate hurried to pull a card out of his wallet.

A few minutes later, he was pulling my chair out for me again, then leading me to the door of the restaurant. His fingertips brushed the small of my back as we walked to the cab, and while we waited, he gave me that same goofy smile, accompanied by a little shake of his head.

"What?" I asked, telling myself to lean into his touch. That's what people did at this moment.

"Nothing, I just wasn't getting the vibe from you. I must have been distracted by, you know, actually being on a date with the girl I'd spent the last couple days building up a crush on." There was that blush again. He was so *cute*. Maybe I just had to fake it till I made it. Little touches were one thing—not everyone just *knew* someone was a good match for them, right?

Yeah. That was what I had to do. Every date this week had been so shrouded in my being pissed off at JJ, and missing him, that my more instinctual reactions to other humans had been dulled. It was possible that all I had to do was clear my mind and give myself over to the attention that Nate, a perfectly nice guy, so clearly wanted to give me.

We stood there in the dim light of the street lamp, waiting for our cab. I shivered against the chill that had crept into the autumn air so gradually I had hardly noticed it until it became unbearable. Immediately, he shrugged out of his jacket and draped it over my shoulders. It smelled like man—a little soap and a little aftershave. Nothing heavy, nothing special, but nice.

He was well-groomed, grown up. No faded jeans or sneakers or wild hair. That was a good thing. That was the kind of thing girls like me wanted in a guy.

His fingers snuck to my side and pressed ever-so slightly into the curve above my hip, and I turned and took a step closer to him, putting our chests parallel to each other. His breath was coming slightly faster than normal, and I smiled. Sweet. He was so sweet, anticipating me getting closer. That was nice, to have a guy so excited about kissing me that his rate of respiration increased. Wasn't it?

So when he gently reached out to brush my jaw with his fingers, then teased them back into my hair, I leaned forward, then pushed up on my tiptoes, with my mouth tilted up to his.

His lips were warm and soft, moving firmly but respectfully against mine. *Tongue, Liz. Give him a little tongue. Maybe that'll do the trick.* I parted my lips, and his tongue darted out across mine, slightly cooler than I would have expected. I wondered if that meant he was nervous. His breath tasted like red wine and the barest trace of medium-rare steak, I noticed, cataloging everything about this kiss with all the detail of an annual checkup.

Okay. The tongue hadn't done it. I sighed, pushing breath out of my nose long and low. He seemed to take that as encouragement, and pulled me in tighter to him, his fingers pressing into the cushiony curve of my side as he did. A small burst of warmth bloomed in my belly. There it was—a little progress, spurned by this little edge of desperation to what had so far been a perfectly pleasant date.

There still weren't any fireworks going off throughout my body, no electric current zinging through my skin wherever Nate touched.

Stop thinking about Jordan, stupid. There's no point in comparing any guy to him. It probably only felt so exciting with him because you knew you weren't supposed to be fucking around with him. Get a handle on yourself. Grow up.

Maybe I didn't want fireworks, after all. Maybe that only came from secret inappropriate relationships, from guys that girls like me were supposed to be dating, from matches made in heaven. Or at least from matches made by the sane, non-asshole members of society.

The cab pulled up, and like a perfect gentleman, Nate pulled away so he could open the door for me. I slid in and forced myself into a relaxed, happy posture against the black leather seat back. He shut the door and slipped his hand into mine again, smiling at the sight of our intertwined fingers resting on my knee. I smiled back.

"I can still tell the cabbie to take you home," Nate offered, his gaze serious with a trace of the excited hopefulness it had held back at the restaurant.

"No," I said. "I'm coming with you. If that's okay."

"More than okay," Nate said, leaning in for a quick peck that honestly took me by surprise. He gave his address to the cabbie, while I texted it to Deanna. Nate may have been Mr. Perfect, but I wasn't stupid. I wasn't going anywhere with a guy I'd just met without telling someone my location.

I gave him a soft smile as the cab pulled away from the curb. I was making the right call. This would be good for me. Not every date was a head-over-heels whirlwind, and not every touch from every guy was supposed to be earth shattering.

It was time I learned that.

CHAPTER 31

JORDAN

MY STOMACH DROPPED to the floor at the same time that bile rose in my throat.

Dammit. *Dammit.* I would have thought that the worst part about seeing Liz hit it off with some other guy would be seeing him touching her, kissing her. Helping her into a cab, which may very well have been taking her to his place for the night instead of hers. Then, after seeing pictures of Nathaniel Perfect, how he looked so natural standing next to her, how he was a perfect gentleman, how he made her look so relaxed and calm, I realized *that* was the worst thing.

Liz being happy with another guy. Yeah, that sucked.

Knowing that Liz had only been so happy with me - if that's what it was at all, compared to being with Mr. Perfect—because I had kept her from being with any guys that approximated normal? Well, that made my gut sink and my chest flood with guilt all at the same time.

It was a miracle I'd made it through the midterm-prep study session I was holding for my students today. When I'd been pacing the room listening to my students work problems, I'd caught one of them zooming in on a picture of Liz and Mr.

Perfect holding hands as they strolled downtown on what I'd started to call the Never-ending Date from Hell. In my head, that is.

For the last five nights, after I'd finished a run or a review session for my students, I'd basically gone catatonic when I got back to Ethan's apartment. There was nothing I could do. Literally everything I could imagine that might make me feel better – drinking myself into a stupor, texting Liz, calling Kiera, writing sappy poetry – would only make things worse. I knew that damn well enough. So I just sat in Ethan's spare bedroom, or occasionally on his couch, sometimes pacing, most of the time running through the reasons I was now totally ruined for dating, all of which were my own damn fault.

I was drowning, not only with the heartbreak of realizing that Liz definitely didn't feel the same way about me as I did about her - how could she when she was enjoying a date with another guy this much? - but with the punch to the ego that the only way I could get her to like a guy like me was by deliberately eliminating the competition.

Feeling dead and empty as a ghost, I once again drifted over to Ethan's couch and dropped onto it with a groan. "Maybe I should contact her boss. See if I can...respond or something."

"Buddy. You are fucking pathetic." Ethan had thrown some nachos together to try to lift my spirits, but despite the delicious smell wafting from the oven, my stomach only turned.

"I know," I moaned into a pillow. "Do you think I should go back to our place? See if she's coming back there right now? He did help her into the cab, but what if the date didn't go well?"

I knew that, at least according to every live feed and picture of #LizDatesMrPerfect, that tonight's date had been amazing. I knew she was headed back to his place, or he to hers. Thank God for Ethan.

"Listen, man. I know you got attached to the girl you were

supposed to be casually hanging out with. It happens." His gaze flicked to Natalia, and she beamed. "But she is definitely not in love with you anymore."

"Yeah, especially since she's going home with Mr. Perfect!" Natalia let out a little whoop. I glared up at her to catch her staring at her phone and giving a little fist pump.

"You know that for sure?" I half growled, half moaned.

"She texted Deanna. The photographer?"

"I know who she is," I mumbled, pressing my face back into the pillow.

"Anyway, your girl is smart. She texted the guy's address to her friend. You know, just in case."

I bristled at the 'just in case' sentiment, even as I realized there would be no 'just in case,' no danger to speak of from this guy. This Mr. Perfect asshole was clearly a little nervous, and a lot in disbelief that Liz had leaned into him so readily, had let him kiss her. But he'd been nothing but respectful.

It had sort of surprised me, too, the first time she'd wanted to be with me. Even that first time, when all she was doing was letting me take care of her, passing the time with a guy she trusted, I hadn't believed she was letting me put my hands on her perfect, creamy-smooth, work-of-art body. Every inch of her was seared into my memory, every breath she took and word she said and sigh that passed her lips.

Yeah, I was a goddamn lovesick fool, and there wasn't a fucking thing I could do about it now.

I'd screwed everything up.

"Alright. This will not stand. Not in my humble abode," Ethan announced. "Listen, man, I'm miserable too. I didn't think Natalia and I agreeing to part ways would hurt so much, but it does. Like hell. But I made that decision, just like you made the one to rig Liz Dates Philly. Now we've gotta live with them."

"So, by 'living with them,' you mean..."

"Drink too much and play video games all night," Ethan finished, confirming my suspicions. Excellent.

I was pathetic. Hell, we were both pitiable, but at least Ethan's heartbreak was only partly his fault. I knew I had to get a place of my own, but at the moment, feeling sorry for myself on Ethan's couch felt like as much as I could handle. I was living the most pathetic bachelor-pad couch-surfing lifestyle possible, with nobody to blame but myself.

Four beers and a few inappropriately loud games of Call of Duty later, I'd all but passed out on the couch. My head lolled back and forth over the arm of the couch, and memories of happier times spent on a couch floated, dream-like, through my head. We'd been so happy—so blissfully in sync—and the only people who would ever know about it was the two of us.

"What a damn tragedy," I mumbled as I thumbed at my phone. I pulled up the Philly Illustrated mobile site, growling at the image of Liz and Nathaniel fucking Perfect that was now plastered across the home page. I scrolled through the short article that accompanied it, and stabbed at the link that said "Feedback for the Lifestyle section?"

Before I knew it, I'd composed an email:

To Whom it me ocncerns:

Liz's dates are funny but it's a shame siznce she loves someone elses probably.

This is Jordan the date-ruiner and there are two sides to every stories. Just so you know. And maybe write about that too.

• *Jordan J*

I clicked on the "send" button and let the phone drop heavy from my hand as I listened to the accompanying "whoosh" sound. I was barely conscious as I felt Ethan toss a blanket over my still-clothed body and turn off the cheap floor lamps that dotted his apartment. "Sweet dreams, asshole," he muttered affectionately, then ambled into his bedroom, probably slumping on top of the covers in his clothes, too.

⊏⊐

I woke to a pounding head, exacerbated by the light streaming in through the uncovered windows. As badly as my head ached and as much as my tongue felt like sandpaper, the only thing that ran through my mind was the memory of waking up to sunlight just like this, in a much better situation—with Liz curled up beside me. I scrubbed a hand over my face, then stumbled to the bathroom, downing tiny paper cupfuls of water.

This whole situation was absolute shit. Yeah, my heart was crumbling, ready to break into a thousand pieces once I read Liz's triumphant column describing in breathless detail how fabulous her date with Mr. Perfect had been. Philly Illustrated had really hit the jackpot with her, asshole roommate -with-benefits aside.

As soon as I thought the words "Philly Illustrated," it all came flooding back – my big stupid hands fuzzy-fumbling with my phone last night, composing a half-sad, half-angry message that said nothing in particular. I bolted to sitting and groaned as a deep, heavy pain settled between my temples. Blinking the pain-induced white waves from my vision took a few seconds, after which I immediately opened my email app, then stared in horror at the email I had apparently written last night. And actually sent.

My awful spelling and belligerent tone in the email was the least of my worries.

Apparently, when I was drunk I turned into the crazy-jealous stalker Liz had dumped me for being in the first place. Which was probably why I was so desperate to read, in her own words, how last night's date had gone.

Don't get me wrong—I was torn. I wasn't sure I could even stomach the idea of reading her damn column, whenever it published, seeing how she'd somehow make even the most perfect of dates sound both amazing and bitingly hilarious at the same time. I wondered if she'd describe what it felt like when he touched her, when he kissed her. She'd never even let any of the other guys get that close to her, let alone—I imagined—look so damn happy about it if they did. I wondered if she'd talk about how handsome he was. The rest of Philly seemed to think so, and I was sure Liz was no exception.

And I knew it could get worse. She could describe how he smelled, how he tasted. Maybe she'd recount the little jokes he used that made her smile like that, maybe describe the suspense of whether he would hold her hand.

I didn't know if I could bring myself to read it.

I didn't think I could ignore it, either.

I sighed heavily and pulled up the page, which already showed the longest column Liz had written to date. Warring emotions boiled up inside me - I absolutely positively did not want to read about this date, especially after what I'd seen on the Philly Illustrated social media feeds, but at the same time, pride welled up in me for what Liz had accomplished.

So much space in a real, big-city publication. She'd worked hard for this, and I knew that even if I never spoke to her again,

I'd always follow her work and feel proud of the journalist I knew she'd develop into.

With one hand cradling my aching head, I pushed my glasses on with the other, squinted at the screen, and began to read.

Liz Dates Philly Special Edition - Liz Dates Mr. Perfect

Well, my darling Philly Illustrated readers, you've really outdone yourselves this time. Actually, you've probably been outdoing yourselves for the past several months, hand-picking an admirable crew of stand-up guys for me to date. Unfortunately, since my friend JJ decided to prank the whole darn city, or at least the portion who reads this column, you've been seeing the most — let's just call them unique *- eligible bachelors the City has to offer. I know it wasn't ideal for finding the perfect match for me, but I sincerely hope that one of you intrepid hopeful young ladies found a special attraction for Neil, Brad, Milton, Trevor, or Alex. Maybe some of you are blissfully single no more!*

This weekend was my long-fated and short-awaited date with Nate, or, as you know him, Mr. Perfect. While I firmly believe nobody is perfect - not even President Bartlett, and you know how much I love him -

I grinned. If her readers didn't know how much she loved President Bartlett, they hadn't been reading very carefully. She'd made a reference to her favorite show - and mine, since I'd met her - in at least five of her columns since she'd started writing.

. . .

- Nathaniel Perfect is about as close to the stereotypical Mr. Perfect as they come. He's five foot eleven, tall enough to let a girl wear heels but not so tall that she needs a step stool to kiss him. Nicely groomed, with bright eyes and a haircut nobody can argue with. He's a college graduate, has a really amazing job, just moved to Philly and plans to stay for the long haul, and he loves his sister and his mom! What's not to love?

The insane thing is that's what we know about him on paper. The truth is that Nathaniel Perfect was an excellent choice for my days-long Marathon edition of Liz Dates Philly, and I know you all are dying to know why.

I was used to the format of Liz's articles by now, and this one didn't differ. She did a great job of promoting the place that had sponsored the date, even when it was the epically ridiculous Uncle Phil's Philly Phun Zone, and dropped in a few facts about the date, along with snippets of their conversation, to keep the human interest portion of the date afloat.

The thing about Liz was that she was always, always kind. Never mean, and only a little snarky - but she also never failed to illustrate exactly why she not only didn't kiss this guy or hold his hand, but why she would not be going on a date with him ever, ever again.

She was a genius at this.

As I skimmed the feature-length article, though, I realized that even though Mr. Perfect was, well, perfect, Liz didn't really include much more about him than she did about any of the guys who'd come before him. Yes, he had an impressive job. Yes, he told her sweet stories about growing up with his family in the country. The pictures Deanna had added to the narrative bolstered the tagline of the whole thing - 'Liz Dates Mr. Perfect' - with shots of Liz smiling, laughing, his hand on her back, and, sometime around four o'clock PM, by my calculations, the guy finally getting enough courage to hold her hand. Liz wrote about those things too, but always in the context of the date location.

The bridge to 30th Street Station is a great place to stroll hand-in-hand with that special someone. Like he was reading my mind, Nate planned just that.

It was a picture-perfect Philly date. The funny thing about being Liz of "Liz Dates Philly" is that I've become used to having my dates planned out, down to the letter. Every other guy I've been out with seems to be perfectly fine with that, but not Nate. And who was I to argue with Mr. Perfect, hmmm ladies? He'd planned the picture-perfect date, complete with candlelight, roses on the table, and a sumptuous dessert cart (One of the top five ways to my heart!) at Morimoto's!

It's been a whirlwind few months, and I'll be forever grateful to all of you for following along with my little journey. How fitting that while I was looking for love in Philly, I not only fell in love with Philly, but also went on my fifteenth and final date with someone who is literally Mr. Perfect!

As my readers have figured out now, though, dating and falling in love in Philly has almost nothing to do with the places you go and almost everything to do with the people you meet along the way. Thanks to our live-blog, my careful readers know that Mr. Perfect and I ended our weekend-long Philly date gazing at the most important thing about any date - the person we spent time with. The places you go and the money you spend are nothing compared to the people you're with and those you'll eventually fall in love with, just like I have.

I'm sure you can guess by now that I'm taking a hiatus from dating around Philly. I've learned a lot and ended the whole experience in the arms of one of the most wonderful guys in the City, and I have you to thank. I'm pleased to announce that Philly Illustrated has kept me on staff, so you'll be seeing me jabber on and on about something or other on a semi-weekly basis beginning in the near future. Stay tuned, and thank you, Liz Dates Philly fans. For everything.

Well, fuck.

If I hadn't known for sure that Liz slept with Mr. Perfect after their first - albeit ridiculously drawn-out - date, now I did. Hell, all of Philly knew.

It had only taken one reader-selected guy and a very long date for Liz to fall in love.

The only reason she could have possibly had to call me again - as a friend with benefits - had just dissolved away before my eyes. With all of Philadelphia reading along.

Some guys might have flown into a rage, or started drinking, or even cried. I just felt... numb. Like I couldn't have forced my face into any expression, even if I tried. Like I was drained of anything I'd felt in the past few months, talking and laughing with Liz, getting to know her, learning to appreciate each one of her features—falling in love with her.

And there it was. A lump rose in my throat just as my phone rang again. I didn't even have to look at the caller ID. "Hey, Kiera. Did you see it? I mean, she's basically in love with the guy already. I'm just...ugh." I hung my head, burying my face in my hands. "Well, hello, loverboy," an older woman's raspy voice came through the speaker. "You sound like someone with a broken heart."

"You're not Kiera," I said, pulling the phone away from my face and squinting at the number.

"No," the voice continued. "I'm Monica. And I think I'm about to be your new best friend."

CHAPTER 32

LIZ

IT TURNED out that Deanna was a really good drinking buddy.

Her apartment was really close to Mr. Nathaniel Perfect's. I thought if I went up to his place—perfectly decorated, perfectly kept, by the way - that I could have another glass of wine, flash some skin, invite some attention from him. Get myself into his bed and, hopefully, get off. For just a few seconds, forget about JJ.

Maybe that was the magic key to activating my emotions, I'd thought bitterly as I finished that glass of wine in record time and set it down a little too solidly on his coffee table. With a smile, he'd reached for a coaster and positioned it under the glass. Even though the wine hadn't been cold.

Perfect.

I'd watched his fingers skate over my crossed knee, just like I'd expected would happen. He'd smiled at me. I'd smiled back and waited for it to come. The feeling, the one that told me that if I didn't keep going I'd regret it, the one that pushed me to touch and taste him, then go for more, and more, and more.

It didn't come, so I scooted toward him and pushed my

fingers through his hair, anchoring his head in place and planting my lips on his in the most passionate kiss I could muster. He groaned, and his hand snuck further up my thigh in what would be a very, very slow path to its destination.

I didn't want to wait.

No, actually? I didn't want it—at all.

I pulled away from him, sitting up straight and scooting backward on the couch as I did. Nate watched me, his eyes full of patience and a little resignation.

"I'd better get going," I said, standing up and brushing off my skirt.

"You sure?" he asked as he walked me to the door. I could see how his pants had started to bulge in front. Not a bad size, either, on a decidedly handsome guy. In another universe, in another situation, I might have just gone for it.

But that would have to be a universe where I hadn't already figured out what it felt like to really fall in love. A universe where I hadn't gone completely head over heels for Jordan Jacobs.

That fucker.

I bit my lip, nodded. "I'm sure. Thanks for a wonderful day. And evening."

Nate raised his eyebrow.

"No, truly. You saved my ass, doing this marathon tour through Philly with me. And you were good company." I leaned in to his side for a second, bumping my shoulder to his.

"Not good enough for a second date, though? Or, I guess, a twelfth one?" I could tell by his soft, patient smile that he already knew. Maybe he didn't feel anything when he kissed me, either. Maybe he did, but was just so damn considerate and attentive that he'd read my body language a dozen times over. I just didn't want him like that.

There was only so far organized, poll-driven dating could get two objectively awesome people in Philly, anyway.

"Do you need a ride?" Nate asked as he picked up my sweater from where he'd neatly placed it across the back of a chair.

"Already called one," I said, waving my phone through the air. Really, I'd texted Deanna, hoping she'd call for a ride. She'd texted back that a car was on its way, and that I could land at her place if I wanted.

With a gentle kiss on the cheek and a squeeze of Nate's hand, I walked out of Mr. Perfect's life and back into my garbage heap of one.

Deanna's couch was too short for me and a little lumpy, but it was close by and it wasn't mine. If I wasn't so damn broke I would get rid of mine and buy a new one. I didn't know how I'd ever be able to sit on it again, to really relax, without being flooded with memories of me and JJ cuddling, kissing, and defiling it six ways to Sunday. If it hadn't been the best sex of my life, I would have tried to erase it from my memory.

Since I hadn't been able to sleep that night, Monica had texted me to take Friday to work from home, do a good job with the final write-up that would appear in Saturday's print edition. After the four - or was it five? - glasses of wine I'd had with Deanna last night, alternately laughing and crying over how ridiculous the past five months of our life had been, I was not going to argue.

Deanna was faring better than I was and headed to the office to work on a larger spread for "Liz Dates Mr. Perfect," complete with sponsor plugs, with instructions for locking up her place when I finally dragged my ass off her couch.

I never did manage to get up. I couldn't stop thinking about Jordan as I tried to make the "Liz Dates Mr. Perfect" write-up sound cheery and enthusiastic. Before I knew it, Deanna was back home, handing me more wine, and quietly inviting me to stay another night. Luckily, I pushed 'send' on my article before I even started to feel the buzz, and lost myself in some Netflix show until I drifted off to sleep again.

I didn't sleep much better that night, but come Saturday morning, it was time to face the music. I waved goodbye to Deanna, who stood watching me from her coffee pot, with a muffled 'thanks.' It wasn't long after that that I pulled myself together, tidied up her place while guzzling water, took a quick shower, borrowed some leggings and a sweatshirt, and got out of there.

As my cab pulled up to the apartment - just *my* apartment now, I reminded myself – my heart sank thinking about how sad and empty it felt. I hadn't heard a peep from Jordan in days, which was bothering me more and more by the hour, even though I'd told him that I never wanted to hear from him again.

I knew I'd yelled at him for being a stalker, but had to know I didn't mean that literally. I'd sort of expected at least one last effort from him.

I realized something was different as soon as I opened the door. The cloyingly sweet scent of glazed blueberry mascarpone scones filled the air. Plates stacked with the round pastries decorated every surface of my tiny home - the counter bar of the kitchen, the little dining table, the coffee table, nestled in the corners of the couch that I'd so dreaded looking at.

The Saturday paper edition of Philly Illustrated sat in the middle of the couch, on top of some folded t-shirts. The headline blared, "Liz Dates Philly: The Final Date—Is Mr. Perfect also Mr. Right?"

I picked up the magazine, gingerly, and flipped through the preview spread, which was basically my social media feed from the week before beside Deanna's photos and a healthy sprinkling of sponsor ads, woven through the write-up I'd managed yesterday. The final paragraph read,

It looks like our Lizzie liked Mr. Perfect enough to follow him up to his place, but did their night have a happy ending?

I chuckled at what I was certain was Alphonso's heavy-handed double entendre. I pulled the paper a little closer to read the last two lines on the page.

You thought the voting was over.... but is there one more choice you can help Liz make? Turn the page to find out...

What the hell? I didn't know anything about more voting. In fact, Monica had expressly promised me that this was all over, which is exactly why I wrote the final column like I had. I might have been drinking, but I wasn't totally sloshed. Monica and I had come to an understanding.

I frantically thumbed to the next page to see Jordan Jacob's engineering department headshot staring oh-so-alluringly at me. My hands shook and my heart raced. We'd agreed to play his involvement in this whole thing down.

I should have known Monica wouldn't be able to resist the drama of getting her hands on Jordan, though. My eyes frantically scattered over the words next to Jordan's picture.

It was a letter. From him to me.

My stomach flipped and I forced myself to take deeper, slower breaths as I read.

Dear Lizzie,

(I know you hate it when I call you that, but since I'm not in the room for you to smack me or glare at me, I couldn't resist. I don't care if you hate it - the nickname is adorable, just like you.)

By now, you and all of Philadelphia know that I artificially stacked the 'Liz Dates Philly' votes for every single one of your dates, to favor guys I was pretty sure you wouldn't get along with. I can hardly even remember how it started. After that first miserable date you went on, seeing you coming home with your ego so bruised and your hopes so low, I told myself I was doing it to help you out—the more incompatible the date, the more hilarious your writing about it would be—God, you're funny, Liz—and the more readers and interest you would get. Most importantly, at least it would be obvious to you that the date going south would have nothing to do with you.

Because, see, I thought you were perfect. I still do. I assume it's plain as day to the rest of Philadelphia, too.

We're roommates, so we did what roommates do. We watched TV together. We cooked and cleaned and explored Philly together, you and I, and I guess I got attached—to you, to the city, to our place, and to the way it all mashed together in a life that made me happy.

Each week, when the vote went up on the Phill-Ill site, I got more and more worried. Would this be the guy you liked more than me? Would I be doomed to finish watching The West Wing without your brilliant commentary? Would I have to go to Joey and Hawk's—the place I think of as 'our place'—alone, like the loser I so obviously am?

My bad voting behavior was driven by that worry. Every time I played my very heavy hand in setting you up with guys I knew were all wrong for you was an act of self-preservation, I told myself that I had to. If I was ever going to have a chance with you, I had to.

It was petty, and it was selfish. You don't deserve that from someone who's supposed to be your friend, who's supposed to be looking out for you. For that, I'm sorry.

But I'm not sorry for falling in love with you.

I know you had a great date with Mr. Perfect last night. Finally, when your devoted readers around the city have a chance to really, truly pick a date for you, the guy is a winner. They've grown to love you, Liz, and to want the best for you.

If you really have already fallen for him, I can't blame you.

If you haven't, though, I want you to know that even though I moved out of our place like you asked, my feelings for you haven't changed. I know it's weird to hear it for the first time in the publication you work for, but Liz, I love you.

I'm in love with you, Liz, and if you think there's even a chance you could love me, if you could forgive me enough to let me prove that I can be the kind of man you deserve, well...

Turn around.

I whipped my head around without a second thought.

Sometime in the course of reading that letter, probably between "Joey and Hawk's" and "I'm not sorry," tears had started to stream from my eyes. They clouded my vision of Jordan, standing in the doorway in his dark jeans and plaid shirt, hair puffed and messed from what I knew, deep down, had been his anxious hands running through it.

My insides twisted, affection pulling them one way, rage tugging them another, as I looked at Jordan waiting for me with his puppy-dog eyes and hopefully arched brows.

After several long seconds, the rage won out, taking over my words. "What the hell is this, Jordan?" I waved the paper helplessly, halfheartedly, in the air. "Are you just—I mean, God! What the fuck am I supposed to do with this?"

"I don't know. Maybe... read it?"

I'd never known a Jordan who wouldn't look me in the eye, whose voice sounded so tired and defeated.

"I read it," I said, my voice breaking even as I rolled my eyes. "You know what I see here?"

He sighed. "That I'm pathetic? That I'm begging you to understand that—"

"That what? Some weird possessive streak left over from when we were kids compels you to mess with every single date I have in Philly? That we sleep together a few times and suddenly I'm not allowed to have a relationship with anyone else without feeling guilty about it?"

"No! Jesus, Liz, no. I just... I don't know. This was the last time I'll say anything to you. You pretty obviously didn't want me to contact you, so I didn't. I guess I just needed you to know. Submitting something with the paper was the only way I knew for sure you'd hear what I had to say. Yes, it was selfish. No, I don't regret it. Because, dammit, you're the best thing that's ever happened to me."

I sucked in a breath, which he seemed to take as permission to take a step closer. I stood in place.

"You're the first girl I ever wanted to spend more than one night in a row with. I guess I just... couldn't stand the thought of those nights ending, is all."

I let my breath back out, long and slow, then raised the paper back in front of me with a still-trembling hand. I read out loud, "I'm in love with you... let me prove that I can be the kind of man you deserve."

He took another step forward, and I felt my desire for him, my all-consuming *want* to be near him, beginning to take over. "Yeah," he murmured. "I mean every single word."

I let out a shuddering breath, and he took two more steps toward me, nearly closing the distance between us. Slowly, he reached out a hand, brushing his fingertips along the underside of my forearm for a torturous second. "Look at me, Liz. Please," he said, his voice breaking.

I knew what would happen if I did. I knew that instinct

would win over, would pull me into his arms, would guide me to where my heart knew I belonged.

I'd spent so long second-guessing every single move I made around him since the day he set foot in my—*our*—apartment. There was one similarity between that moment and this one—I had nothing to lose.

So I took the final step, letting my toes touch his, and tilted my chin up so my lips were a breath away from his. Jordan's eyes fell closed as his hands slowly, reverently, moved up to cup my face, his long fingers brushing my hairline.

"Oh, Liz. Thank God," he breathed before capturing my lips in a soft, tender kiss.

My lips parted of their own accord, letting me sigh into his mouth, and he swallowed my breath like it was the most delicious thing he'd ever tasted. I pressed up on my toes, turning the kiss into something desperate, claiming. His arm circled my waist, pulling me up on my tiptoes and tight against his chest, while he nipped at my bottom lip, then soothed the little hurt with a swipe of his tongue. My fingers itched to wander under his shirt, but I pulled away to slow myself down.

"Your writing sucks," I murmured against his mouth. "Or, you know. Alphonso's does."

"How did you know? Is it that obvious that he re-wrote half the thing?" he growled, still holding me tight to him, his fingers hooking into my belt loops and digging into the skin there, like I would fade away if he didn't.

"Nobody else would use the phrase 'the kind of man you deserve.' Definitely not you," I said, giggling into his mouth. God, I'd missed the feel of him so much in just a week. It was insane.

He pulled back, a look of mock scandal on his face. "Excuse me," he said, "but I can be romantic!"

"I know. But I wouldn't love you so much if you even thought about writing something that cheesy."

His grip on my waist gentled, and he reached up to stroke my hair, pressing a feather-light kiss on my lips. His forehead touched mine, and he closed his eyes with a gentle smile. "You love me?" he asked in low voice, his breaths coming heavy and hot now.

"I'm pretty sure I do, yeah. But if you really want to seal the deal, taking me to bed would probably do the trick."

As soon as he saw the teasing quirk of my lips, he dipped down, catching the backs of my knees with a strong forearm, and had me hoisted in the air, bridal-style. "I think I can manage that," he panted before sprinting both of us into my room. I squealed and kicked the door shut behind us.

CHAPTER 33

JORDAN

"WHY DID SHE DO IT?" Liz asked between licks and bites to my abdomen that were quickly taking away all rational thought. Her fingers started to brush right under the waistband of my jeans, her thumb flicking at the button.

"Do what?" I managed.

"Monica. Why did she let you publish the letter?" She flicked the button open and slowly pulled the zipper down, then sat up and tugged my jeans and boxers all the way off. She was still wearing leggings and an oversized sweatshirt, with no makeup and her hair a mess. I had never seen a more gorgeous sight in my whole life.

She knelt between my legs, wobbling a little bit on the unsteady mattress, and then leaned down.

"You're not gonna like it," I groaned as her tongue circled the head of my cock, making my head feel fuzzy as every one of my neurons focused between my legs. Her glistening lips had already started to work up and down my shaft, just the way she knew I loved. She pulled away with a pop, and I whimpered. She raised her eyebrows.

"You want me to keep this up? Tell me."

"Okay," I said, covering my eyes with my hand. "She asked for a vote on this, too."

Liz sat bolt upright, her eyes wide. "What the hell *for?*"

"Everyone who voted that we'd break up for good got entered for a chance to win a gift certificate at Joey and Hawk's."

Liz rolled her eyes. "I should have known. More ad buys. And what did the people who voted we'd get together get entered for?"

"Oh my God," I said, suddenly mortified. Last night I'd been so focused on this last chance to communicate with Liz, to pour my heart out to her, that I didn't really care how embarrassing the trappings of the thing were.

"Jordan? Tell me."

The wetness Liz had licked onto my cock was drying, making it cold. If there was ever a time to fess up, it was now. "A year's supply of condoms."

But instead of ranting about how ridiculous it was, how cheap it made her look as a journalist, how nobody would ever take her seriously now, Liz just threw back her head and laughed. For a second, I was worried she was finally cracking under all the stress of the last few days.

"What?" I asked after a few seconds of my hard-on starting to wilt. Nothing to accomplish that quite like a girl kneeling over you and laughing.

"Just...I don't suppose you thought about stacking *that* vote, hmmm? Because we're gonna need all the condoms we can get."

I half-rolled my eyes and smiled at her. "No we're not. Because there's not going to be anyone else for me," I murmured curling my fingers under her shoulders and giving her a little tug. "C'mere," I managed before pulling her lips to mine.

We kissed for a long time, our tongues meeting in languid swipes, tasting and mapping each other's mouths, like this was the first time we'd kissed and like we had all the time in the world, all at once. With each passing second, I grew harder, and she got wetter, until my cock was gliding through her lips and I thought I would combust. "Liz," I groaned, and either she read my mind or was thinking the same thing, because her hand darted down to ease my cock to her entrance.

In the next breath, she'd lowered herself fully onto me. God, I fit so perfectly inside her, and her wet heat felt so delicious surrounding me, I never wanted this to end.

Maybe it wouldn't have to.

We rocked together like we'd done it a thousand times, and would do it a thousand times again. The thought was so over-whelming that I pulled her back down to me for a sloppy, searing kiss, and she whimpered as she responded in kind.

When we finally finished, moaning incoherent things into each other's mouths, Liz collapsed on top of me, gasping. "Love you," I murmured into her hair, marveling at how warm and full it made me feel just to say the words I'd been thinking and feeling for so long.

To think that I'd almost been too cowardly to say them at all.

"I know it's kind of forward, since we just got back togeth-er," she panted into my neck. "But...I was going to ask you..."

"Yeah?" I asked, breathless all over again. "Anything."

On shaking arms, she pushed herself up, her hair falling in curtains around us. "Well...what would you think about moving in with me?"

I grinned as my fingers danced over her ribs, tickling her in retribution for that most welcome of little teases. She collapsed on me again in a fit of giggles, and I captured her lips with mine while I was still grinning. Our teeth clacked together and neither of us could catch our breath, but I didn't care, and I had a pretty good feeling that she didn't either.

It was good to finally be back home.

***

Sign up for the Alessandra Thomas Newsletter for information about new releases and sales

ACKNOWLEDGMENTS

First and foremost, as always, thank you to Lyla Payne, my ride-or-die, who reads every single thing I write and tells me how to make it better. Thank you for being by my side in this crazy romance-writing world from day one. I couldn't do any of this without you.

Julianne Daly, my faithful copyeditor, went through this book with a fine-toothed comb so that no serious grammar or spelling atrocities would be committed in its pages. I am appreciative; my readers, even more so.

Denise Grover Swank, thank you for volunteering your love, time, and energy to give this book one more editorial once-over, plus a shiny new cover from Estella. Your belief in me is a source of encouragement every day.

Dear readers, thank you for showing up to lose yourselves in these stories. A special shoutout to those of you who have been with me since book one. I may have taken a short break from publishing, but I never stopped writing new stories for you to read one day. I'm so grateful to you for spending time with Liz, Jordan, and all the characters in books still to come.

ABOUT THE AUTHOR

Aless is the bestselling author of several steamy romances who swears she was in her twenties yesterday. Since that's sadly untrue, she spends her time writing fun, sexy stories about men and women falling in love under the most unlikely circumstances.

When she's not writing, you can find her with a spoonful of ice cream in one hand and a romance novel in the other, snuggled up with one of her giant dogs.

ALSO BY ALESSANDRA THOMAS

Picturing Perfect Series

Picture Perfect

Subject to Change

Drop Everything Now

***

Sign up for the Alessandra Thomas Newsletter for information about new releases and sales